HUYTON HUYTON
TWO DOGS FIGHTING

HUYTON HUYTON
TWO DOGS FIGHTING

JOHN O'NEILL

authorHOUSE

AuthorHouse™ UK
1663 Liberty Drive
Bloomington, IN 47403 USA
www.authorhouse.co.uk
Phone: 0800.197.4150

© *2015 John O'Neill. All rights reserved.*

No part of this book may be reproduced, stored in a retrieval system, or transmitted by any means without the written permission of the author.

Published by AuthorHouse 11/20/2015

ISBN: 978-1-5049-9394-4 (sc)
ISBN: 978-1-5049-9393-7 (hc)
ISBN: 978-1-5049-9395-1 (e)

Print information available on the last page.

Any people depicted in stock imagery provided by Thinkstock are models, and such images are being used for illustrative purposes only.
Certain stock imagery © Thinkstock.

This book is printed on acid-free paper.

Because of the dynamic nature of the Internet, any web addresses or links contained in this book may have changed since publication and may no longer be valid. The views expressed in this work are solely those of the author and do not necessarily reflect the views of the publisher, and the publisher hereby disclaims any responsibility for them.

In loving memory of my brother

James O'Neill

Chapter One

Dot Harper jumped up and down on Longview School sports field waving her arms in the air with excitement. The only thing John Kelly was excited about was the sight of her chest bouncing up and down under her white school t-shirt. She had just won the girls hundred yards sprint, and John had won the boys race only minutes before.

John had been crazy about this girl since his first day at Longview and now it was his last, and he couldn't believe his luck that he was actually celebrating it with her as part of the school leaver's sports team. "Okay, stand really close in now... That's it! Hold... and smile."

John was ecstatic as Dot, wearing a grey and white figure hugging school tracksuit and smelling of her fresh perfume put her arm around his waist as he stood with his arm around her shoulder, while they posed for a picture for the local paper. He put all thoughts of her having anything more to do with him after the celebrations right out of his head.

As rumour had it Dot Harper was *only* interested in older men, one man in particular known as Eddie D. Nobody ever seemed to know what the D stood for, but John reckoned it was for dirty bastard because he liked to get his leg over with the younger girls.

Dot had been secretly dating Eddie D for months. He was a director in his father's construction company, divorced and at thirty-six he was twenty years her senior with a receding hair line and bulging waistband. All Dot saw was his expanded wallet and big silver Volvo that he picked her up in when he took her to stay in fancy hotels. He lavished her with expensive gifts and clothes, all of which she kept hidden in her best mates house, Wendy. She was dating Eddie D's best mate Brian Murphy, who was similar in age to Eddie and also had the cash to flash. Like Dot, Wendy was a city girl and like many city girls their age, once she got dolled up, she knew how to turn any man on with that knowing look and come on smile.

Dot was the one that Eddie D couldn't resist and she made him feel like he'd died and gone to heaven. Both knew these girls where still only young, "fifteen goin' on fuckin' fifty" Brian used to say. But Eddie D didn't give a shit because there was something special about Dot. Something that had him falling in way too deep, and he knew if it ever came out he was seeing her, her family would come after him and his name would be mud, something Dot and Wendy understood only too well.

They lied to their parents every time they stayed at a hotel, each saying she was staying in the other girl's house. They were all skating on thin ice, which only added to the thrill. Eddie D was determined to find a way of keeping it under wraps until Dot was old enough to tell everyone where to shove it. That day wouldn't be too long a wait because as a school leaver she wasn't too far off her sixteenth birthday.

Dot was not into young boys, Eddie was a grown man and John Kelly was just a school boy. John knew she'd not as much as give him a second glance. Instead he consoled himself with the fact that she'd had her arm around his waist. John Kelly on the other hand would have sung it from the roof tops if could still smell her perfume on his t-shirt, as he told his parents and older brother Jimmy just how fantastic his last day as a pupil at Longview school had been.

There on the kitchen table was a copy of the Liverpool Echo opened on the school's sports section, and showing the picture of John Kelly and Dot Harper under the heading 'Longview School, Pair of winners!'

"Yeh, they're a pair of winner's lad" John went beetroot as Jimmy was taking the proverbial piss as he looked at the size of Dot Harpers chest, and raucous laughter reverberated around the kitchen table from the gang of lads John and Jimmy had been mates with for as far back as they could remember.

"That'll be enough of tha' carry on in this house, thank you very much!" said Ma Kelly who was standing next to the cooker, up to her elbows in flour as she was baking. This was something she done every week always making sure there was enough to go round, with plenty left over for unexpected visitors. "Sorry Mam" Jimmy knew he'd over stepped the mark and was suitably shamed faced when his mother shot him a look that let him know she was disgusted.

She and old Joe Kelly had reared their lads on traditional catholic values, so there was no room for that sort of talk in this house. It wouldn't be tolerated. They had done the best by their sons, devoted themselves to bringing them up properly. They were proud at the way they'd turned out. At nineteen Jimmy worked with his dad in construction and now John had left school and was almost sixteen, he was due to follow suit as an apprentice plasterer.

Jimmy was also a newly married man and trying for a baby with his wife Jean, who worked as a nurse with her older sister Colette in Whiston hospital. Ma Kelly wouldn't stand for him being disrespectful in that way. "It's a good job your father isn't here to hear you talk like tha', he'd wipe the bloody floor with yeh". Old Joe Kelly would indeed have wiped the floor with him, if for nothing else for speaking like that in front of his mother.

Joe had worked hard all his life and was now coming up to retirement and working on his last big refurbishment for Knowsley Golf Club. It was his final pay out and he had invested all his savings into the project. When it was finished he would be able to pay outright for the bungalow in the up market district of Rainhill, on the outskirts of Liverpool, and still have plenty left over to furnish it. Not many people could afford to buy their own home let alone pay for it in cash in the sixties. But Joe had been working towards this dream all his married life. He had paid the hefty deposit, and soon the outstanding balance would be cleared and it would be something that was all theirs.

He was older than his wife by twenty years, so he was looking forward enjoying a bit of peace and tranquility away from the daily grind of city life with her. Finally he would have something of value to leave behind to their two sons. Right now their two sons along with their four mates couldn't get out of the kitchen quick enough, as there was nothing worse than Ma Kelly when she had a cob on.

Big Harry was six foot two, built like a brick shithouse and had hands the size of coal shovels, but whenever Ma Kelly got a 'cob on' he was the first out of the door, closely followed by Dominic McGuire. Thanks to the support and guidance of her and her husband Joe, these two lads had enlisted in the British Army as soon as they were old enough to leave home and get away. They spent every home leave with the Kelly's.

Big Harry's mother was an alcoholic and a bloody nightmare. Sweet as pie one minute, and ready to fight the whole street the next minute. She was a piss head. All the other kids laughed when she staggered home from the local boozer that was more like home to her. The house she lived in was tired and neglected. Big Harry's dad was a G.I and had long since returned back to the State's. She lived alone and it showed.

Dominic McGuire's life wasn't much better. His mother was known in every ale house from one end of the dock road to the other. He'd never known who his father was because his mother had been with that many men, and she didn't know either. That was why Ma Kelly and her husband Joe had taken these two lads under their wing from they were nippers, with a warm meal, a friendly welcome and a clip around the ear when needed.

Their open door also attracted Danny Owens and Arthur McNabb, who also thrived on the easy banter and warmth of the Kelly home which was a million miles from their own miserable lives. All of these lads were the same age as their own son Jimmy, but one way and another all of them were much harder than him and John put together. They'd had to be to survive and not many would be foolish enough to cross them.

They were known all over Huyton for being hard bastards and that guaranteed the Kelly brothers total protection and respect. Although it had to be said that there was fuck all *'soft'* about Jimmy or John.

John had a temper from when he was a little lad and was renowned by everyone for bearing a grudge. Though younger than Jimmy by a couple of years in some ways he was far more the leader of the two, something that worried Ma Kelly and her husband Joe. He was a good lad and good son, but unlike Jimmy who had always been a bit of a homing pigeon, John couldn't wait to fly the nest and see the world.

Like the Kelly men, Danny Owens worked in construction as a plumber but with no thanks to his mother who'd lived her life in the bingo chasing after 'the big win' that never happened. His father was no better, a waster that spent most of his time in Walton Jail for petty crime. It was Joe Kelly who'd kept this lad on the straight and narrow and he loved him for that.

Arthur McNabb on the other hand, had a very strict upbringing and he was pushed every foot of the way to make something of his life. So much so, his parents by passed all warmth and affection for rigid learning. It was something Ma Kelly and her husband Joe made up for in abundance with bowls of scouse and peawack soup, fatherly advice or a motherly hug which was never very far away when needed. It was no surprise though that Arthur became a copper, with ambitions of working undercover in the anti-terrorist unit.

At long last, John Kelly had finally left school and could make something of himself like the others. Even though it meant resigning himself to the fact that Dot Harper would be forever out of his league and would soon be a thing of the past. He couldn't wait to get the school leaver's dance out of the way and become a working man like his brother Jimmy and the other four lads.

Chapter Two

Val Harper displayed the cut out picture from the Liverpool Echo on the wall just above the mirrors in her hair dressing salon, so it couldn't be missed. As one customer after another sat in the salon chair to get their hair done, she beamed with pride when they commented on it saying what a good looking girl her daughter Dot was, and how happy her and young John Kelly looked together. However when one customer said "Tha' girl in the picture goes out with my ex husband" Val was completely caught off guard and stared at her in stunned silence.

The woman continued, knowing full well she was talking to Dot's mother. "They're in the 'SHE' nightclub every Friday night together". Yes, she knew exactly what she was doing and she was enjoying every minute of it. "Yeh, she's a right arl arse cos he's nearly 36 like, but when she's all done up with her slap on she doesn't look much younger".

Val Harper felt a sickening knot in her stomach as she struggled to take in what was said. "No, you must be mistaken love. Tha' girl in the picture is only fifteen and she doesn't go drinking in any nightclub, and I should know, I'm her mother!"

This time she really sent the boot in "Well I hope for your sake you're right. But I've gorra tell yeh girl, Eddie D likes 'em young, and I should know, cos I was only fifteen when he had me."

Val Harpers instincts was to slap this woman right in the face there and then, and throw her out of the shop, but something inside told her not to. Because something inside told her this woman was telling the truth and her daughter was in big trouble.

"If he's touched one hair on her head I'll kill the bastard. No man leads my daughter astray and gets away with it!" In all the years they'd been married Val Harper had never seen or heard her husband Norman so angry or so worried. She'd churned all day wondering how she'd tell him. Wondering how he'd react. Now she knew as she sat across the dinner table from him, their evening meal not touched.

It was Friday night and Val Harper hadn't said a word to Dot as she left the house before her dad had got home from work, saying she was sleeping over in Wendy Bingham's house. It was something she'd done every weekend for months. Val and Norman Harper didn't mind or worry about it, because her and Wendy were best friends and had gone through school together. Now it was clear that she'd been lying through her teeth.

There was only one thing for it, Norman Harper and his brothers headed straight to the She Club in Liverpool city centre. They had been there for over two hours nursing their drinks, not wanting to get drunk. Just as they thought they had been wasting their time, they spotted Edie and Brain arrive and head to the bar. It looked like they were on their own, but then the barmaid opened a bottle of champagne and four glasses.

Norman knew they were waiting for the girls to come and it was not long before Eddie was joined by a long legged blond with her tits half hanging out. The relief washed over him "Thank God he's with that slut and not my daughter". Then she turned around laughing and he could see it was indeed his daughter. His baby Dot was dressed like a woman twice her age and flirting with Eddie D.

He could scarcely believe his own eyes as he walked towards them, his 'little girl' dressed like common tart and enjoying being touched up by an older man. One sharp punch to the gut and the dirty bastard went down like a sack of spuds. Norman Harper went in for the kill then and kicked ten kinds of shit out of Eddie fuckin D, as his daughter looked on in horror *screaming*.

Blood poured from Eddie's nose and his lips blew up like the size of a balloon. Three bouncers came running from different parts of the club and after dragging him off Eddie the bouncers pulled Norman outside as he yelled and roared insults and threats to Eddie D, who was still struggling to get up off the floor.

Once the bouncers got Norman outside, they pinned him up against the wall. Luckily his brothers came to his rescue to explain the situation. They didn't want to hurt this man. They had teenage daughters of their own for fuck's sake and would have done the same. So they calmed Norman and Dot down, and then sent them on their way.

Val Harper was beside herself with worry when Norman turned the key in the front door. He shoved Dot in the living room before entering himself with Eddie D's blood all over his shirt. The sight of witch made her panic "Oh my God! What's happened? What the fuck 'ave yeh done?" Still white, livid Norman Harper ignored his wife and went straight into the kitchen and picked up a dirty wet dish cloth then returned to the front room and threw it straight in Dot's face.

"Wipe that shite off your face and get up them fuckin stairs now! And if you ever see tha' dirty sleazy bastard again I'll fuckin kill him!" Dot ran up the stairs and threw herself on her bed crying uncontrollably. Not because she'd been found out, but for the look she seen on her dad's face. The hurt and disgust she seen in his eyes. The disappointment she knew she'd caused both him and her mum.

But why couldn't they understand, she was only doing what other girls her age do. She was only having fun and Eddie D didn't deserve to have the shit kicked out of him for that. It wasn't fair so they could both fuck off! She decided there and then that she wasn't going to stop seeing Eddie D, no matter what them or anybody else said.

Eddie D sat nursing his thick lip, as he sipped on a cup of tea, starring at the now famous picture of Dot with John Kelly in the Liverpool Echo. Although it had been some weeks since the bust up at the She Club, Eddie was still carrying the scars. He was also missing Dot more than he thought possible. The only contact he had with Dot was through Wendy. He had not seen Dot at all and he was missing her badly. Then suddenly he had an idea. It was perfect! He was playing with fire and taking a big risk, but he didn't give a toss as long as it meant he could carry on seeing Dot.

The school leavers' dance was due and as a school leaver John Kelly was bound to be there. Dot may have been well and truly grounded but she'd be allowed to go to that. So Eddie and Brain persuaded Wendy to visit Dot and talk her into copping off with John Kelly. Dot was unsure and couldn't understand how Eddie could even suggest it or why he wouldn't be jealous. But the truth of it was as a successful businessman he didn't see how a school leaver, not quite sixteen, could pose a threat to his and Dot's relationship.

He wined and dined her and showed her the high life and she loved every minute of it. So he was confident she wouldn't let go of any of that for some wet behind the ears school leaver called John Kelly.

"Oh my god Dot, it's perfect! It'll take the heat off you an Eddie until you're sixteen. Then you can do what you want". Wendy really egged her "come on, if nothing' else it'll be a good laugh, plus, your mum and dad will start trusting you again if they think you're with someone your own age". Dot began to see the bigger picture and agreed to give it a whirl.

Friday night and Longview School Hall was packed to the rafters. With all the school leavers, everyone was dressed kill, none more so than Dot Harper and Wendy Bingham, they looked stunning. John Kelly couldn't take his eyes off Dot thinking 'If only' when she looked right across the crowded hall and smiled at him his stomach done summer salts as he smiled back.

Then suddenly he realized Wendy was standing right in front of him. She handed him a scribbled out note from Dot, inviting him to a family party with her the following Saturday. John took the note, glanced at it quickly then looked back at Wendy. Trying hard not to show his shock he said "How come she's isn't taking her fella?" Wendy smirked in his face making him feel uncomfortable "They split up. She's free and single now, so are yeh gonna go or wha'?"

Her smirk was fixed and still unsettled him, he felt like she was taking the piss, but he couldn't pass up on an opportunity like this. So trying not to appear too eager he agreed to meet Dot at the Harpers family home at seven o'clock the following week.

As soon as Wendy relayed to Dot what John had said the two of them started laughing and left the dance. But John stuck around to tell anyone who'd listen that he'd finally copped a date with Dot Harper. But once outside Longview school gates, Dot Harper and Wendy Bingham ran to a nearby side street where Brain Murphy was parked up and waiting for them. They jumped into the back of the car laughing

"Quick! Drive fast in case someone sees us!" Brain grinned at Wendy as he turned on the ignition and sped off with her and Dot ducking down on the back seat still laughing "Come on then, share, how did it go?". He couldn't wait to see if they'd put their plan into action. "Oh my God! He's such a Div!" Wendy was hysterical laughing as Dot added "He fell for it hook line and sinker!" Brain joined in the laughing as he drove them to a pub in nearby St Helens to meet Eddie, so him and Dot could spend a few quality hours together without being seen by anyone.

Chapter Three

By the time Saturday evening came around, John Kelly was a bag of shite as he pressed the doorbell at the Harper household. He stood anxiously waiting for it to be answered and he was relieved when Dot opened the door and like himself was casually dressed. She was in a pair of tight blue jeans and plain white top and her long blond hair was neatly tied back in a ponytail. She looked gorgeous and he felt as if her bright blue eyes looked right into his soul as she smiled 'hi-ya, come in'.

Her welcome was warm and after getting him a drink and immediately introducing him to her parents and relatives, he began to relax and enjoy himself as Dot kept up the small talk and even got him up to dance. Norman Harper was relieved to see Dot with the lad she had been pictured with in the Liverpool Echo. *At least they were the same bloody ag*e, he thought. He was impressed that this young man was due to start work with his father soon, as an apprentice plasterer.

By the end of the night John was thrilled as Dot asked if he'd like to see her again. He jumped at the chance. Before now he thought she hadn't even noticed him. Now she'd just kissed him goodnight on the lips at the front door. As he began his walk home feeling ten foot tall, Dot closed the door behind him and turned to Wendy Bingham who was waiting in the hall grinning. They gave each other a high five then burst out laughing.

It wasn't long before Dot and John started spending all their free time together, and she was playing him to perfection. He was like putty in her hands. She knew how inexperienced he was, and enjoyed teasing him when they were alone together kissing and cuddling for hours. She really liked the way he looked at her, liked the way he looked down her top when he thought she wasn't looking. For her, this was an exciting and thrilling game. She laughed and joked about every time she got the chance to see Eddie. Dot had the best of both worlds and she was learning to enjoy it.

For John, this was real. This was love and he believed Dot when she said she was still a virgin. He respected her when she said she wanted to stay that way until she got married. He now thought the rumours he'd heard about her had all been lies. She wasn't that kind of girl at all. She wasn't anything like what people had said she was. She didn't deserve any of the insults and name calling. She was decent, and not in his wildest imagination would he have recognised her as the scantily clad girl who liked being chased around hotel rooms by Eddie D.

Sport was the one thing they did have in common. They both loved it and loved running and keeping fit. They started jogging together a few times a week. Val Harper's customers often said how they had seen Dot jogging with her new fella. So within a few short months things in the Harper household were back to normal and Eddie D's name was a thing of the past.

Dot asked if she could sleep over at Wendy's house again, because John was going to watch his beloved Everton play away in London. Val and Norman Harper agreed to start trusting once more, albeit with much reluctance and great anxiety.

John went to every Everton home and away match of the season. His brother Jimmy joined him, as did Big Harry and Dominic McGuire when they were on home leave from the army. Danny Owens and Arthur McNabb also joined them when they could.

After one of the away games in Blackburn, while they were all waiting to be served in a local chippy, they found themselves surrounded by a dozen or so Blackburn supporters looking for trouble. Quick as a flash, big Harry decked three of them. One was doubled up holding his stomach and another had blood pouring from his nose. It was enough to put the shits up the rest of them as they all left the chippy far quicker than they came in it.

As they all made their way home to Liverpool, Big Harry was celebrated as 'man of the hour' modestly. He insisted it was all down to his army training and being a black belt in Karate. It was something he'd always encouraged John to take up, but was something until now John wasn't interested in. But if it meant he could handle himself like Big Harry just had, he was game for it.

John was relieved Dot didn't mind him joining the local karate club, as it was on a Wednesday night, the night they normally went jogging together. She saw it as a chance to spend more time with Eddie D. The more time Dot spent with John Kelly, the more she spoke about him to Eddie D, and he was getting pretty fucked off with it. It was jealousy pure and simple. It was beginning to gnaw away at him, driving him to spy on them when they went jogging.

Dot with her long blond hair tied back in a ponytail, wearing a figure hugging tracksuit that showed all her curves. Laughing and joking and having a good time with him, John fuckin' Kelly. Eddie brought these two together for a reason, to keep the scent off Dot seeing him. Now they were getting close, too close. So it was time to tear them apart and the sooner the better before it all backfired and he lost Dot to this little shit.

Big Harry and Dominic McGuire were due back at army camp and set to be away for a few months. The lads decided to throw a bit of a do in the Kelly household before they left. Mar Kelly made plenty of scran to eat and old Jo made sure there was more than enough ale to go round. There was quite a turn out. Jimmy turned up with his wife Jean and sister-in-law Colette. Big Harry and Dominic McGuire arrived wearing their army uniforms. Arthur McNabb never wore his coppers uniform unless he was working, and Danny Owens never wore anything else but a suit jacket and jeans.

The neighbours were all used to a good do in the Kelly's and drifted in and out as the night went on. Music played and laughing could be heard up and down the street as old Jo told one good yarn after another and had everyone in stitches. These were memories in the making and the lads loved it. They loved the crac, the camaraderie, the sense of real bonding felt by them all. They didn't have to be blood to be family. These lads had grown together from little nippers and now they were men, real men, hard men. Hurt one and you hurt them all.

By the time John turned up with Dot on his arm, the party was in full swing and everyone was well oiled. The sight of them walking through the door still turned heads. Dot looked stunning, no wonder John was hooked. She was beautiful and her smile lit up the room. She stayed at his side all night refusing all offers to dance in place of giving him all her attention. She made him feel ten foot tall, and he loved her so much he thought he might burst with pride.

At the end of the night John took her home in a taxi. As they got out and John paid the driver, they didn't notice the yellow Consul Capri parked a few hundred yards up the road with its headlights turned off. Eddie D was sitting behind the wheel watching them, he was seething. The scheming bitch was wearing the expensive dress he had bought her only the week before. She was all over John before they both disappeared inside Dot's house.

When John didn't come back out again, he nearly burst a blood vessel before driving away convinced they were sleeping together. But John was fast asleep on living room couch and covered up with a blanket that Val Harper threw over him. She insisted on him staying because it was late to go home and he'd had too much to drink.

Eddie D was still livid when he picked Dot up and drove them to a pub on the outskirts of the city. His expression was cold and uncaring and he didn't say a word as he drove. After pulling into the car park of a county pub, he got out of the car and walked ahead into lounge. Dot followed unsure of her ground. She'd never seen him like this before and didn't know what to expect or how to handle it. She sat at a table and waited while he went to the bar to order their drinks. He placed a large gin and orange on the table in front of her then sat down with his pint.

"Do you think I'm fuckin' stupid?" Dot was shocked and before she could even answer he went on "I saw you with tha' cunt Kelly the other night. Wearing' the dress I bought you to wear for me. Not for some shitty arse fuckin apprentice yeh fuckin' prick tease!" She didn't know what to say. She knew it better be good, better be convincing. Anything else and the money, the expensive gifts and clothes, the nights out in fancy restaurants and plush hotels would all be gone. Eddie D wasn't the sort of man to be made a fool of, no matter how much he idolized her.

"Have you been fuckin' spyin' on me?" She had him on the back foot now and knew by the surprised look on his face he wasn't expecting her to fight back. He was flustered "No, I was drivin' past yours the other night and I seen yeh, all over him like a fuckin' rash!" She slammed him "You fuckin' started this! I had my mother waiting up for us and you're the one who wants me to make it look real!" She had him banged to rights and like putty in her hands he softened as she continued. "You're the one I wonna be with, and you're the only one who sees me undressed".

She knew what she was doing as she gave him that smile, that come on look, the one that made him take her by the hand and lead her to the hotel room. She had two men, one rich and one poor and both were in love with her.

But jealousy is a terrible thing and Eddie D had made up his mind. No matter what she'd said, he was convinced she'd slept with that little cunt Kelly. So it was time for him to be taught a lesson and taken right out of the fuckin picture.

Michael and Maurice Higgnet were identical twins in their early twenties, both six footers with blond hair and blue eyes. They lived in Widnes, a town some ten miles from Liverpool. They were both coppers in the Merseyside police force based in Liverpool just like their father and that wasn't the only thing they had in common with him. Word on the street was they were all bent, the similarities ended there as their father was a senior officer. They were a pair of meat heads and both as thick as pig shit and living off his reputation for being ruthless.

Eddie D sat at a round wooden table drinking with them in the Deans house pub in Prescot. Telling them how this little cunt Kelly was shagging Dot. How she denied it, but he was no fool and knew she was lying. The twins were all ears, listening to every twisted detail. Until one of them spoke, but Eddie didn't have a fuckin clue which one he was. "We know wha' you're askin', but wha' kind of money are yeh talkin'?"

Eddie wrote down a figure on a beer mat and pushed it across the table. "Half up front, half when the job is done". The twins approved of the sum on offer and Michael was the first to give his hand to Eddie over the table. Eddie gripped it tight as they shook on the deal. "I don't care wha' you do or how you do it. Just put the little cunt out of action and take him off the scene".

Chapter Four

Life for John had never been better. He was in a secure job that he enjoyed and had a stunning girlfriend who he loved, and old Jo and Mar Kelly thought the world of her. He lay awake in bed at night dreaming about his future, dreaming of the day when he'd get down on one knee and ask her to marry him. Dreaming of them making love for the very first time. She was his first love, the love of his life, and in his heart she would be his forever love.

Dot on the other hand was becoming unsettled. She was fed up with Eddie D trying to control her. Fed up with his jealous outbursts. Fed up with him asking her to run away and marry him. It was intense and she felt like she couldn't breathe. Eddie realized she felt suffocated by his attention to everything. He knew he was spoiling things and at the risk of driving her away. So he met Wendy Bingham for a pub lunch behind Dot's back to talk about it.

Wendy thought Dot had been exaggerating when she said how jealous Eddie had become of John. Now she could see it for herself as he grilled her "I just wonna know the truth! Are they sleeping together?" It was pointless him even asking the question as he didn't believe the answer when she told him *no*.

Wendy had always believed anyone sincere or nice was a bore and a phony. She had always thought anyone caring and kind was weak. She had never grasped that difference between naivety and stupidity, or the quality of trust coming before gullibility. On every count it was how had she seen John Kelly, so she had no sympathy for the position he was in with Dot.

No respect for John's feelings, and she believed he deserved all he got for being so stupid. Little wonder she was agreeable when Eddie D asked if she could persuade Dot to go away with him to Scotland to get married. He would obviously make it worth her while. She jumped at the chance to make money.

Wendy visited Dot at home and at work in her mum's salon, at every opportunity she got. Taking advantage of the friendship and trust between them she probed for information to take back to Eddie. She started planting the idea of marriage and began piling on the pressure for Dot to commit to Eddie. "Just think you'll be seventeen soon old enough to marry Eddie. Yeh lucky cow! You won't want for a thing".

Dot shocked her though, as she admitted she'd grown fond of John and had become so close to him. She actually enjoyed being with him more than Eddie. Wendy was horrified and couldn't understand why "Are you mental! Why?" Dot was serious and more sincere than Wendy had ever seen her before. "All Eddie wants is sex sex and more sex. He even 'got a cob on an accused me of goin' off him, because I wanted him to take me to the pictures, and not bed". Adding "John respects me, he doesn't even try it on". Wendy couldn't resist a swipe "He's probably queer".

Dot was immediately defensive "No he's not!" Wendy was shocked and gave a phony laugh "Oh I'm only messing". Then she decided to change tack, she pointed out all the benefits to marrying Eddie D "He's a director in his dads business, he's got his own house, and he gets a new car every year. It'll be years before John's served his time as a plasterer. Even then he'll end up working for someone like Eddie. He'll never be able to provide like Eddie can".

Dot thought she's got a point. She knew she would have a fabulous lifestyle with Eddie and be made for life. She still felt as sick as a pig, as she knew how much she had led John on. She knew he was madly in love with her. She knew he really was a good lad and deserved better than her. But she had developed feelings for him. Now it all felt so messy and she didn't know what to do.

As Dot's seventeenth birthday drew closer John spotted a beautiful watch in the jewelers. It was expensive and would take up most of his spare cash, but he didn't care as it was special and Dot was worth every penny. Wendy let Eddie know behind Dot's back that John was buying her a watch for her birthday. So he made it his business to buy the most attractive and expensive watch he could find. There was no way was he going to be up staged by fuckin apprentice. He also decided as he couldn't be at her official birthday party, he'd propose to her that week, before it happened. So he could scupper any chance that little cunt Kelly might have of doing the same.

On the night of the actual party, John turned up at Dot's house with his brother Jimmy. Dot was over the moon when she opened the front door and clapped eyes on him in a new suit. He looked like a different fella, older and dead smart. He gave her a card and present and when she opened it, seeing it was no match for the diamond studded watch Eddie D had given her a few nights earlier, she pretended to be thrilled. Wendy knew that was going through her head as she watched on with that smirk on her face that John couldn't stand.

But it soon disappeared when John showed the inscription on the back of the watch that read 'love you loads'. Overwhelmed Dot threw her arms around him 'I love you too'. In a funny kind of way it was true, she did. Wendy realized it too and could see her big pay out from Eddie D fading away before her eyes. So she decided to act fast.

Sitting in the Hillside pub a few days later, she told Dot that Brain had booked a cottage for two weeks in Scotland and she was dead excited. "You and Eddie come with us! Just tell your mum and dad you're invited on holiday in Cornwall with my mum and dad". Dot was tempted. "Go on, we'll 'ave a ball! Eddie will spoil you rotten!" Wendy was right. In the build up to going away Eddie D went out of his way to spoil Dot at every opportunity. He even booked her driving lessons, saying when she passed her test and things were out in the open, he'd buy her a Mini Cooper. Dot's resistance began to weaken.

It was Wednesday night and John was at his usual karate club when Brian picked up Wendy and Dot. But to Dot's surprise instead of taking them to their usual out of town boozer in St Helens, he drove them down Huyton Lane and turned onto a piece of land just before Huyton Village. Eddie D was standing with a smile on his face as they pulled up. He'd been expecting them and was standing in the middle of a construction site. When they all got out of the car, Dot was even more surprised. Eddie was standing where three large four bedroom houses were being built. One was for sale, one belonged to his dad, and the third was for him and Dot to come back home to from Scotland.

This was Eddie D's proposal for getting hitched in Gretna Green, even though she knew her parents would go berserk and possibly never speak to her again. Dot knew this was a great opportunity. Yet deep down, she wasn't happy. She needed time to think. She'd treated John so badly yet he was in love with her. All this had to come out, and when it did, she knew he would be devastated and never look at her again.

When she first started out with Eddie's plan it all seemed like a good idea, a good laugh, now it had all gone too far and it was horrible. It was no longer a game, no longer funny, they'd messed around with John's life and he didn't deserve it. Things were about to get a lot worse because the Higgnet twins had decided it was time to pay John Kelly a visit, and Dot had realized she might be pregnant as she hadn't had a period for over five weeks.

John was pleased Dot wanted to go away on holiday with Wendy and her family. It gave him the opportunity to go to Jersey to visit Danny Owens, who was working over there as a plumber's mate. Big Harry and Dominic McGuire were both due home leave from the army. The plan was for the four of them to get together and have a lad's holiday.

In the build up to it all, Dot met Eddie in secret and he took her to a well-established Jeweller in St Helens. He bought her a beautiful gold bracelet. Then he slipped a fabulously expensive engagement ring on her finger. It fitted perfectly, thanks to Wendy, who had sneaked her ring size to Eddie weeks earlier. It looked stunning and made her feel like a million dollars. "Just think, when we come back from Scotland you'll be wearing a wedding ring next to it". Eddie was excited, but Dot didn't answer him.

Dot knew with the possibility of carrying his baby, she had no choice; she'd have to marry him. Eddie D had no idea that she might be pregnant. He knew in his heart she was growing up fast. He knew she was no longer the naive young school girl he fell like a ton of bricks for. He knew that she had turned into a beautiful young woman and if he didn't get her hitched to him now, chances were it would never happen and he'd lose her to that little cunt Kelly.

Dot still hadn't finished with John, and she couldn't shake off how bad she felt over the way they had treated him. She couldn't eat because of the feeling in the pit of her stomach. She cried herself to sleep every night at the thought of his hurt. Her guilt was gnawing away at her and she was totally confused and unhappy. Brain Murphy was driving her and Wendy to Scotland on the Saturday, but Eddie D was traveling there alone a day earlier, saying he wanted to make sure there'd be no last minute hick up's before the wedding. So she had one last chance to see John and say goodbye to him properly.

Chapter Five

Old Joe Kelly was dressed in his best suit and on his way to the golf club to collect his pay cheque. All his work there was completed and had been passed by the local building inspectors, and the golf club committee. Joe was hard working man and a perfectionist, something he was known for throughout the building trade. Only the highest standard of work would do for him, and that was why his name went before him. People respected him for it. And the fact that he was an honest and reliable man, who was as good as his word.

The only problem Joe encountered on this job had been a leak that lasted a whole weekend. Somebody had gone through one of the water pipes with a nail and caused a little surface damage. It took less an hour to fix but it meant he couldn't decorate until the plaster had dried out, and that meant the job was delayed by ten working days.

It was nine thirty on the dot and Joe was sitting in the waiting room of the treasurer's office, anticipating his pay out. He planned to take it straight to the bank to deposit, then go to the solicitors to arrange the final payment off his bungalow. The Treasurer, Tom Sloan, opened the office door with a smirk on his face, and invited him in. Once inside Jo was surprised to be confronted by two additional committee members. 'Unfortunately Mr. Kelly, we've had to enforce a late penalty clause'. Tom Sloan then handed Jo the pay cheque adding 'Ten days day's equals a two thousand pounds penalty'. Joe was gob smacked and looked at the cheque. Sure enough it was two grand down and written out for a poxy one thousand pounds. Now he understood why the other two members where there. It was in case he knocked the shit out of Tom Sloan.

"No. No fuckin' way!" Old Joe was white livid "I'll blow the fuckin' place up before I'll let you get away tha, yeh robbin' shower of bastards!" Joe shocked himself with his own outburst, but this wasn't just a matter of being two grand down. His whole future depended on it. His lifelong dream of a retirement bungalow for him and Mar Kelly now hung in the balance. "This is fuckin sabotage!" adding "Nowhere in that contract did it state a two hundred a day penalty for delay's". Tom Sloan held his stare at old Jo as he pulled a copy of the contract that Joe had signed, out of his desk draw and handed it to him. There in the small print was the figure of a two hundred pound a day fixed penalty clause.

Joe felt like he needed to sit down but remained standing and defiant instead "Listen, I discussed the penalty clause with the club secretary, Ted Brown, and he said it was a nominal twenty pounds a day. Big fuckin' difference don't yeh think!?" Tom Sloan grinned "That was the last contract Ted Brown worked on before leaving the club to immigrate to Australia. So what you're sayin' can't be verified. So, it's time you took your money and left the premises Joe". It was a set up all right and old Joe knew it as he made his out of the office in a state of shock and bewilderment.

John Kelly and his brother Jimmy were in high spirits as they walked into the Hillside pub to have a celebration drink with their dad. But when they arrived they were shocked to him sitting alone and staring into space with an empty pint glass in front of him. "I'm gonna go round there and kick the fuckin shit outta the lot of em" Jimmy was almost frothing at the mouth with anger after Joe told him and John what had happened. John was in just as much a state "No one does this to you and gets away with it".

But the last thing Joe Kelly wanted was his two lads getting hurt or in trouble with the police. They were no match for the two goons with the treasurer, so he calmed them both down and forbid them from doing anything. One of the hardest things Joe had had to do then was face the builder, Brian Brossly, and let him know he couldn't go ahead with the purchase of the bungalow. But even harder still was going home to face his beloved wife and crush all her dreams.

It was Friday night, and Eddie D had long since left for Scotland, while Val and Norman Harper had gone out for the night to their local pub. Dot had the ideal opportunity to be alone in the house with John for a few hours. The knot in her stomach wouldn't go away and as she waited for him to arrive. She started to think she should have written him a letter. It would have been a lot easier, but she wanted to give him something real, something special. So when the shit did hit the fan he'd have it to hold onto.

When John did arrive he was still feeling low about what had happened to his dad earlier in the day. As Dot led him up the stairs to her bedroom like she had done many times before when her parents let them spend time together playing records, this time instead of playing music she started to undress him. All thoughts of his dad and everything disappeared.

Dot began kissing him gently on his neck and moved slowly to his chest. His body felt muscular strong and firm. Not like Eddie's flab form and bulging waist, and when she finished undressing him she could see unlike Eddie he was very well endowed. Even though he was still a virgin he knew exactly what to do after she finished undressing herself and lay next to him. It all felt different to anything she had ever experienced with Eddie, and she realized it was because John was actually making love to her. Every touch, each caress, the closeness, it all made her feel special, so wanted, and afterwards he held her in his arms.

She had never felt so safe or loved in her life. When Eddie finished he'd just roll over and reach for his fags, leaving her feeling used and cheap. Only now did she fully realize it was because he was in lust not love. He was obsessed and wanted to own her like one of his many other possessions. He was incapable of loving as John did.

Days earlier Wendy had been taking the piss because John still hadn't tried it on, and Dot barked "it's because he respects me!" But when Wendy laughed and barked back "well tha won't last when he finds out how long Eddie's been knockin' you up" she shocked herself and Wendy by bursting into tears. She stunned Wendy even more when she said she might be pregnant. But when she added she was only a few weeks overdue, Wendy told her to stop worrying as she herself was often late, as it was common to be irregular at their age.

As she lay in John's arms feeling contented and loved, Dot hoped and prayed that Wendy was right, she couldn't bear the deceit any longer. Her parents were due back from the pub, so she didn't have enough time to confess everything. She didn't want to just blurt everything out, rush it like it wasn't that important, or bad. No, John deserved better than that and she wanted to do it properly. As they stood at the front door kissing, John picked up on Dot's mood she seemed quiet, pensive, but he thought it was because they had just made love. This was all new to him and thinking it was for Dot too. He reasoned maybe that was the way girls were afterwards.

So he told her he loved her more than life itself and with tears in her eyes she replied 'love you too'. In that instant she made up her mind to tell him everything. Hoping against hope he would forgive her and give her a second chance. Hoping against hope she wasn't pregnant. Hoping against hope they had a future together. As she realized she really did love him and she was sure of it now, she was sure she wanted to be with him not Eddie.

So she asked him to come back at ten the following morning. She wasn't due to set off at noon, so John assumed she wanted to spend a little more time with him before he waved her off. But she wasn't going anywhere, she was staying put to drop the dreaded bombshell and hoped she could survive the fall out. As John began his walk home he was ecstatic, convinced Dot wouldn't have given herself to him unless she loved him. So he made up his mind then and there that he'd ask her to marry him, and he hoped his poor dad would be cheered up a little by his plans.

As continued walking he didn't even notice the two men standing at a bus stop. It was Higgnet twins, as he walked passed them Maurice called out his name. He turned back around to see who it was and was met with a baseball bat being smashed full force into his face and the lights went out.

Chapter Six

Old Joe and Mar Kelly could scarcely take it in. "Your son has been involved in a road traffic accident, a hit and run, we need to get you to Whiston Hospital right away". Two young policemen were standing in their front room with concern etched on their faces. Ten minutes later, old Joe and his wife were standing in the intensive care unit at the side of John's bed as he fought for his life. They were numb with shock and disbelief as he lay motionless and rigged up to life saving equipment and tubes.

His head seemed bigger than its normal size and his face looked deformed. His eyes were just slits swollen and closed, and dry blood was clogged and crusted around his nostrils and mouth. "That's not my son". Panic and fear gripped every part her being as Mar Kelly collapsed to the floor. But the police had found John's provisional driving license in his pocket. The consultant confirmed as well as multiple fractures to his arms and legs, John also had head injuries and a broken jaw. For the time being, he was in an induced coma and critical.

Dot had tossed and turned all night going over and over the best way to tell John everything and how if he gave her a second chance she would never let him down again. But, if she was pregnant how she planned keeping it but would never let on to him, or Eddie, that it was Eddie's. She knew that was wrong, knew it was still deceiving him, but she didn't see she had any other choice. If Eddie D knew she had his baby, he would never give them a minute's peace or ever let them be happy together.

But what if all this backfired? What if it proved one horrible big mistake to come clean and tell John and he didn't want to know? What the heck then? Well she wasn't going to stick around to find out. She wasn't going to be crucified for it and loose Eddie as well and all the trappings of a plush lifestyle that came with him. She knew it was mercenary, but she had a plan B and that *was* Eddie D.

Eddie didn't know a thing about this plan of hers, and even if John tried to blab about it and make waves when they all got back from Scotland, she knew she could square it with Eddie. She could wrap him round her little finger and she knew it, especially if she was carrying his child. She hated that she could be so calculating, so cunning, so cold. Yet she felt shame deep within her being, but she was in a mess, a fuckin horrible big mess. She reasoned she was simply trying to make the best out of that horrible situation.

It was turned ten thirty and John still hadn't arrived, and by the time it got to eleven, she knew he wasn't going to either. She began panicking and was angry with herself for misjudging things so badly. She convinced herself that now John had got what he wanted; he'd clearly lost all his respect for her and didn't want to know. Her fate was sealed.

Eddie D had spent all of Friday night knocking back the whisky and smoking expensive Cohiba cigars at the hotel bar, making sure he gave the bar staff generous tips with every drink he ordered. Making sure they'd remembered him. Making sure he secured himself a water tight alibi for when John Kelly was beaten to a pulp and left for dead.

Fate had kindly intervened for John Kelly. A man out walking his dog along Knowsley Lane found him, and ran to the nearest phone box and dialed the emergency services. Now he was critical and in intensive care, he had survived the beating, and made it through the Friday night. His family was at his bedside, praying that with youth and fitness on his side he would pull through.

Old Joe sat bewildered in the relative's room, as he held Mar Kelly's hand reassuringly. She sat just as bewildered and quietly weeping. Jimmy's wife, their lovely daughter-in-law, Jean, was on duty, she had volunteered to sit with them, gently telling them the new developments. The consultants were agreed. It was no road traffic accident. No hit and run that had left John Kelly so unrecognizable to his own and fighting for his life. He had been the victim of brutal and vicious attack, and a weapon or weapons had been used on him.

As she always did in times of joy sorrow, Mar Kelly turned to the Blessed Virgin and she prayed with more fervor than she had ever before prayed in her life. After all if anyone could understand her heartache and pain as a mother, the Blessed Virgin could. She had suffered the agony of seeing her own son bleeding dying and gasping for life. She had suffered the unimaginable agony of seeing her own son being murdered before her very own eyes.

It was enough to make any mother snap and loose her mind, snap and lose all her faith in man and God. Lose all her hope in life itself. But the Blessed Virgin held her son in her arms and she held her nerve and her faith. Mar Kelly promised to follow her example, as she pleaded for her own son's life to be restored and healed to a full recovery.

A week had passed by since the attack on John Kelly. Instead of him being on holiday in Jersey with Big Harry, Danny Owens and Dominic McGuir, they were with him in the Liverpool Royal and keeping a bedside vigil. Big Harry and Dominic were on leave from the army and Danny Owens had flown over from Jersey into Liverpool airport. He jumped a taxi straight to the hospital as soon as he got news of what had happened. They took it in turns with Mar Kelly, old Joe and John's brother, Jimmy, for one of them to be at John bedside at all times.

Although he was no longer critical in coma, he was still very poorly. Mar Kelly knew her prayers were being answered and she couldn't have been more relived or thankful. John had been moved out of intensive care and was now on a general ward. He was still in shock and couldn't remember a thing of what had happened. Despite extensive enquiries the police were still none the wiser, but everyone was agreed two things. Where the fuck was Dot and why hadn't she been to the hospital to visit John? Everyone's shit detector was on high alert and the general consensus was that she knew something about John's attackers. It was a sure bet Eddie D was behind it.

Val Harper was inconsolable and Norman Harper stood shaking with rage with the telegram still in his hand 'I've married Eddie'. Right up until that point they still thought Dot was on holiday with Wendy Bingham and her family. "I'll kill the cunt! I will. I'll kill him!" Days earlier a customer having her hair done in Val's salon had told her about the terrible attack on John. By then word on it had already spread all over Huyton. Now as Norman Harper stood almost frothing at the mouth with rage, he knew in his heart *this* was why young John Kelly had been done over. It was all down to his daughter marrying Eddie fuckin' D.

They'd been waiting for Dot to come back home off holiday before telling her about John. They wanted to be with her when she was hit with the shock of it all. They wanted to be sitting with her at his bedside as she took in the fright of the hideous mess he'd been left in. They wanted to support her as she sat absorbing the gravity of the situation. But all the time the heartless little bitch already knew, but unlike Norman Harper, Val Harper refused to believe her own daughter could ever be that cruel.

Norman Harper and his wife Val turned up at the Liverpool Royal hospital, without Dot. They were shaky and white faced as they sat with John's family and friends in the relative's room, and told them the dreadful news of Dots marriage to Eddie. "So that's it. I've washed my fuckin' hands of 'eh! She's no daughter of mine, and she never will be now either, the heartless little bitch!"

Old Joe and Mar Kelly appreciated their visit and their honestly. They couldn't help but feel for the terrible position Dot had put them both in. However as one mother to another, Mar Kelly was saddened that Norman Harper could disown his own off spring and leave

Val unsupported in her worry fear and heartache, leaving their only daughter continued to be corrupted and used by Eddie D.

Whoever attacked John Kelly would pay for it tenfold. That was something John's brother, Jimmy, and all the lads agreed on as they sat drinking in the Hillside pub waiting for Arthur McNabb to join them from work with any info he'd managed gather. And when he arrived he didn't disappoint them. "Word in the station is the Higgnet twins know Eddie D well, done a few bent deals with him in the past like. And here's the interesting bit… they've not long got back from a weekend break, in Scotland".

The atmosphere was suddenly charged with pent up anger as Arthur knocked back a neat Whisky then continued. "They go cycling every Saturday morning along a remote dirt track by a disused railway line close to where they live in Widnes. It's just the sort of place where a terrible accident could happen". Jimmy interrupted the flow of conversation as he lifted up his paint glass, and after swallowing what was left of his lager in one gulp looked at them all with steel in his glare and said "Let's do it then. Let's do it right now and kick the fuckin shit out of them?" They all agreed but Arthur's experience as a copper reined them in "Nah, we need as much info as we can get first, and I know just how we can get it…" They all looked at him in anticipation of what he was going to say next when he grinned and added "But the next round's on Jimmy first!" Everybody burst out laughing.

Nobody had seen or heard anything of Dot since she returned home from Scotland married to Eddie D. She hadn't even had the courage or decency to face her poor mother, Val Harper, who was still out of her mind with worry over her. Everybody was disgusted that she could be behind the terrible beating that John Kelly had suffered weeks earlier and was still recovering from in hospital.

The truth was until Wendy Bingham visited her in the new house, and told her about all the rumors flying around Huyton, she was completely oblivious. She didn't know a thing about the attack and she was as horrified as everybody else when she found out. She was also frightened because she knew nobody would believe she didn't know anything about it.

Mar Kelly was taken aback when she heard the faint sound of sniffing coming from behind her as she sat at John's bedside. She was even more taken aback when she turned around and seen Dot; the girl she'd hoped to call daughter-in-law the girl she'd hoped would give her grandchildren, standing there, on her own she, like butter wouldn't melt as she cried into her tissue.

Brazen faced that she was, Dot had devastated everybody including her own family, when she run away to Gretna and married Eddie D. Eddie D who she'd obviously been carrying on with behind John's back all along. Using him as a cover in her game to stop her parent's finding out, proving all the rumors, every last sordid one of them had been true after all.

Now she had the brass neck to turn up at the hospital and put the water works on. "My God, you've got some nerve comin' here". It was the first time in Mar Kelly's life she actually wanted to hit someone, but for the fact her son was laying in his hospital bed, doped up to the eyeballs and fast asleep, with his arms and legs still in plaster she'd of done it. She'd of ragged the fuckin head off the treacherous little bitch! Instead she kept it low but the hostility in her voice wasn't wasted.

As Dot stood shaking with fear and upset, and out of guilt took everything that was thrown at her. "You've got some explaining to do and God help us Dot… If I find out you or that piece of shit you married had anything to do with this. I'll swing for you myself, so help I will".

Tears rolled down Dots cheeks as she looked at John in disbelief. He was still in a deep sleep and in traction. It looked as if most of his body was in plaster, and his poor lovely face was black and blue and badly bruised all over. Deep down in her heart she knew Eddie was behind it. She kept going over and over the day she married him. Remembering when she walked back into the lounge bar after getting changed into a new outfit but returned earlier than she was expected and unwittingly walked into Eddie D who was having a drink with the Higgnet twins.

She didn't know who they were at the time, or why they were there, but she knew it was for some kind of wrong doing. She overheard Eddie mocking "Poor bastard, we'll have to buy him a decent pair of crutches". Laughter filled the room then and Eddie patted one of them on the shoulder saying "Job well done lads", as he passed him a wad of cash. As soon as they saw her and she joined them they made their excuses and left.

Now looking at John she realized he never stood a chance of turning up to see her on the morning she left for Scotland. Eddie had obviously planned it all to the very last minute. So while sick with nerves thinking he'd got what he'd wanted and lost all respect for her, he was in fact already fighting for his life, and Eddie had secured himself a rock solid alibi.

None of it was ever meant to be like this. It was all just exciting and meant to be a laugh, a bit of fun. It was never meant to turn out this frightening and horrible. Mar Kelly's voice interrupted her thoughts. "Right, your ten minutes are up and God knows it's more than you deserve. So you can go now… And don't be in a rush to come back cos you're not welcome".

Mar Kelly was cold and cutting. Despite herself she'd given in to the girl's tears and groveling apologies, but she was sorely disappointed by her lack of explanation and information. Still, she reasoned with herself, every time John woke up the first person he asked for was Dot, and he couldn't understand why she wasn't there. And he was too poorly to be told the truth. That she hadn't gone on holiday with Wendy and her family. She'd gone to Gretna Green in Scotland and fuckin married Eddie D. He loved her so much and he when strong enough to be told that particular gem, only God himself could say how he'd take it.

Chapter Seven

Southport beach is terrifying at three in the morning. Especially after you've had a sack shoved over your head and been hog tied and thrown into the back of a navy blue transit van to take you there. "Right you piece of scum it's time to talk". Big Harry was standing next to Danny Owens looking down at Brian Murphy kneeling in the in the cold damp sand. He was trembling from head to toe aware that Dominic McGuire and Jimmy Kelly were both standing behind him.

His heart began thumping hard against his chest and convinced he was having a heart attack. He started pissing his pants with fear as he felt himself sinking into the sand. Big Harry nodded to Jimmy Kelly who in turn ragged the hood off Brain Murphy's head. Then Big Harry shone a torch into his eyes. "Wha' D'you know about Eddie D and the Higgnet twins attacking John Kelly?" Brian could hardly think straight with fear as he squinted into the beam of the torch.

"I don't know wha' you mean. I don't…"

He didn't get the chance to finish his sentence before Big Harry twated him full force in the face with the torch, and Jimmy shoved the hood back over his head. Then all four men dragged him along the sand screaming like a pig as blood gushed from his nose almost choking him as it ran down the back of his throat.

Arthur McNabb remained behind the wheel in the Transit van. As a copper used to driving at full speed on emergency call out's and police chases, he was the one who could get them back off that beach at brake neck speed, and he wouldn't need the headlights on to do it. He watched carefully as the silhouetted figures of the four lads dragged Brain right to the tip of the sea coming in. Then pushed him flat onto the sand where the incoming tide felt freezing cold as it lapped over his feet.

Big Harry then flashed the torch once and Arthur McNabb drove the van right up to them.

"High tide is in one hour. Time to meet your maker"

Big Harry's tone was mocking before shouting at the others "Quick! Get back in the van!" And as they did what he ordered he could hear them laughing as they drove away.

As Brain Murphy lay on the wet sand with his hands and feet still tied behind his back, and the blood still coming from his nose soaked into the sack covering his head. He heard the sound of the van drive off into the distance… Then the terrifying sound of the sea as the tide came in and lapped over his ankles and moved a little higher up his legs with each new wave.

And convinced he was at the very isolated and terrifying end to his life. He did indeed pray. That God would forgive his selfish and wasted life. Forgive his uncaring disregard for the needs of others. Forgive his cruel streak and cheating nature. His whole life flashed before him as he began drowning in his own fear as well as the sea. Seeing what a selfish son and brother he had always been. He'd brought nothing but trouble to his family, and now it was too late to tell them he was sorry. Too late to tell them he did love them. Too late to put any of it right and too much to bear when he screamed at God

"Get on with it and fuckin take me!"

Jimmy and the lads sat in the van watching the tide coming in. None of them had ever done anything like this before in their lives. Sure the army had trained Big Harry and Dominic McGuire how to kill a man. In battle and in war, but not in Civvie Street, and the police had trained Arthur McNabb how to get a confession out of a man, but not like this.

They were all in a little shock at what they were doing. At the fact they were all actually capable of reducing a man to nothing and leave him to meet his maker, alone and in terror. It was frightening but at the same time the awful truth was there was something thrilling about it. Something thrilling having power over another man's life and death. They had opened the gateway to the darkness that lurks in each of us, and like a dog once it's had the taste of blood. Hereafter they would be forever dangerous, and bonded by their dark secrets as well as their brotherly love for each other.

What seemed an eternity was in fact less than ten minutes when Brian Murphy again heard the sound of the Transit. Only this time it was coming towards him and stopped right next to him and the four lads jumped out of the back of it. They dragged him out of the water that had already covered his chest and was seeping its way up his neck, and they bungled him into the back of the van. He was hypothermic and dithering and his soaking wet clothes weighed heavy and stuck to him as they dripped all over the floor of the van. The stench of his own shit overwhelmed them all as he cried like a new born under his hood.

Jimmy Kelly again ragged off his hood, and then untied his wrists and feet. Then Big Harry stood glaring at him with disgust and utter revulsion before breaking the silence "Talk". Humiliated and petrified Brian Murphy told them everything they wanted to know about Eddie D paying the Higgnet twins to do in John Kelly.

Everyone was stunned. Old Joe Kelly had died in his sleep. No illness. No warning. He'd died, just like that, nodded off in his favorite chair with a solicitor's letter in his hand and never woke up. Nobody knew he'd even been to a solicitor, but he had. To extract what was owing to him from Tom Slone and names, on the Golf Club Management Committee. He wanted to fight them the proper way, because he didn't want his lads trying to sort it out for him and coming unstuck. But the letter stated the Golf Club had refused to pay him any more money and they would contest any court action taken against them.

Poor Mar Kelly was beside herself with grief. She was beyond words. She was so angry and heartbroken. In a matter of weeks she'd lost all hope and dreams of ever moving with Joe into a lovely retirement bungalow in Rainhill. She had lost all hope of seeing her son John marry the girl of his dreams. And now she had lost her beloved Joe forever.

She couldn't even let John know. Not yet. He was still far too weak from the beating. The doctors had said it would be a long road to recovery, and they were right. He was still physically weak and psychologically he was even weaker. Telling him about his Father's death *and* Dot marrying Eddie D would undo every bit of good work the doctors had done. It would set him right back and hinder all progress. So after much discussion with her eldest son Jimmy, his wife Jean, and her four lovely 'adopted sons', it was agreed. Telling John anything at this stage wasn't an option.

Old Joe Kelly was given a fitting send off by all his family, friends and neighbours, with a requiem mass at the local parish church followed by a burial at Huyton cemetery. Everybody went back to Mar Kelly's house for a do that Joe Kelly himself would have proud of, as they all shared stories of what a great man he'd been.

In the weeks that followed the funeral Mar Kelly spent most of her time in church or visiting John at the hospital. And she felt sure her prayers were being answered as John seemed stronger on every visit, and more alert as his meds were reduced. But he still couldn't remember anything about the attack. Nor could he understand why his dad had stopped visiting him so abruptly, and Dot had abandoned visiting him altogether.

So to save him further confusion and the distress it was causing him, it was agreed by all concerned agreed it was time to break the bad news on everything that had happened.

Jimmy and Mar Kelly were subdued as they sat around John's hospital bed.

Mar Kelly had just broken the news to him that not only was his dad dead but he was also buried. And not only did Dot go on holiday, she eloped to Gretna Green and married Eddie D.

Days earlier the police had visited him he told them he was unable to recall the attack. And as they were unable to gain any witnesses information or leads they had no option but to leave their investigation on file, but would open it up again if they got any new leads.

With no grasp of why anybody would want to beat him up and leave him for dead. No help from the police in catching whoever it was that done it. He was totally bewildered and felt like the world was against him. But finding out about the loss of his dad and Dot marrying Eddie on top of it was all was just too much.

At first he lay there in stunned silence, then he began sweating profusely and breathing heavily. It was a panic attack made worse by the fact he was still in plaster and couldn't move a muscle. His head was reeling, filled with unfathomable information, filled with confusion and his heart felt like it was breaking in two. Realising he was in a state of panic and shock, a state of raw grief, the nursing staff once again sedated him.

Chapter Eight

It was Saturday morning and with not a cloud in sight, it was just how the Higgnet twins liked it. Clear blue skies all the way as they rode their bikes towards the dirt track that led down the embankment to the disused railway track. But neither twin had seen the wire tied at head height until it was too late. Luckily they weren't decapitated as the wire cut deep into them as it abruptly stopped them in their tracks, and bounced them off the bikes.

They both landed on their back and Michael was knocked unconscious. Maurice on the other hand was badly stunned and gagging to breathe as he tried to roll over onto his hands and knees to get up. So he didn't see the two figures walk out from behind the bushes. Nor did he see the scaffolding bar that smashed down on the base of his spine shattering it instantly. It was Big Harry and Dominic McGuire and they then turned their attention to Michael and handed out the same punishment to him.

Their alibis were secure as they'd booked into hotels rooms in London the night before, and ordered breakfasts for each room, just like they always did when they followed Everton away. Then they left Jimmy Kelly and Danny Owens at the hotel and they left in the early hours. Arthur McNabb sped them back to Widnes, and now he was parked up and waiting for them as they slipped out of the bushes and straight into the back of his car, and within minutes he had them speeding back up the motorway to London. As Maurice and

Michael Higgnet, were left sprawled on the dirt path, unconscious and damaged for life.

Once back in London they met Jimmy and Danny at the ground Everton were playing at. Watched the match together and headed back to the hotel bar for another night of raucous laughter and flirting with the bar staff. So if need be they'd all be remembered and could prove to the police they couldn't be in two places at the same time.

The pressure was on for Big Harry and Dominic McGuire, as it was almost time for them to return to camp to be then posted on a six months tour of duty in Germany. So they decided to tie up as many loose ends as they could before leaving Huyton. So with Jimmy Kelly, Arthur McNabb, and Danny Owens, they walked into the Huyton Golf Club like they owned the place and headed straight for the bar. And as they crossed the room people stopped talking and you could have cut the atmosphere with a knife as they struck fear into everyone there. Especially Dot and her face drained of colour as they leaned against the bar waiting and to be served and stared right at her.

Only minutes before the conversation on everyone's lips had been about the terrible incident involving the Higgnet twins. Rumours were rife some saying vandals had attacked them. While others suspected it was probably somehow connected to the attack on poor young John Kelly, so it was some sort of punishment or revenge. Not that many cared either way cos as bent coppers the Higgnet twins were pretty much despised by most.

Brian Murphy on the other hand knew for sure it was Big Harry and the rest of his company that had left them both paralyzed. God knows they'd terrorized him to the brink of extinction, to get the information they needed on what the Higgnet twins done to John Kelly. But he knew better than to let on about that to anyone, or he'd just go down in local folk law as a dead grass. Dot didn't need Brian Murphy or anyone else telling her for that matter. She already knew, instinctively, that it was a punishment beating for what they'd done to John Kelly, and privately she too was glad that they got what they deserved.

Big Harry and the others walked away from the bar with their drink's and deliberately sat as close as they could to Dot and Eddie D, who were making up a foursome with Brian Murphy and Wendy Bingham. Dot was convinced they were there to stick it to Eddie before leaving. She could feel the panic in her rising as her mouth dried up and she began trembling, and feared her legs would buckle under her as she submitted to Big Harry's gestured to join them at their table.

She was the colour of boiled shite and trembling from head to toe but the first words out of her mouth were 'How's John?' So she had bottle they had to give her that. More than could be said of the shithouse she married. Cos he stayed sitting at his own table and left her to fend for herself as she stood there wearing the big gold wedding ring he'd put on her finger, right next to her very expensive looking engagement ring. "The poor bastard thinks you still love him and can't believe you've betrayed him by marring shit head over there". Still trembling she looked genuine when she said "I don't know what to do".

So through gritted teeth Jimmy added "Well I do. So here it is. You go back into that hospital. You tell him you don't love him. Then you fuck off and you don't ever fuck with his head or his life again. Have you got that?" She nodded 'I'll go in tomorrow' Jimmy looked her up and down like she was a piece full of shit "You better, cos that's the only way he'll see you for the dog you really are and get strong again and on move on… Now fuck off!"

She'd never felt so low or humiliated in her life, but as she walked away she suddenly stopped dead in her tracks and looked back at them all but looked Jimmy straight in the eye "Just for the record. You're dead wrong. Cos I do love him… and more than you'll ever know".

Everyone shuffled in their seat uneasily as Jimmy spat back in anger "then why marry that prick over there?'

Her reply shut them all up "Cos I got pregnant and had too, that's why!"

Jimmy's sister-in-law Colette was on duty and at John's bedside trying to get him to eat. Her heart went out to him as he poured out his grief to her daily, not realizing she already knew the whole story "you've got to eat to get well John, otherwise you'll never get out of this place". But depression had set so even though all the plaster had been removed from his arms and legs, he didn't care. Especially as Big Harry and Dominic McGuire were now back at army camp. So that was two more people he loved and was now missing.

Colette was back in the office and answered a timid knock on the office door. She wasn't surprised to see Dot standing at the other side of it as she'd been tipped off that she was coming in.

"Follow me and make it brief, he needs his rest".

Colette's tone was as snotty as she could make it, as she walked briskly ahead of Dot and pulled the curtains around John's bed to give them some privacy.

Dot took one look at John sleeping and broke down. She didn't know where to begin and wanted to hug him so much it hurt. Even though he was asleep it was as if he sensed she was there, because he opened his eyes looked straight at her and he broke down too.

'Is it true? Have you really married Eddie D?'

By now she was sobbing and all she could do was nod her head.

"Why though? I don't understand. Did I do summit wrong?"

She didn't want to hurt him anymore than she already had but she knew she had to follow through on her word, because she could see for herself that Jimmy was right. If she didn't, John would never get well again and move on.

"Look, it wasn't you ok. It was me. It was all me".

It was killing her but she was determined to sound as cold and uncaring as she could, determined to make him angry towards her because she knew that anger would make him strong. And if it helped she was even willing to make him hate her, and eventually hate her he would.

"Well I don't care. I'll forgive yeh… Cos I still love yeh…I still wonna be with yeh"

She felt sick to her stomach and knew it was time to be cruel to be kind

"Look, gerra grip, stop making' it harder on yourself. It's not about what you want. I shouldn't have led you on ok. I know tha now…I'm sorry ok. But it was just a laugh, it didn't really mean anything".

He lay there staring at her in disbelief. "Why have you come in to see me then?"

It was time to deliver the killer blow. "I wanted yeh to hear it from me first… I'm pregnant". Mission accomplished.

He was devastated "Gerrout! Fuck off! Go on, gerrout!"

Colette quickly pulled back the curtain from around his bed and glared at Dot.

"It's time you left" Dot felt the shame of what she'd done burn right through to her very soul. She turned her back on John and walked away from him for good, as the tears streamed down her face.

Chapter Nine

It was over a week since John had been told by Dot that she was pregnant. Colette and the doctors feared on top of everything else he'd to deal with, it would set his recovery right back. But it had done the complete opposite, and Jimmy was right all along. He had seen Dot for the bitch she really is and now that he had it had done the trick, and he was getting stronger every day. So much so, Jimmy told him about the solicitor's letter they found in his Dad's hand when he died, and also told him about terrifying the information they got out of Brian Murphy, about who beat him up. So he knew now it was the Higgnet twins and that they were paid to by Eddie D, for no other reason but pure jealously.

But now they had been paid back for it tenfold by Jimmy and the lads. The more John heard, the more he wanted to hear. He was piecing together every last detail, making sense of it all, realising how he'd been played all along by Dot. The more he worked it all out, the angrier he got and soon became hell bent on revenge.

Before being beaten up he was a naive and fun loving young man who was in love for the very first time. He was his father's proud young apprentice and he looked up to his big brother Jimmy and the rest of the lads as his idols. He was happier than he'd ever been after leaving school and finally becoming one of them. The kid brother of their own little gang and they all loved him as he loved them.

But that naïve and fun loving young man was gone forever. So too was Dot, and his father, who was unbelievably dead. Dead and buried and he hadn't even got to say goodbye, hadn't got the chance to show his last respects to his own Dad. He wasn't having it, wasn't having any of it. Now in place of his fun loving nature ice ran through his veins. As he decided he didn't yet know how or even when, but if it took him the rest of his life he'd have his revenge. He'd have Mr. and Mrs. Eddie fuckin D on a plate. D for dickheads, D for doesn't ever fuck with me and think you can get away with it. D for fuckin dead, and while he was at it, he'd have the cunts that ripped his Dad off too.

There's no mistaking a copper's knock, especially when it's a Jack from the CID, or plain clothes detective as the police preferred to call them. But when Wendy Bingham opened the front door to the house she'd moved into with Brian Murphy. This was no ordinary Jack. It was Superintendent Ralph Higgnet, all plain clothes and off duty, and one of Merseyside's best known bent coppers. He was on his own and barge and his way right past Wendy and walked straight into the living room. 'Okay, let's cut out all bull shit and get straight to the point. You tell me everything I wonna know and I'll let you live in peace… Now who put my two sons in wheelchairs for life?'

Brian sat with his head down. He wasn't getting dragged any further into this one, but Wendy could see Ralph Higgnet wasn't the sort of bent copper who'd walk away without anything. And word on the street was he was making everyone's life a misery with impromptu visits. So she reasoned with herself it was ok and safe to compromise, give him just enough to keep him off their backs without putting them at risk with the Kelly brothers and co.

"We only know what everyone else knows and it's only rumors like but…" If she'd have known what had happened to Brian Murphy in the early hours one morning on Southport beach, she'd of shit herself and kept her big fat gob shut. Brian wanted to shut it for her right there, right then, but it was too late. She'd already dropped all the names out of the hat; even Andy McNabb's who was a fuckin bent copper himself. Brian though she had more sense, thought she was savvier, what the fuck was she thinking of naming fuckin names like that?

Then again, it was his own fuckin fault, yeh he blamed himself completely, becasue that's what you get when you think with your dick. That's what you get when you shack up with a girl who's not long walked out of the fuckin school gates.

She might have been fifteen going on fifty when they first met, and now at almost seventeen she might be as good as any mature woman in the bedroom department. But she was still just a kid, a young girl, a fuckin liability. He jumped up off the couch "Right, that's it. We've got nothin else to say and them names are on everyone's lips. So go and put pressure on someone else cos we don't know anything".

Ralph Higgnet smirked, he knew his two sons had something to do with young John Kelly being left for dead in the gutter. But he wasn't the least bit bothered by that. He'd just got enough to be going on with for now so he tipped them a nod 'I'll see myself out'. Turned his back on them and left as quickly as he'd arrived.

Arthur McNabb didn't bat an eye as he sat on a straight back chair in front of the finely polished conference desk answering to his Superintendent Ralph Higgnet, who was determined to get to the bottom of who destroyed his sons lives and why?

He wanted to know the ins and outs of a cats arse. What was the word on the street about Eddie D and Brian Murphy? What was their connection to John Kelly and his brother Jimmy? And what the fuck did any of it have to do with Big Harry and Dominic McGuire? Clearly there was a lot of talk going on all over Huyton and clearly this bent bastard was piecing it all together. So one by one Arthur McNabb answered all his questions and told him what he wanted to know. Adding "John Kelly's attack was unprovoked and completely undeserved, and he's lucky he survived. So those responsible had to be punished". Ralph Higgnet was stunned for a moment "are you saying what I think you're saying?".

Arthur McNabb grinned.

"I'm saying it would be wise to carefully consider the consequences of any arrests and charges brought to bear on those you think are responsible".

"I beg your pardon?"

Ralph Higgnet was gob smacked. He couldn't believe the audacity and sheer nerve of the man. Sitting there in his office, as cool as a fuckin cucumber and warning him not to charge the scum that crippled his own sons.

Calm as you like Arthur McNabb added "The attack on your two sons happened around about the time I watched Everton's pre-season friendly with your so called suspects, in London."

He grinned again before continuing "good match too as I recall. You'll have no trouble getting our stay down there verified by the hostel staff".

Ralph Higgnet was raging.

"If you think you can sit there and tell me you're somehow involved in the attack on my two sons, and then warn me off the case you're off another fuckin planet man!".

Arthur tut tutted. "Listen you prick, your two sons are as bent as you are and there's a fuckin big long line of con's and inmates bearing very big grudges against the lot of you. Every last one of them are onside and ready to blow you all out the fuckin water" Ralph Higgnet didn't alter his stark expression but a brief show of panic flashed in his eyes as Arthur McNabb stared at him menacingly before grinning yet again and giving him his final warning.

"You really are gonna have to close the file on this one".

He then stood up and walked towards the office door and stopped as he put his hand on the handle.

"Oh, and don't go gettin' any crazy ideas, cos if anything happens to me or my brothers as a result of this chat - your whole family will suffer… beginning with that half a million pound mansion you all live in being burnt out. That's a promise."

He then opened the door and casually walked out grinning to himself this time, as no such plan of action was in place. It was pure bluff.

Arthur McNabb confirmed all Ralph Higgnet's suspicions that Eddie D had taken Dot from John Kelly, and paid his two sons to frighten him off her permanently. Yet they let him jump through fuckin hoops and be humiliated to find out the truth of that. They could have told him themselves. After all they'd lost the use of their legs not their fucking brains. They could have saved him all this fuckin agro. If they weren't cripples already he'd fuck cripple them himself.

Well fuck them. Fuck the two of them. Their actions had led to Arthur McNabb laying down the law to him. A senior ranking police officer and in his own fuckin office too. And it would be impossible to make any charges stick on Big Harry and Dominic McGuire. Any effort to try would result in his whole family being destroyed. As they'd all be burnt out and he and his two sons would all be exposed as bent coppers.

They'd all be finished for life. Beside the loss of career and status, it would also mean the loss of all pensions and that was one serious wedge. It wasn't ideal and it certainly wasn't what he wanted, but this problem had to away and the only way to achieve that was by getting rid of Arthur McNabb. But it had to be in a way that smoothed every one over, pleased all concerned.

Even though it galled Ralph Higgnet more than words could ever say, he decided to give McNabb what he'd always wanted and arranged for his transfer to the Met in London. So he could finally work with the anti-terrorist unit dealing with the IRA, and he hoped to God that he'd get blown to kingdom come while he was at it.

Chapter Ten

Six months had passed since John's attack. After undergoing an intense programme of physiotherapy to strengthen the muscles in his arms and legs, he was finally physically fit enough to be fully discharged. Mentally though it was a different matter. His mind remained in turmoil by all that had happened and once back home in his mother's house the loss of his father hit him like a ton of bricks.

The grief was all consuming and made worse by his clan moving forward with their lives. Big Harry and Dominic McGuire were still serving in Germany with the Army. Arthur McNabb had been working undercover with the anti-terrorist unit in London. Danny Owns was still working over in Jersey, making a good living as a Plummer. Rumor had it even Brian Murphy had fucked off to Cardiff to work. He felt he couldn't even get close to his brother Jimmy as he spent every spare minute he got being a good husband to Jean. Jimmy was working on a piece of land that he'd bought in Huyton Village, building a four bedroom house for them.

Everything was different and nothing would ever be the same again. His life had changed forever and so had he. Right now life felt pretty empty and bleak. He had far too much time on his hands to think and pine away for his Dad, and Dot. She seemed to rub salt in his wounds as her and Wendy Bingham 'tear-arsed' around Huyton showing off Dot's brand new Mini Cooper like they didn't have a care in the world.

Unable to stand the sense of loss and emptiness any longer and encouraged by his mother and Jimmy, he decided to go back to Blair Hall. He'd spent many happy times there with the lads learning Martial Arts. The Sensei, an Irish guy called Jimmy Mac, kept a close eye on him as he spent hours at a time doing press up's on his knuckles to build up his upper body strength. But at the end of one such session he sheepishly approached John and told him because of his recent injuries to his arms and legs, the club insurance wouldn't cover him to compete at competition level.

John stood glaring at him for a moment, disappointed by his apparent lack of understanding and attitude "I've been workin' my bollocks off to make sure nobody will ever get away with tryin' to kill me or put me in hospital again. Not to win some fuckin fancy rosette and nice colored belt… So fuck you and fuck your insurance!"

Much to everyone's surprise, on top of his small construction business, Old Joe Kelly had salted away a modest amount of money to leave behind to his wife and two sons after he died. So Mar Kelly and Jimmy both encouraged John to use some of his share to go to Jersey and stay with Danny Owens. The trip would help get him strong enough to move on from all that had happened. To their relief John agreed. He did need to put the past behind him and it was good idea.

He travelled by Ferry and when he arrived in Jersey, Danny was waiting for him with a huge smile on his face as he disembarked. The first thing they did was hug "you're a sight for sore eyes you are lad, yeh look great!"

John was made up to be given such a warm welcome and instinctively knew he'd done the right thing leaving Liverpool for a while, as they walked away together laughing and joking with Danny carrying his kit. He knew with every step he took this was just what he needed and he couldn't wait to book into his room at the boarding house.

The owners were a middle aged couple called George and Margaret Davenport, and they also owned a row of small shops and the local chippy.

Danny had already told them all about John's attack before he arrived, but they knew better than to talk about it when they met him. Instead they shook his hand and gave him the warmest of welcomes. John took to them instantly and paid them for a four week stay in advance. The boarding house was situated very close to the harbor where he spent most of his time strolling. He soaked up the sun and day dreamed about owning a fantastic yacht like the ones the bobbed up and down all along the harbor. He was completely smitten and Jersey had begun the process of healing his heart.

Danny joined him most nights after work for their evening meal from the chippy, or the local pub where they downed a couple of pints. They laughed together about all the good times they'd shared growing up in Liverpool. It was the first time he'd felt happy and relaxed since before the attack.

It was a typical Friday night, as Danny went out and pulled a different girl. Most of his conquests were holiday makers and went back home on the Saturday morning. So he never had to see them again, which was just the way he liked it. But thanks to Dot, John's trust was well and truly shattered in women. So he spent Friday night going to George and Margaret Davenport in their local pub that overlooked the harbor.

They liked John. He was a very warm and friendly lad and he was also very respectful towards them and well behaved, unlike a lot of the young holiday makers that had stayed at their boarding house. They could see he'd obviously been brought up well, but they could also see he was troubled as his sadness, his grief, showed in soulful blue eyes. John couldn't help but tell them how much he'd fallen in love with Jersey and how he envied Danny living and working there.

George smiled "Nah, no need to envy the lad. Just try your luck at the building site fifteen minutes up the road? I'm sure you'd get a start there and we could always come to an arrangement over a permanent room for you, couldn't we Margaret?"

She smiled in agreement. "Of course we could". That was it. It was like a light had just been turned on and he didn't have to think twice. He was going to get a job and live in Jersey and nothing was going to stop him.

Mar Kelly and Jimmy were over the moon to see John back home and looking so tanned and healthy. They'd missed him like mad and listened with delight as told them all about the impressive yachts that took pride of place in the harbor and belonged to millionaires. How beautiful fresh and clean Jersey was in comparison to city life, and how lovely George and Margaret Davenport were to him. They hadn't seen him this animated and happy since before his attack and losing his dad and they couldn't have been happier. Then he dropped the bombshell.

"So I've decided, I'm goin' back over there to work and live".

Mar Kelly's heart sunk as a flood of questions flowed from her lips.

"Work where? Doin what? And where will you live?"

All questions John knew she would ask and he had all the answers ready.

"I start on a building site for an Irish fella called Billy Walsh and his two son's Shamus and Shaun". She interrupted "but you're only an apprentice". He reassured her that didn't matter, because after a lifetime of training from his dad he knew he could keep up with the best of them. She knew that too. Old Joe Kelly had often told her with pride just how good he was at the plastering. Jimmy was made up

"So are you gonna live with Danny?"

John shook his head "Nah, I've gorra good deal off George and Margaret so I'll 'ave me own room at their boarding house".

Mar Kelly knew he youngest son had gone away a young lad and come home a man. He'd grown up. He'd gone away hurting and sad and with no hope of a future. He'd come home bright and full of hope and promise and she knew it was her time to let him go.

She also knew as only a Mother could that her son, her youngest son, who she brought into this cruel and unjust world and held so tightly, nurtured so lovingly, would never be the same again. Would never be that lovely innocent and naive little boy. That gentle and caring lad, who's every hurt she could kiss better and make go away, because he was man now and all those childish ways had gone. But more than that, something inside him had gone.

She could see it in his beautiful blue eyes. Something inside him had died and she knew it would never come back, just as she knew he would never come back to Liverpool to live. Her youngest boy had changed forever and there was hardness in his heart, and she knew he hadn't even realized it himself yet. She just hoped and would pray to the Blessed Virgin he wouldn't discover it by hurting others.

As soon as John arrived back in Jersey he felt like he was back at home and soon settled into his new life. He loved working on the site with Billy Walsh and his two lads and they were suitably impressed by him because he knew his trade alright, there was no doubting that.

Outside of work he was fitting right into the local community too. He helped George Davenport every Saturday morning to unload the potato delivery straight from their farm to their chippy. In return for the gesture George and Margaret stood him a few pints every Saturday night in their local, the Rose and Crown. It was during one such get together they told him they had a sixteen year old daughter called Lesley who was at an all-girls private boarding school in England. They had great plans for her to go on to University. And they looked forward to introducing him to her on one of her term breaks.

After his experience with Dot, he didn't care how nice these people seemed or how lovely their daughter might be, he was still off women and only interested in being just friends with any girl. Something he eventually confided when he told them all about Dot, and he was relieved when they totally understood and respected his feelings, still not realizing Danny had already told them everything.

The one thing that was annoying John was the site agent; a guy called Tony, who as far as John was concerned seemed to be an alright fella, but he couldn't organize a piss up in a brewery. John had to constantly chase up the electricians and plumbers to have the houses ready ahead of him, because he couldn't rely on Tony telling them. But even if he did, the tradesmen didn't take any notice because they thought Tony was a complete knob. How the fuck he got such a responsible job was a right conundrum.

Until Shaun Walsh explained Tony was the rich nephew of the Burgess Family who owned the Channel Island Development Corporation. It was one of the biggest development companies on the island and the south of England, with a host of other companies including the Channel Island Building Society.

Tony had dropped out of University. His aunty and uncle, Rene and Edward Burgess, who were major shareholders on the board of directors, put him there to get a taste of the real world. It also allowed him to earn a living. However he was like 'a round peg' in a square hole and it was painful to see. Made worse by the fact he blamed everyone but himself for his short comings and giving out wrong completion dates to prospective buyers.

It was late Friday afternoon and most of the men had finished for the weekend and gone off-site. John was still there making a brew, when in walked Tony with a very attractive well-dressed woman. She looked in her forties and was as posh as fuck. They ignored John and walked right past him to the desk and Tony took the site plans out of the draw and opened them up. It was impossible not to hear their conversation as Tony fed her bull-shit about a plot being ready to move into for the February.

John shook his head, it was two weeks before Christmas and most of the contractors were due to finish the following week and as most of them lived on the mainland, they wouldn't be returning until the second week into the New Year. So he couldn't resist putting his ore in

"Last week in March love. That'll be the earliest you can expect to move into that plot".

He then walked out of the site hut with his mug of tea. Tony was embarrassed.

"Who was that?"

"Typical Scouse 'know it all!"

But she wasn't impressed. For this was Rene Burgess and when on site she was his Director, not his aunty. She was furious as several of her friends had purchased properties and Tony had given them all inaccurate information and the wrong moving in dates. But all had said the young Scouse plasterer had been very helpful and worth his weight in gold in sorting out their enquiries and problems.

But for the fact he was her nephew she'd have fired Tony there and then. She instead chose to do a little homework on John and got Tony to give her all his details and address.

Margaret Davenport was delighted when she opened her front door.

"Rene! What a pleasant surprise! Come in, come in".

The two women kissed cheek to cheek and Rene followed as Margaret led them the kitchen for coffee.

"I've got a favour to ask".

Straight to the point as always Rene continued.

"One of your boarders is one of my plasterers. A Scouse, called John Kelly. What do you know about him?"

Over coffee Margaret told her everything that John had been through before moving to Jersey. How Dot had shattered his confidence and trust in women. How Eddie D paid the Higgnet twins work him over and they left him almost for dead in a gutter. How his dad had died and was buried while he was still in a coma.

"Yet all things considered Rene, he's a lovely young man; hardworking, respectful and reliable too. He's not only on time with his rent he's always in advance with it".

Adding "George and I have grown quite fond of him to be honest, and I think he's grown close to George because he sees him as a father figure after losing his dad". Rene had heard all she needed to know.

Chapter Eleven

John was enjoying his usual Saturday night pint with George Davenport as they waited for Margaret to turn up from one of her ladies guild meetings at her local church. When she walked laughing and joking with Rene Burgess. John couldn't believe it. "Shit!". George looked at him shocked "What's the matter?" He picked up his pint fast and tried to talk behind it "See tha' posh bird who's just walked in with Margaret, she was on the site yesterday getting messed around by Tony".

George smiled but he didn't have time to answer as Margaret and Rene joined them, and George stood up to greet them like Rene was the fuckin' queen. "Rene, it's been a while. You're looking as fabulous as ever". They kissed cheek to cheek before he turned to John.

"This is John, who as you know works on one of your sites".

She then looked at John and smiled.

"John, meet Rene Burgess, your employer".

He laughed as he added "She's one of the major shareholders on the site you work at."

John couldn't hide his surprise or embarrassment as he stood up to shake her hand "Please to meet you love and er…"

He didn't get a chance to finish his sentence when Rene smiled.

"Its fine John, I know you thought I was a customer yesterday".

Just then Margaret helped them all out. "Right then, why don't you two boys go and get the drinks in before Rene and I die of thirst".

A few drinks later when they were all relaxed and having a good time Rene asked John what he thought the problem was with Tony.

"He's a nice enough fella but he doesn't have the respect of the others because they know he doesn't really know any of the trades".

She nodded.

"Okay, so what would you do if you were in his position?"

He thought about it for a moment.

'Well, I'd call them into the office and tell them I expected all remaining units ready for plastering no later than the second week in January or they'd be out, and new contractors would be in".

She was impressed and John had her full attention as he continued.

"They know plenty of contractors would jump at the chance to get on the books of Channel Island Development Corporation. So believe me, they'd have that work done to deadline".

At that point George piped in "Rene dear, have you come here to grill John or for a catch up with old friends? How's that old fart of a husband of yours? Still working in the New York office?"

Rene left her conversation with John in mid-air as she began engaging with George and Margaret. But she couldn't help eyeing John up for the rest of the night.

She liked the way he was able to assert himself and hold his own in company that was not only much older than him, but also much more cultured and affluent. He was younger than her other lovers and far less educated, that was obvious, but he was much warmer and more real.

Every one of them had been players and simply said what they thought she wanted to hear because she was so wealthy, so fabulously rich, and they were out to use her as much as she used them. But this fine specimen of Scouse rough was far too genuine for that, and he'd run a mile if she made a pass at him. So she decided there and then she'd enjoy taking it all very slowly and play the seduction game.

It was Monday morning and John didn't have a clue why Tony had just shouted across the site for him to come to the site office. Once inside he was surprised to see Rene standing there "Morning John, I'll get right to the point. You have a very good working knowledge and background in the building industry, and Tony could do with somebody like that to show him the ropes. So as of today I'm making you the site Foreman. It will be reflected in your pay packet of course".

John was shocked "But worra bout…" She interrupted him "Don't worry about Billy Walsh. I've had a word. So, you now work directly for Chanel Isle Development Corporation and not contracted through Billy and he's fine with it". She didn't just want him for Tony. Her sites were set on having him for herself and by fair means or fowl Rene Burgess always got what she wanted,

John was ecstatic and couldn't believe his luck and pointed out to Tony now was the perfect time for them to make their mark. Tony starred at him for direction "How?" John grinned "Tell everyone you want them in the office to sort out their Christmas bonus. They'll soon appear. When they do, tell them if they haven't got the remaining units finished by the end of the last week in January, they're out! Then tell them you'll have new contractors brought in to finish the work to schedule".

Tony looked like a rabbit caught in the headlights but he followed through on everything John said, and at the end of the week when everyone knocked off for the Christmas break. John and Danny caught a flight back to Liverpool. Both were in really high spirits, as Big Harry and Dominic McGuire were home on leave and Arthur McNabb was also home from London. Danny was also made up because he knew as long as John was working directly for CIDC as a Foreman, he was guaranteed to stay on the pay roll.

When they arrived back at Mar Kelly's the atmosphere was fantastic! It was hugs, kisses, and presents. Everyone was laughing as Danny took the piss out of John saying 'he was only made Foreman because he kissed the arse of the boss's wife and she was some posh middle aged bird!'. John roared with laughter adding "Listen, I'd kiss the arse off me fuckin arl granny if she put me salary up by tha' much!"

Mar Kelly hadn't laughed so much or felt this happy since before losing Old Jo. It was a blessing and a tonic to have them all home at the same time. But the time seemed to fly past. Once through

Christmas day and the wonderful Christmas dinner cooked up by Mar Kelly and Jimmy's wife, Jean, New Years Eve was upon. They all went to the 'She Club' to bring in the New Year.

They all took the piss out of Arthur McNabb because while they were all clean shaven and in their best suits, he'd grown a full beard and had took to wearing a flat cap as part of his undercover role. But behind all the piss taking they respected him and his job, which had him working on a building site in the middle of London so he could ingratiate himself into the Irish community there. The upshot being he was on two salaries, one off the site and the other off the police.

So he'd started to accumulate quite a big bank balance. The 'She' was bouncing as it held over five hundred and was full to capacity with the sound of steamers and horns repeatedly going off over the sound of the music. At some point John made his way to the gents so he could get back to the lads in time for midnight. As he started to squeeze his way back to the dance floor, there standing right in front of him as large as life was Dot.

It was as if every celebratory sound disappeared into the background and time itself stood still. He felt the power leave him and the colour drain from his face as his mouth dried up and he began to tremble. "Can we talk… please?" He couldn't believe her audacity but he was incapable of speech and just nodded. "Quick, come this way". She grabbed his hand and led him away from the basement disco through a maze of party goers and drunken revelers up to the middle floor cabaret area, and by sheer luck managed to get them into a small booth. It was still loud but at least here they could talk here.

John sat looking at her still speechless "Look, just let me finish before you say anythin', ok?" He nodded. "I admit I did only get with you keep my parents off the scent of me seein' Eddie… But it backfired on me because I started to have genuine feelings for you John". He went to speak but she put her finger over his lips "Please, let me finish, yeah?" Again he nodded. "It all went wrong, really horrible and wrong, and I wanted it over. Over between me and him, not me and you".

He was churning inside and couldn't stop himself 'Why the fuck are you tellin me all this shit?' She looked him in the eye "I need you to know when we spent our last night together an I asked you to join me early the next day, it was cos I needed to talk to you… I was goin to tell you everythin John, and I was goin to ask you to give me a second chance cos I'd fell in love with you. But when you didn't turn up I didn't know what to think… Because I honestly didn't have a clue you'd been attacked".

At that point she put her hand on his and squeezed it "I had nothin to do with tha John and I'm so sorry for everythin, I'm ashamed too, and for what it's worth, I want you to know I'll probably pay for it all for the rest of my life. Cos I'm in a loveless marriage with a man I can't stand but I'll stay with him for Michael's sake". John frowned "who's Michael?"

He felt like he'd been kicked in the guts when she said "my son". He'd heard as much as he could take. He believed her when she said she knew nothing about his attack. He believed her too when she said she was sorry and that she did love him. But none of that altered the fact that she had still played him good and proper. Even when she knew exactly how much he was in love with her.

How much he was still in love with her and he hated himself for it. He wanted to hate her too and God knows he'd tried hard enough. But he just couldn't. He hated Eddie D though. He'd always hate him, and even if it took him the rest of his life he'd see the day of that flash bastard. And he'd make him live to regret the day he ever crossed John Kelly. But tonight was New Year's Eve. A time to let out the old and bring in the new. So Dot could fuck-off back to her loveless marriage and her son. He was fucking off back to Jersey and he couldn't wait.

5…4…3…2…1…Happy New Year!

The place erupted to a cacophony of sounds, bagpipes, party poppers and streamers, even the fog horns from the ships on the river Mersey could be heard over those singing *'Should old acquaintance be forgot for the sake of auld langsyne'*. Everyone was kissing and hugging and wishing each other all the best, and there out the corner of his eye John could see Dot crying. She was pissed and had eyes like a panda with her mascara was running.

As Wendy Bingham who was just as pissed tried to wipe them and drag her onto the dance floor to celebrate. So he picked up his glass of neat Whisky held it up to the ceiling and said "this one's for you Dad" then knocked it straight back put the glass back down on the table and said to Jimmy "I'm gettin off. See you back home lad".

As he went to walk away Jean grabbed his arm "Are you gonna be alright John?" He'd never felt so sad in all his life yet in a weird sort of way he'd also never felt more certain that he was going to be alright. He looked back at Jean with a smile full of sadness. "She had a son". He then kissed her on the cheek "but don't worry I'm ok with it" then rolling his eyes to the ceiling added "me dad's watchin over me". He then winked at her warmly "see you back at me mam's" and he left the club and his past behind.

It was the second of January and everybody was making tracks back from where they came. Mar Kelly was flustered as she stood at the door with Jimmy and Jean waving them all off.

Arthur McNabb was back off to the smoke to continue with his undercover work. Big Harry and Dominic McGuire had been selected for a special training assignment that was supposed to be 'hush-hush'. But they let everyone know they'd soon be flying off to South America, spending two days on Christmas Island before going to a British Garrison base in Belize.

Danny Owens was heading back to Jersey with John. So it was hugs all round with tears from Jean and Mar Kelly. The lads felt like shedding a tear themselves but for Mar Kelly's sake they stayed strong as they finally all parted ways.

John arrived back in Jersey energized and rearing to go in his new role as Site Foreman and Tony was really pleased to see him back on the site. Not least of all because John's directive had worked. All the subcontractors were pushing ahead with their work, joined by Billy Walsh and his two sons who were pushing on with the plastering.

The result being the whole development was back on track and set for a March completion date.

Rene dropped by for a progress report and was delighted with the results. So she gave Tony the green light for him and John to start on the next twenty units. John was over the moon and keen to make the most of the opportunity to impress saying "the ground workers are able to start on the foundations right away. But I think it's best if we get shut of the shirkers. I can bring in a gang of brickies from Liverpool". Adding "They can get digs near to the site and be here eight am prompt every day. They're not frightened of hard graft and won't mind putting in a six or seven day week".

Rene liked his ambitious streak, but looked at Tony. "What do you think?" Tony was excited by John's ability to make things happen and get the best of out the workers. "I agree. It would be good to have some new faces here, and it would send out a clear message to all the contractors. If they're not good enough and hold us back. We replace them. Simple as that".

Rene was delighted with Tony's new found confidence and enthusiasm for the job and she knew it was thanks to John. She could see there was a healthy respect building up between the two of them and they made a good a team. So she gave them the go ahead. She'd barely stepped foot on the site office and John was on the blower to Liverpool. He immediately arranged for a 'two and a four gang' of bricklayers to join him in Jersey by the end of the month.

Ray Hall was the contracts manager for CIDC and was in charge of all the construction that was carried out on the island, and Rene made a point of introducing him to John personally. Ray quizzed him a little about his previous experience in the building trade, and was really impressed by his working knowledge. As it was clear he knew exactly what he was talking about and his background was obviously steeped in construction. It was clearly in his blood.

Rene was delighted to hear such comments and coming from Ray Hall. It was high praise indeed, and the more she heard and seen of John, the more determined she became to make him her very own personal project. John in the meantime formed a strong working relationship with Tony, and the two of them went from strength to strength. The bricklayers arrived from Liverpool and were doing a brilliant job and the new development was forging full steam ahead.

When John got on the phone and requested twenty thousand more bricks he was surprised by Ray's response "You have got to be joking! You only took a delivery of the last lot two weeks ago". Ray wasn't best pleased but John insisted everything was fine and he just wanted the superstructure on the new development to be finished by April.

But Ray sent in the quantity surveyor to have a good look around the place unassisted, to make sure everything was above board. He was relieved and impressed in equal measure when he read the surveyor's report. As not only was everything as it should be. The work was to the highest standard and the whole development was ahead of schedule. Adding the Foreman seemed to have an outstanding work ethic and the ability for getting the maximum effort and standard of work from his men with the minimum of ease. Ray conceded John had well and truly secured his future with CIDC. And with the way Rene had been eying him up, that wasn't all he'd secured.

John was sitting in the chippy eating a fish supper, when in walked a slim and very attractive girl with dark shoulder length hair and big brown eyes. She looked about seventeen and was drop dead gorgeous. She was with her friend who in comparison was a bit nondescript and the two of they were laughing and chatting as they stood waiting to be served. It reminded him of how Dot used to be with Wendy Bingham, but he immediately put that thought right out of his head.

This was a new year and a new start and that's how he intended to keep it. Then he heard Betty who worked behind the counter call her Lesley. So he mouthed the words to Betty 'is tha' George and Margaret's daughter?' She smiled and nodded and as she took their money and passed them their chips she said "Oh by the way Lesley love, that's John who stays at your mum and Dad's boarding house and works for Rene Burgess".

The girls smiled a little, as they took their chips and John stood up smiling ready to speak to them. But they walked straight passed him without so much as a side glance. He felt a fool and couldn't help himself as he shouted after them "nice to meet you too". Betty giggled "take no notice John, she's just a little shy".

John liked Betty. She was a big hefty woman with short grey hair and a round face; she was warm and friendly and was always smiling. She was one of those motherly types and she'd made him feel welcome from his first day on the island. He'd spent many an evening nattering to her over a fish supper, and was always amazed by how much she knew about so many living on the island.

There was never anything malicious in what she said, quite the opposite in fact as she was always considerate in her opinions and didn't tend to judge. But she was honest and told it like it was and it's fair to say she'd worked in that chippy for that many years not much got to Betty.

"She seems more like a right stuck up bitch to me".

Betty gave her usual warm smile.

"No lad, she's not. But I'll tell you who is. Rupert Burgess. That's Rene's grandson, he's no manners or respect either. He's just very rude and arrogant and he's a bloody bully too. If Lesley's home from boarding school, he must be home from Uni. So if you get to meet him be forewarned, he's as nasty as dish water".

John smiled. "Ah don't worry about me Betty, cos I can take care of myself girl".

Nonetheless, he was grateful for the heads up'. Over his next few visits to the chippy he made it his business to sit around get the rest of the low down on Rupert Burgess. And there was a fair old bit of history surrounding his boss Rene and Rupert Burgess... he was most certainly a force to be reckoned with.

It appeared Rene Burgess was the step-grandmother to Rupert. Edward her husband had married once before. His first wife died tragically in childbirth, leaving him with a son, also called Rupert. The war came along and Edward was very much caught up in it. So his sister Margo took on young Rupert, who was two years old at that time. Margo's health deteriorated and she was forced to move in with her best friend, Rene.

Poor Margo died of a massive heart attack. With Edward away at war, Rene kept full care and custody over Rupert for the following four years. When the war ended and his father Edward returned, he was devastated at the loss of his sister Margo. Edward was consoled and comforted by Rene and they eventually fell in love and married. Edward insisted on sending Rupert to boarding school, something Rupert desperately didn't want to do and he deeply resented both his father and Rene for it.

Rupert grew cold towards them and resentful; he felt he was a burden. He became disturbed and rebellious, and who could blame him? His life had begun at the cost of his own mother's life. He believed the strain of his poor Aunt Margo caring for him was too much for weak heart, so he had killed her off too. Then his father returned and put a wedge between him and Rene and that rejection was felt all the stronger when they sent him away to boarding school.

So he deliberately failed at everything he done. When he was old enough he left home, rejecting all security and wealth to live as a farmhand. It was the biggest insult and hurt he could afford them. He then met a young woman called Lilly who he married without informing his father or Rene and she had his baby, a son, who he named Rupert. But he soon realized he needed more than a farmhand's wage to give the child a secure future so he joined the British army and was eventually posted to Northern Ireland, where he was shot dead by a member of the IRA.

Edward and Rene were said to be heartbroken but never spoke of their pain except to each other. Then when their only grandson Rupert was just two years old his mother Lilly died in a car crash. Again they were devastated, but again they never spoke about it outside of the family and they reared Rupert.

They showered him with as much love as they were capable of and gave him a life that most people would only dream of, read about in fancy magazines, or see in the movies. He was unlike his own father, who rejected the family fame and fortune, in search of true love and happiness. Rupert Jnr was an obnoxious spoilt brat, who thrived on both the name and fortune of the Burgess Empire. John was amazed by it all and glad that Betty had put him so clearly in the picture.

Chapter Twelve

By midsummer the construction that John and Tony were working on was almost complete. Rene was like the cat that got the cream as Ray Hall gave a progress report to the CIDC Board of Directors. "Thanks to John Kelly, our new Foreman, we're three months ahead of schedule and can now go ahead on the next development. For which I propose we use him again". A lengthy discussion followed on the pros and cons of Ray's proposal, as the new development was renovating an old army hospital they owned into an orphanage to be leased to the Government. It was quite a prestige's job.

But it was finally agreed to give John the opportunity of working on it with Tony. His work record was outstanding and it was time for CIDC to invest in some fresh young blood. John was over the moon as he shared the news with Margaret and George in the Rose and Crown on their usual Saturday night out together. He was all the more made up because their daughter Lesley was with them. This was to become a regular occurrence He could see Betty was right - she was shy, and he liked her a lot. He was doing his best to impress her with the responsibilities of his new role as Forman.

George and Margret gave one another a knowing look. They could tell that the youngsters were getting closer, as they were increasing spending a lot of time together. Margret was not surprised when Lesley told her she was taking a year out before going to university and she would help out in the family business. Her little girl was beginning to grow into a beautiful young woman. She was secretly pleased to be spending extra time with her before her daughter flies the nest.

By contrast, Rene was dining out with her husband Edward in their favorite restaurant. "Well my dear, I've been wondering what's put the spring back in your step, now I know". He knew the signs. He'd seen it all before many times. She picked up her glass of wine and deliberately looked at him like she was bored. "Really?!" Edward smiled "Yes really. I must admit it was a good move to put him in with Tony… But have you slept with him yet, this new young Foreman of yours?" Rene smiled "John. His name is John. And no I haven't as it happens". Edward laughed heartedly "I do hope you're not losing your pulling power my dear".

She hated it when he was like this. "Oh do shut up Edward". They had an understanding.

They'd always had an understanding. He slept with his mistresses and there had been plenty over the years. She slept with her lovers, mostly young pretty boy lovers. She often lavished gifts on them, before getting bored and moving on to the next one. But there hadn't been any of late and she knew it was it was because of her age and she was beginning to feel insecure. So it didn't help when Edward made ridiculous comments, especially as he seemed to get better with age and was never short of a beautiful woman.

They were as interested in him now as they had ever been. And he was twenty years older than her, which she deeply resented. Still she knew no matter how beautiful the women were in Edward's life or how exciting the young men were in her own. She and Edward would never part as they were bound together by the love of a boy who grew up to be a brave young soldier, who was shot dead by a member of the IRA.

Bound together by the sorrow and loss, his unforgivably early death had brought to them both. Bound too by the guilt they shared for the confusion and rejection he felt from them all his life. Such things were enough to rip any two people apart, but not these two, because they really did love each other. Not in a physical sense, that had been sorely lacking from the start. It was why they'd agreed to let that particular need be met by others.

For the love they did have for each other went far deeper than any sexual relationship could ever bring. They were also bound together by an international business empire and hundreds of millions of pounds. Wealth acquired through vast amounts of inheritance on both their parts, including gold bullion and great works of art, legitimately given to Edward to hide in his Swiss bank accounts at the start of the war. This was to prevent it being stolen by the Nazis. But many of its rightful owners and their descendants had lost their lives in the concentration camps.

What Edward was unable to return to the rightful owners, he invested into his bank and companies, with the proviso any legitimate claims made on it would be honored. And every last unclaimed penny along with all other assets and businesses was to be left to their grandson Rupert, who boasted about the fact to anyone who'd listen.

John sat on the small harbor wall and gazed out to sea while he waited for Rene to arrive and he couldn't help but drift back to his old life in Liverpool. It already seemed like a life time ago. One minute he was a school leaver just on sixteen and dating his first crush. The next he was in hospital, she was married to Eddie D and his poor dad was dead. Then to top the lot she had a baby boy.

It was still crazy to think about that time. Life was flying past and now he was an eighteen year old Foreman in Jersey of all places. He felt more at home here than in Huyton. Especially as Danny Owens, one of his lifelong friends was still with him here. But he still loved going back to visit his Mar, Jimmy and his wife Jean, that was the best feeling in the world. But like them all he missed Big Harry and Dominic McGuire, who as far he knew was still doing well in Belize, as was Arthur McNabb in London.

He thought back to Dot and how cruel and deceptive she'd been. Then he smiled to himself as he thought of Lesley. How different she was. How shy and gentle she was. She was back at boarding school or college or whatever the fuck they called it. And he was actually missing her. Especially the way she'd eye him up as he helped her dad unload the Jersey Royals for the chippy every Saturday morning.

He played up to too it making sure he was always bare chest and in his shorts. Carrying two 'forty-eight pound' sacks of spuds to her dad's every one sack. He'd grown to love her company and loved the stories she told him on a Saturday night in the Rose and Crown. All about her skiing holidays and sunbathing with her best friend Brenda, on Brenda's parents eight berth yacht. It was all a different world to the one he came from, but she seemed as interested and as fascinated by his world as he was in hers. Brenda mind you was a different kettle of fish. She was always a bit aloof and moody, but Lesley was lovely and he knew she wouldn't hurt a fly.

"Penny for them" Rene's voice brought him back out of his trance and he got up on his feet as quick as he could. "Sorry I didn't notice you standing there". Rene smiled "This way handsome". She then turned and walked in the direction of Moonbeam, her private yacht. John followed thrilled to be asked to look at the timber decking as it needed its annual check.

The sun was beating down as John stood on the upper deck with the skipper. He was bare chest in white shorts and nothing on his feet, and was thrilled surveying all around him as they left the harbor. Rene had arranged a surprise cruise around the island and as the cool sea breeze jutted across his face and gently blew his natural wavy blond hair he felt wonderful. Rene stayed in the galley and the skipper who'd worked for the Burgess for over ten years and had seen this scenario played out so many times before, smiled inwardly as he admitted to himself John was different to her usual toy boys.

He was a nice fella, genuine, and as yet hadn't even realized this was all part of Rene's big seduction. She'd prepared a picnic of delicate food and fine wine and had laid it out on the timber decking that was perfectly fine and not in any need of an annual check. That had simply been a rouse to get John on board. They'd been out of the harbor for thirty minutes when she called him to join her and he left the wheelhouse to join her with an apology. "Sorry, I didn't join you sooner Rene. I've never done anything like this before so I just wanted to enjoy the whole experience".

She smiled, as she was pretty much thinking along similar lines but for different reasons. As they sat in the heat talking and drinking, laughing and eating, she eyed up every inch of him. His flaxen wavy blond hair and golden tan, his perfect white teeth and bright sparkling blue eyes, his smile that was full of warmth and lit up the whole of his face. He was a sight to behold with broad shoulders and a firm lean waist. She eyed his solid strong legs and she couldn't take her eyes off him.

The Captain knew exactly where to stop, as he'd done it so many times before then he made himself scarce. John hadn't even noticed, but Rene had and she knew this was her time to make her move. "You need some lotion on or you'll burn, want me to rub some on for you?" Who could refuse an offer like that? She looked stunning with her dark tan and beautiful slender body in a sexy black bikini. Her tits and legs were fabulous and she just oozed sex appeal and smelt amazing.

As he lay on his flat stomach she started on his shoulders rubbing the lotion deep into his flesh. Then she slowly worked her way down his back. It felt incredible and by the time she got to his thighs and started massaging them he could feel himself getting more and more aroused. Then leaning over him she whispered "turn over" and as he did she was thrilled by the sight and size of his erection as she sat astride him.

Her heart pounding as she leaned forward to massage the front of his shoulders and chest, and felt his hardness underneath her causing her to gasp a little as she pushed herself against it before moving off him and slowly pull down his shorts and take him into her mouth. He had never felt anything like it in his life; it was mind blowing and he just exploded. Rene was thrilled especially when shortly afterwards he pulled her towards him and began kissing her passionately.

She tingled and wanted him inside her there and then. He stood up and took her by the hand and led her to the galley bedroom. By the time they got there he was hard again and ready for her. With no experience behind him it was pure animal instinct, pure passion and lust. As he entered her he drove her wild, and she cried out and whined with his every thrust.

From that first day of wild passionate sex together on the Moonbeam, John spent every Saturday afternoon with Rene doing the same thing. And they made the most of any other opportunity they got to be together. He had entered a world he knew nothing about and she made him feel like a real man and he couldn't get enough of it. She had finally found herself a younger man who made her feel like a real woman. John actually wanted her for her, and not just her money. She couldn't get enough of him. They were a mismatch made in heaven and genuinely cared for each other and shared a mutual fondness and affectionate.

Unless on any of the building sites. Then it was business as usual and with Rene remaining professional at all times and treated him as no more than the site Foreman. For which he understood and didn't mind, but he did worry about Edward finding out and eventually said as much. Rene smiled "John Darling, Edward has his lovers and I have mine. That's how we work. So relax and enjoy it for what it is". He was gob smacked. "Where I come from if a man so much as made a pass at another man's wife, it was enough for him to do time for it". She was amused and laughed "Well thank heavens it doesn't work that way here".

'Why don't you marry Lesley?' They were naked and lying side by side on the bed after an afternoon of love making. It had been this way every week for a couple of years at least and neither one of them had tired of other. So John was shocked "Wha? Why would I want to do tha?" Rene gave him one of her knowing smiles "because you're in love with her". It was true. He was. Outside of work and during the times he wasn't with Rene he spent all his time with Lesley and they'd grown very close. They'd never made love; in fact Lesley was still a virgin and not embarrassed to admit it.

"That" she was proud to say, "is something I'm saving for when I get married" and unlike Dot Harper, she was telling the truth. Rene knew all of this and she knew all there was to know about John's past.

He'd opened up to her over the years and hadn't left a thing out, such being the trust between them. "John darling, she's a brilliant girl and very much in love with you too, and unlike Dot she'd never hurt and betray you. She'd make a very loyal and supportive wife. It would be wonderful".

After they parted John spent the rest of that evening and the following week giving the matter some serious thought. Lesley was kind and caring and also a very understanding and compassionate young woman. Although she'd been wealthy all her life she wasn't a snob, unlike her best friend 'stuck up Brenda'. No, Lesley was far from being that, just like her parents, and Rene, who were all very down to earth. Brenda was contrived, with big ideas and ambitions. Though he doubted she'd ever achieve any of them as she was too lazy.

Lesley on the other hand had left University and worked hard helping her parents to run the boarding house, the farm, and their various other business ventures. And the more he thought about marrying her, the more it felt right and he knew he wanted to spend the rest of his life with her, so he decided to propose.

Truth told he was a bag of shite, as he picked her up to take her to their favourite restaurant. His nerves got the better of him, as he spoke continuously about anything and everything on the way there. Lesley looked at him quizzically "You're in an odd mood tonight, what's the matter with you?" She was like that, always able to pick up on his mood and could often read him like a book. He was just thankful she'd never been able to read him over his long term relationship with Rene. But he thought that was probably because Rene was in her late forties with Rupert, her grandson, who was a similar age to himself.

So he supposed it wouldn't cross Lesley's mind that he would even look at Rene in that way. But look he did and much more besides, he was crazy about the sex they had together. If Lesley agreed to marry him, he told himself all that would stop. But some things in life are easier said than done, and with Lesley believing in no sex before marriage. He reasoned maybe it would be easier to stop all that after the wedding. But there was no denying he would miss it like mad.

Half way through their main course John looked into Lesley's big brown eyes and smiled "You do know how much I love don't you?" She laughed quietly "Of course I do and I love you too". He smiled then he reached into his jacket pocket and brought out a small dark red box and opened it to show off a beautifully stylish diamond engagement ring. He held it up to her as he asked "Will you marry Lesley?" Her face flushed and her eyes lit up as she stared at the ring and then back at John and gasped. "It's beautiful. Yes, yes, and yes, I will marry you!"

Chapter Thirteen

George and Margaret couldn't have been happier as they stood filled with pride watching John and Lesley pose for the photographer. Lesley looked radiant in her beautiful white wedding dress, and John beamed with happiness and pride as he stood next to her looking very dapper in top hat and tails. Brenda was matron of honor and John's brother Jimmy was his best man. Mar Kelly, who had aged lots since losing Old Jo, was supported by her daughter-in-law Jean.

While Big Harry, Dominic McGuire, Arthur McNabb and Danny Owens all stood with Ray Hall, Billy Walsh, and his two son's Seamus and Shaun. Talking about the construction business in between having a good crack about the pit falls of tying the knot. The atmosphere and mood was light and celebratory and being enjoyed by all, including Rene and Edward with their grandson Rupert and his new wife Francesca, as the champagne popped and flowed like Niagara Falls.

For a wedding present George and Margaret gave the happy couple a large three bed roomed bungalow. It was set in its own grounds and had a thirty foot lounge and separate dining area. But their honeymoon was to be a surprise. In the week following the wedding, the Liverpool lads left John and Lesley to enjoy their new found wedded bliss. The lads enjoyed spending time together and having a good old catch up. They were staying at the boarding house owned by George and Margaret, but went to the Rose and Crown every day for a good scran, booze up, and the odd game of snooker.

It was during one of these sessions that Big Harry and Dominic McGuire said they'd had a belly full of the army and wanted out. Arthur McNabb admitted he was sick of living under cover in the smoke. Harry got excited "We should all start up our own security business. We'd be fuckin brilliant!" He wasn't joking, he and Dominic McGuire were trained killers and with Arthur's training he could take a man down in two seconds flat, and none of them were short of cash. It was doable.

Arthur confided he was pretty much over the whole undercover experience and missing Liverpool. Not least of all because he'd had a breakthrough in establishing IRA funding going on in the Capital. It was sensitive information and too detailed to go into at length, but he trusted these lads. After all they went right back to early childhood together for fucks sake. Old Jo Kelly and his missus had kept them on the straight and narrow, especially Big Harry and Dominic McGuire who were a pair of fuckers. Real hard cases they were and everybody knew it.

But here, together like this, and closer than family he had no qualms in letting them know the heat was on and he thought his days were numbered. He'd established IRA contacts that had trusted him enough to let him in on times and dates of money transactions going straight into the IRA coffers. So he was in it up to his neck and if his cover was blown he knew he was a dead man.

So transferring back home Liverpool had never felt more appealing. Especially after hearing that bent arl bastard Ralph Higgnet, kicked the bucket within weeks of retiring. Big Harry and Dominic had had enough of the fuckin jungle and destroying cultivation camps. So it was agreed, Arther was transferring back home to Liverpool and the lads were coming out of the army and setting up a security business together.

Lesley really was shy and not only did she get undressed in the dark, she also got into bed with a long nightdress on. It all felt very strange and John couldn't help but think about how different she was to Rene and even Dot before her. Rene walked around the yacht naked almost every time they were together, and even though he'd only slept with Dot once, she was very confident of her body. But his new wife, his Lesley, was pure and she was very nervous and shy. He loved her all the more for that and was as patient and gentle as she needed him to be.

Yet he fantasized about the sex he'd had with both of the other women, especially Rene. He hated himself for it, because deep down he knew that it wasn't going to stop. Rene was like a drug and he just had to have her. For the first time he allowed himself to understand why Dot had enjoyed being with an older partner. Why she had found it so hard to stop it. Why being a cheat wasn't as black and white as he thought.

It annoyed him, because he didn't want to be anything like that bitch that played him and as a result he was almost killed. He didn't want to think of himself as a cheat but he was. But he wasn't cruel like Dot was and he'd never do what she done. He would never hurt his beautiful new wife - his lovely Lesley, whom he wanted to spend the rest of his life with. So he would make sure she'd never find out about him and Rene.

Big Harry and Dominic McGuire had returned to their army base stationed in Wiltshire. They'd done a stint in Ireland, a stint in Germany, and they'd even done a special mission in Belize to thwart the drugs trade out there. Now time served, there was almost an end and they couldn't wait for their discharge. They loved the camaraderie of army life, but they were sick to the back teeth of the rest of it.

They couldn't wait to return to Civvy Street and get the security business up and running in Liverpool. Let's face it, steeped in guerrilla warfare and armed combat, not to mention martial arts, a security business was right up their street and would be a piece of piss.

The newlyweds though were still enjoying time off together. They had been walking hand in hand along the harbor, sharing their dreams for the future. They were agreed, they wanted to start trying for a baby right away. But Lesley's father George, had asked John to take on the name Davenport and it wasn't sitting easy with him "But it's only for business purposes John, you don't ever have to refer to yourself as Davenport if you don't want to".

John understood that and in some ways he actually didn't mind, but he didn't want it to be forever because he wanted his name and his father's name before him to live on in his own son, and Lesley understood and respected that. "Ok, as soon as we have our first boy we'll tell dad we're reverting back to your name of Kelly". John smiled and gave her a quick kiss on the lips "you've just got yourself a deal Mrs. Davenport- Kelly".

They laughed and chatted easily as they made their way back home to their beautiful new bungalow, where Lesley's mum was preparing lunch for them. But when they arrived at the bungalow Rene's car was parked in the drive. John felt himself tense up inside. This was the first time since his wedding day he was to be in Rene's company and he was dreading it.

His stomach turned over as they walked through the door. He didn't even know who to feel guilty on for fucks sake. Rene because she knew by now he had consummated the marriage or Lesley because he knew in his heart of hearts his relationship with Rene was far from over.

"Surprise!". Margaret and George were all smiles and standing close to Rene and Edward who were also smiling, and a small buffet was laid out on the kitchen table. The shock on John and Lesley's face made them all burst out laughing. "John darling, don't look so worried, here enjoy a glass of wine". Rene kissed him on the cheek as she handed him the drink. He knew she was letting him know everything was alright as he took it off her. Then it was kisses handshakes and hugs all around and Rene poured the wine for everyone and they tucked into the food.

Edward let everyone know he'd bought a new yacht. It had ten double berths, a huge galley, a movie room and bar, plus a speed boat fitted. It also had a crew of six as well as a cook and waitress who doubled as the cleaner. The glossy pictures of the boat that he passed around were fabulous; it truly was a glamorous vessel and emblazoned on her bow was the name 'The Blue Lady'.

"We're delighted you like her, because we'd like to take you both on a cruise for your honeymoon". Edward was smiling, and so too was Rene as she stood linking him. Fuckin' hell! John couldn't believe what he was seeing. He couldn't believe his own eyes. He couldn't believe her fuckin front. Standing there arm in arm with her husband, while offering the man she's shagging behind his back, a cruise with his new wife for fuck's sake.

What was she thinking? What the fuck was she playing at? Acting like it was the most natural thing in the world. But that was just it, to her and Edward it really was the most natural thing in the world.

Everyone was smiling as Lesley and John looked at each in shock then back at their company in stunned surprise before Lesley gasped "I don't know what to say". She was thrilled and wanted to accept right away, but she could sense John was uncomfortable and tense as she looked at him with a smile and urged him to speak. "What do you think John?" He was panicking inside thinking how the fuck do I get out of this one? "What about work? I can't just leave without giving Ray Hall and Tony some notice".

They all laughed warmly "That's all sorted John so don't worry, besides, you'll be with the owners of the company so I hardly think anyone will make an issue of it". Edward was warmly reassuring him, as he could see the worry in his face. "That's it then. We'd love too. Wouldn't we John?" Lesley's smile lit up her face as she looked at him and he felt sick as a pig and rotten to the core as he heard himself hesitantly say "Yeah, definitely, thank you. Thank you all".

John put his glass to his mouth and took a huge gulp of wine that he still hadn't learnt to like the taste of, but he didn't give a fuck because on this occasion he'd of gladly knocked back a glass of shite if it took the edge off his discomfort and guilt.

As everybody chatted and enjoyed themselves, Rene gradually made her way over to him as he poured himself another glass of wine in the kitchen. She smiled warmly "Happy?" He nodded "Yeah, I am actually". Then he whispered in annoyance "What the fuck are you playing at?" She was amused and dismissive "Oh stop looking so worried darling, I won't be sneaking into your room for a quickie… Edward's friends will be on board for a business trip, so just enjoy it".

She then gave him a mischievous wink and pinched his bum before turning her back on him and walking away to join the others with a smile on her face. He couldn't help but smile to himself and be turned on by her confidence and the sexy way she moved her body as she walked away from him.

The Blue Lady was moored in the harbour and John was carrying luggage for him and Lesley up the gangplank when Rene shouted down from the upper deck "The deck hands will carry your luggage John". He couldn't be arsed with all that palaver, so carried on. Then immediately after boarding Lesley went walk about with Rene.

Rupert, and his wife Francesca, arrived on board. He and John had met for the first time when John worked on the renovation of the old army hospital into the orphanage, and like all other construction jobs before it and since. John had got the best from the builders and they completed every development to the highest standard and ahead of schedule.

Far from being pleased, Rupert dropped in on every site John worked on and stuck his big fuckin nose in where it wasn't wanted, making things difficult for everyone but especially John. Who'd realized from the word go that Betty from the chippy was right - Rupert Burgess was one nasty bastard.

Francesca was all smiles as they came on board. But Rupert stood fuming at seeing John, and he couldn't understand. What the blazers was his grandmother thinking of inviting him. So he decided to make his feelings clear.

"Oh it is good to see that Grandmother has hired someone we know for this cruise. Our luggage still needs bringing on board. Now go fetch it".

John resisted the urge to twat him on the spot and knock him clean out. Choosing instead to lean into his face and wipe the smarmy smile right off it

'Listen posh boy, speak to me like tha' again and I'll rip your fuckin tongue out. Now go fetch your own cases you lazy fat bastard'.

The deck hand heard every word and struggled to conceal his pleasure and grin as Rupert stood white faced with shock and fear, and Francesca stood with her gob wide open like she was catching flies.

The other guests had flown in from America and had arrived at the quayside by Rolls Royce. Lifelong friends and business associates of Edward, they were Ester and Benjamin Epstein with Violet and David Greenburg. And once on board The Blue Lady they were all ready to sail to one of the finest harbors in the world, Puerto Buenos, where the filthy rich loved to be seen to party.

Then crowds of people gathered along the quayside and even other yacht owners stopped to look on in admiration as The Blue Lady pulled out of port. Rene and Lesley were standing on the top deck and felt like a million dollars as they smiled and waved to everyone, and there stood right in the middle of them with a smile from ear to ear and feeling like the dog's bollocks was John, with one arm around Rene and the other around Lesley. And as Danny Owens watched on from the quayside and couldn't help laughing out loud at the cheek of the lucky bastard.

John was back off his month long honeymoon and Danny Owens couldn't wait to see him because work hadn't been the same without him. As much as he didn't mind the Walsh brothers in small doses, he was irritated by being joined by them every day, just as he was now in the Rose and Crown for a few pints after work.

"How long has your man Arthur been a copper back on the mainland?"

Danny concealed his alarm at the question Shaun Walsh had just put to him and laughed it off as ridiculous.

"Arthur a copper? You're fuckin messing aren't yeh, he can't stand them. So where did yeh get that idea from?"

Shaun was matter of fact "I overheard him talking when he was at John's wedding". Danny's concern was rising.

"Nah, you've obviously got the wrong end of the stick there soft lad, he was probably telling stories about when we were all younger, little fuckers we were, always getting into some sort of lumber with the police".

Shaun looked at him disbelievingly.

"It's odd that because some of the fellers when we left Ireland with work in London, doing the same thing as us like on the building, our Seamus visits them on a regular basis".

Danny could guess where all this was leading.

'In fact, he was der just before John's wedding and said he seen a fella in de boozer who was a dead ringer for your man Arthur'

Danny was feeling the heat "Nah, I don't think Arthur has even been to London to be honest". He tried to make a joke of it and laughed.

"He must have a fuckin doppelganger"

But Shaun didn't see the funny side and just looked him straight in the eye "Doppelganger or not, he was drinking with all the Irish lads off site an I can tell you that for nothing'. They wouldn't take too fuckin' kind now to drinking with the filth".

This was not good. This was not fucking good at all. So Lesley was not going to be a happy bunny him contacting Arthur so soon after them getting back off honeymoon. But some things are more important than what a man's wife thinks for fuck's sake, so she'd just have to live with it.

Apart from Rupert being a bit of a twat trying to belittle the crew members and be rude to John in equal measure, the honeymoon had been amazing and true to her word Rene didn't put John in any awkward situations. Instead she spent most of her time with Edward and their guests mixing business with pleasure, as they arranged for the fair distribution and sale of many of the spoils of war that Edward had held in trust for the best part of thirty years.

So the bride and groom were given plenty of privacy to enjoy being newlyweds' just sunbathing, eating good food and drinking cocktails and fine wine, that John still didn't like. But when it came to the bedroom department Lesley was still shy and a little nervous. So John was more than just surprised but really made up when she enjoyed letting him make love to her in the shower.

A first for them both, and afterwards as they lay in bed together and she drifted off into a deep contented sleep as she lay in his arms. He lay there thinking about his past and how odd it was that the worst time of his life, had now led to the best time of his life because without doubt. If Dot hadn't of played him and Eddie D hadn't of got him worked over and almost killed. He would never in a million years have moved to Jersey and met Lesley, who he now loved so much he could never imagine his life without her.

And he wondered at just how different Lesley was to Dot and Dot was to her and Rene for that matter. Yet even now as he lay with Lesley resting in his arms. He had to admit to himself that Dot had made her mark and still owned a small piece of his heart, because she was his first love and the first girl he made love to and he'd never forget that. But he'd never forget Eddie D either or forgive him, and he was as determined as ever that if it took him the rest of his life.

He'd get his revenge on that horrible bastard and all the cunts who shafted his poor dad. Then he pulled Lesley closer into him and lovingly kissed her gently on the lips as she slept, and thanked God he'd found her. Because he knew they loved each other in a way that nothing would ever or could ever spoil. Because they had promised to love each other for better or for worse, and for as long as they both shall live. And he knew with great certainty they would never break that promise to each other and would rise above every problem life threw their way.

Chapter Fourteen

Now John's month long honeymoon was over and he was back at home and sitting in his kitchen with Danny Owens and he was dead set on tipping Arthur off right away. Danny could go but the chances were that they would be watching him to see if he went missing and that would only confirm their suspicions.

"We've got no option. We can't take a chance on ringing him cos an odd on his phone is tapped. And we're not fuckin' leaving him like a sitting duck" so it was agreed. John was going to London to tell him to get the fuck out of there cos his cover was blown.

Arthur McNabb was drinking at the bar in the Elephant and Castle when he felt someone tap him on the shoulder, and when he turned around to see who it as he immediately knew something was seriously wrong. Because there large as life a twice as ugly was John Kelly standing right in front of him, in a flat cap and glasses and wearing old jeans, a well-worn brown leather jacket and working boots.

"What the fuck?" John shut him up right away. "Get me a bevy and we'll talk when we leave here".

Within five minutes they'd knocked back a swift half and left. As they walked to the next pub John told him Seamus Walsh had seen him weeks earlier talking to a copper in a pub, and Shaun Walsh had quizzed Danny Owens about him.

"I might be wrong lad, but, I'd treat it as your cover's been blown and get the fuck back to Liverpool". They slipped into the next pub through the side door by which time Arthur had clocked they were being followed by two men. So they downed another swift half in a quiet corner of the pub. Then Arthur deliberately shouted across to the barmaid to ring a cab to take them to the Liverpool match being played that day.

Twenty minutes later they were in a taxi and heading for Highbury. After driving just over a mile away Arthur asked the cabby to pull over next to the tube station. At which point they made a quick exit and vanished into the crowd, and once sure they'd lost their tail. Arthur led them to a cheap getaway car that he kept parked miles away from where he lived, for situations such as this.

On the drive back to John's car Arthur told him of other uncover coppers that had disappeared without trace. That was how the IRA worked. They kidnapped and tortured them until they got the info they needed, then it was bingo! And they were bumped off and their bodies never recovered.

As they parted John sat behind the wheel of his car with the engine running and Arthur thanked him through the open door window.

"I won't forget this John. You've risked your life comin' here cos if they'd of took me, they'd of took you too".

John winked. "No bother, just get back home to Liverpool as soon as you can, ok?" Arthur understood the very real danger he was in and the weight of John's concern for him as he nodded sagely. And as John's pulled away from the curb he gave him one last look and winked as he put his head out of the open window and said "be lucky" before driving off and heading back to Jersey.

In the time it took John to get to London duck and dive with Arthur and return to Jersey, he'd managed to piss off both Lesley and Rene. Lesley because he'd left without telling her where he was going and Rene because he'd stood her up. She'd waited all day on her yacht, Moonbeam, where they spent every Saturday together. While Lesley spent the day with 'stuck up Brenda' browsing and shopping followed by a long liquid lunch, while all the time thinking John was working.

From the day he'd arrived home from London the atmosphere was heavy and had been for over week as Lesley kept up the silence treatment, and John couldn't stand it a second longer "Look love, I've said I'm sorry, and I am. But I couldn't tell you before I left for your own good". He'd told her everything several times over but it made no difference, because even though she understood Arthur had to be warned about the danger he was in. She still wasn't happy.

"But you're still not getting it John, what about the danger you put yourself in?"

He'd tried to explain this from every angle but she was still going on "Well I'm home now and safe, so it doesn't matter' She screamed at him 'but it does John! It bloody well does! She broke down crying I'm pregnant!"

John walked around work like a dog with two dicks, he'd often wondered what it felt like to be having a kid, now he knew and it was incredible and he just hoped and prayed he'd have a son. The only damper on the horizon was Rene. She was still smarting from him standing her up and she blanked him every time they had to be in the site office together.

If he asked her a question, she ignored him completely and directed all her answers to Ray Hall who was feeling very uncomfortable and asked John what he'd done to upset her. "Its personal Ray. That's all I can say, but if she keeps this up she can go fuck herself!" Ray was shocked but he didn't press for any other info, but he added he'd never seen Rene seethe so much in all the years he'd worked for her.

But as far as John was concerned it had reached the point of ridiculous. She wasn't his fuckin wife for God sake and he wasn't willing to put up with it any longer. After all, she had Edward and he didn't make life awkward for her.

He didn't have to wait long for the opportunity to put her straight as she once more ignored a question he put to her about work, in favor of answering it to Ray Hall. He'd had enough! So after slamming down his mug of tea on the office desk he looked her straight in the eye. "If you wonna get shut of me, fine. Just say. But don't think you can sit there playin' Mrs. High and fuckin mighty with me, cos it doesn't fuckin wash ok!"

He grabbed his jacked off the coat hook on the back of the office door and looked at Ray. "Sorry for putting you in this position Ray, but you're free of it now mate cos I'm fuckin off to the Rose and Crown". And as he walked out of the office he made it his business to slam the door behind him.

Rene had been used to getting her own way and seeing the lovers in her life come to heel and roll over. So it was quite a shock to her system when not only did John leave her waiting for him on her yacht like a fool. He actually stood up to her shouting and swearing and all in front of Ray Hall. She wasn't having it. Just who the hell did he think he was?

It had turned five o'clock and John was on his second pint in the Rose and Crown, and was just wondering if Ray Hall would join him after work. When in walked Rene, and made her way straight over to John "Calmed down now have we?"

He was still in no mood to put up with any of her shit "Wha D'you want?" He infuriated her.

"Don't be so bloody rude and get me a gin and tonic". She plonked her arse down on the seat next to his, while he went to the bar. After sitting with their drinks in silence for a short while, John broke the ice. "I'm sorry I didn't turn up last Saturday".

Relieved he'd finally calmed down, finally showed her he cared and was sorry, she smiled "I'm all ears".

So he told her every last detail about the Arthur situation and his cover being blown. She was gob smacked and totally on side. She hated the IRA with a passion and with good reason. They shot dead her stepson Rupert when he was just a young man. Something she'd never spoken about to anyone except Edward, until now. The antiterrorist unit had a tough job on their hands, a terrible job, and she was proud that John had risked his own safety, his own life for Arthur.

He showed courage by going all the way to London to warn him to get the fuck out of there as soon as possible. She was also glad he'd discovered the Walsh brothers were IRA sympathizers.

"They're now working on the last contract they'll ever get with CIDC or anyone else in Jersey for that matter, and I'm just the right woman to make sure of that".

John was impressed, he hadn't seen this side of her before and he liked it. She then stood up "Fancy another?"

He gave a huge smile "Go on then". As she walked to the bar he laughed to himself thinking 'it's not often you get a sexy millionaire woman to go to the bar and get the ale in'. And by the end of the night they'd both got the ale in that many times they'd had a right skin full and were pissed, they were really happy too. Happy they were back on speaking terms. Happy they'd found yet another new understanding. Happy because they'd missed each other more than either of them cared to admit, and now they were back together.

And that didn't get in the way of them celebrating the fact that John was going to be dad. Okay it was an unusual set up. At least it was to John, but it worked. To Rene it was all quite common. But to them both, whether they wanted it or not, this had developed into a passionate love affair and affectionate friendship. No matter how much John kidded himself that they would have to end it. Deep down both knew no matter how much they tried they never would.

It was too far involved and far too easy to get away with. Beside when it came to sex Lesley still wasn't the adventurous type, but with Rene nothing was off limits and he was content to indulge. They met each other's needs in the most exciting ways. And the fact that neither one of them posed a threat to the others marriage, made it all the more impossible to bring to an end.

Chapter Fifteen

Everyone was over the moon that Lesley had given birth to a beautiful baby girl named Rebecca, who was the living image of her dad. But John felt disappointed. He loved Rebecca more than he thought was possible and he was proud of her, and Lesley who he now loved more than ever. But he desperately wanted a son and he wanted the Davenport to be replaced with his own name of Kelly. He wanted his Father's name before him to live on in his own offspring. Lesley comforted him, "We'll keep trying until we have us a beautiful son".

All things considered the christening was a modest and quiet affair, with 'stuck up Brenda' as the godmother and Danny Owens as the godfather. John's family couldn't attend because Mar Kelly wasn't up to the journey from Liverpool and Jimmy couldn't get the time off work. Big Harry and Dominic sent their apologies too. They were worked off their feet with the security business they'd set up. Since Arthur McNabb had got his transfer out of the smoke and back home to Liverpool, he was helping them out as much as he could. Ideally they wanted to expand but they didn't have the extra finance they needed to do it.

Once the weekend of the christening was over life pretty much went back to normal. Lesley decided to be a stay at home mother and John worked his nuts off to provide for them. Something he didn't have to do, because in reality they were exceptionally wealthy. But he'd never sponged off anyone in his life and he didn't care how much money any of them had, and that included Rene. He would do what he'd always done and work hard to pay his own way in life and provide for his own family.

Ray Hall and John were completely caught off guard when Edward Burgess walked into the site office, all smiles with his grandson Rupert and a middle aged man they'd never seen before. Ray immediately put his mug of tea down on the desk and stood up and John followed suit.

"Good afternoon gentlemen, let me introduce you. This is Mr. Terrance Humphries, MD of the Channel Island Building Society, a subsidiary of the Channel Island Development Corporation that I own". He smiled broadly as John and Ray shook his hand, "Call me Terry" and they immediately warmed to him.

"Now if one of you men would be kind enough to pour us all a nip of the whisky you keep in that desk draw of yours, I'll get straight to the point of why we're here".

John hated being in Rupert's company and right now was no exception as he sat there looking like he had a bad smell under his fuckin big nose every time he sipped at his whisky. "Right gentleman, I'd like you both to go on a fact finding exercise with Terry, to Liverpool".

John's face lit up and Edward smiled. "I thought that would appeal to John". Amused they all laughed a little apart from Rupert. He'd never been one for smiles never mind a fuckin laugh. Edward explained that Lord Sefton's Croxteth Park Country Estate on the outskirts of Liverpool was being sold off for twelve million pounds. It's surrounding areas took in the affluent West Derby district on one side.

It was also just a stone's throw away from the notorious rundown council estate nick named 'The Boot' and that meant if they put the bid in, they got that too.

They could make the properties so wide ranging they could attract sales from all those aspiring to better themselves, regardless of their budgets. This was set to become the biggest private development in

Europe. A well-established company called Brossly Homes had gone for it and they'd got the outline permission to develop the site. But it was deemed too high a risk by the commercial banks so they were struggling to rise what they needed to keep it.

Consequently their broker approached CIDC adding on an extra three million pounds for the development of the roads and main drains services. John was chomping at the bit. "I know Brian Brossly, my dad had all the plastering contracts for his sites, and our Jimmy still does". He then told them how many cowboy companies had been and gone in the area, but Brossly Homes had stayed and had an extremely good reputation.

This was just the sort of local knowledge Edward needed. The meeting lasted for over two hours and by the end of it Ray was up for the challenge and John was rearing to go. So Edward made a phone call to have them booked on a flight for the following week. He booked them into the world famous Adelphi Hotel in the city centre, along with Terry Humphries, so they could make a three pronged approach to their fact finding mission.

As they sat in the airport, Ray shared his enthusiasm for the job with John and confided in him. "This could be the making of me John. Edward has invited me onto the Board of Directors with CIDC. I've been working towards that for the past ten years".

John was genuinely happy for him and understood his sense of achievement as he congratulated him. "Cheers, but I'll be honest with you though John. There's no disputing you're very good at what you do on the building side of things, but we both know you'd never be a part of any board meeting if you weren't shagging Rene".

John was shocked and didn't see that one coming at all, "Hey hang on a minute". But Ray didn't hang on "No, listen mate, you've only been with the company a few years next to my ten and you're already on most of the board meetings".

John had heard enough. "The fuckin tea lady goes to every board meeting. Does tha mean she's a threat to you too?" Ray burst out laughing "Piss off you big headed shit! I'm trying to say you've done well. But if you use your head you can do even better".

John looked at him uncertain of what he meant "Listen to me, you're a good man and a hard worker and you're in a unique position because of your relationship with Rene. So make the most of it while you can, because this is the biggest private development in Europe. Build up a good business reputation for yourself, that'll get you into senior management with any company. Because to some extent you're being used John, especially if it all goes tits up with Rene".

They both laughed, "You know what I mean".

John nodded in acknowledgement "Just make sure you do a bit of the using too. That way if she gets bored with you like she has with some of the others, at least you'll still be able to get a good job anywhere and provide for that lovely wife and child of yours, like any man should".

John was taking in every word. "I'll always have your back mate". He then stuck out his hand "I just hope you'll always have mine". John nodded as he shook his hand and winked "Always".

After boarding the plane, John sat back to enjoy the flight to Liverpool. He closed his eyes, to deliberately block any conversation with Ray and Terry. Ray was a good fella, he knew that. But he was still shocked by everything he'd just said. Even though he knew there was more than a grain of truth in it, he was feeling unsettled.

He supposed all the other builders thought along similar lines with regards to Rene. Fuck them; Edward knew the score and he was fine with it. So it had fuck all to do with anybody else. But if he was honest with himself there were times when he did feel like Rene and Edward were playing a game with him.

But then again, when he was on his own with Rene he also felt genuine warmth and affection from her, and even though she never told him so he also felt her love for him. Not as Lesley loved him. That was different. That was pure and clean and it was special. Then he smiled to himself as he thought back to the night before.

Lesley poured him a large whisky and cuddled up to him on the sofa. "Come on, I'm off to Liverpool for a week tomorrow. Have one with me". She looked into his eyes and smiled. John was confused "ha? Worra you smiling at?"

'I'm so proud of you and I'm really happy you're getting this long term opportunity on the County Park development, because…" She tailed off mid-sentence and just carried on looking into his eyes. "He was totally confused "What? Worra you smiling at?" She then gave him the biggest warmest and most beautiful smile and said "We're going to have another mouth to feed". It took a second or two for it to sink in; "You're joking?" She shook her head.

"No. I'm due the end of the year".

He threw his arms around her and started hugging her tight and kissing the face off her.

"I love you Mrs. Davenport-Kelly".

She smiled her special love filled smile "And I love you too Mr. Kelly, and I will do my best to give you a son". They both laughed and John's hopes for a boy soared.

He opened his eyes still feeling the love and pride he'd felt the night before. Terry and Ray had both nodded off and the flight was nearing its end. He left them undisturbed as he pondered on the future. The new Croxteth Country Park Development would take up to twenty years to complete. He could work on it for the duration if he played his cards right, but took Ray's advice just in case.

He supposed Edward would be well gone and kicking up the daisies before the end of the development, because he was already well into his late sixties. Rene too, she'd be in old age and retired by then because she was well into her late forties. And that meant that lazy fat bastard of a grandson Rupert would inherit the fuckin lot and take it over. John had no doubt, at that point he would be the first to be kicked out of the door.

Terry dealt with the City Council officials while John took him and Ray to a few of the local estate agents to gauge house types and prices in the area. Then they moved on to a site at Westbrook to meet his brother Jimmy. In turn Jimmy gave them a tour of the site to show what type of properties were being built there, and what sort of prices they were going for and it all pretty much tallied with what the estate agents had said.

Jimmy then gave them a potted history of Brossly Homes and Brain Brossly in particular. Pointing out he ran a very professional outfit that worked to the highest standards. The money his properties sold for reflected that, adding "it has to be serious money before Brian considers the sale of anything".

John invited Jimmy to join him for a pint in the Adelphi Hotel, but Jimmy declined saying he didn't drink through the week because of work the next day. But the truth was much as he loved John and was both happy for him and proud of what he'd achieved, he was also a little jealous. Jimmy resented the fact that while he was off making a life for himself, he had been the one left to look after their mother since their dad died.

Much as that was a labour of love, he'd had no choice in the matter and no support from John either, in fact these days he didn't even bother to ring them up much. And now John was staying in the Adelphi Hotel and calling it a fuckin business trip like his shit didn't stink. He was too important to even have a chippy tea with his own family. And only Jean, his beautiful wife Jean, who had suffered so much hurt and disappointment at not being able to conceive. Who'd helped him look after his mother like she was her own, only she knew how he truly felt.

As their time in Liverpool drew to an end, John fixed a night off work for himself and met up with Jimmy, Big Harry and Dominic, and Arthur McNabb. They started the night in an old Italian restaurant called Franco's, as it was their favourite place to eat and they were big spenders whenever they went there. Something Franco hadn't forgotten as he opened his arms wide in a gesture of warm welcome when they walked through the door "My boyz! Is a long time since I see you, where have you all been hiding from?"

They were over the moon to see him as they got hugs all around off him "Come, sit at my best table and allow me, first drinks on Franco". It was like they'd never been away and they loved the warm welcome this guy always gave them. The laughter and banter reverberated around the restaurant, as they exchanged stories on how well they were all doing.

When John broke the news that Lesley was having another baby, the old camaraderie was still there with back slapping, hand shaking, toasts and good wishes all around. Even from Jimmy whose private pain of still not being a father after years of marriage, he kept to himself. And by the end of the night nothing felt more certain than when they all agreed, time and distance hadn't so much as touched their bond.

And they were still so tight together you couldn't so much as put a cigarette paper between them, and the old adage of one for all and all for one still applied. Something that would come in very handy and benefit them all once John was back in Liverpool and working on the Croxteth Country Park Estate.

Chapter Sixteen

It had been a long tiring week and the last meeting with Ben Adams, the Chief Planning Officer with the Liverpool City Council had just concluded. He'd given them the grand and very impressive tour of the whole estate, with its vast and beautiful meadows. So beautiful in fact it seemed wrong that one day it would all be a housing estate, forcing John to openly ask the question "Why has the Council give permission to build on such a beautiful green belt?"

Ben Adams waxed lyrical about it all being Government sanctioned when Lord Sefton died, he had no heir, only a young wife, and with death duties of over ten million pounds, money her ladyship didn't have. It was decided to take what was there and sell off half to developers, but keep Croxteth Hall separate and spend money restoring it to its former glory.

Following the grand tour they'd been shown the plans for the estate, and although the whole site only had outlined planning permission, it was plain to see in every aspect this really was a massive project. Their last day ended over a meal and couple of bottles of wine in the hotel, to have a final discussion about all their findings. And they were agreed that every meeting they'd had, at every level, had all been favourable.

They spoke facts figures and information including Brain Brossly and his company Brossly Homes, and the potential property types; detached, semi, and terraced. Again agreeing by any standard it had been long exhausting but very productive week, and all of it had been a resounding success.

There was no doubt it Edward Burgess and Rene wanted the whole development and would not only outbid anyone to get it, they'd crush them out of business existence if they had too. If that meant bending the law, and damaging lives to do it, then so be it. A lot of hard work was on the table for them all, and that meant John would be back and forth to Liverpool for the foreseeable future.

Life couldn't be more exciting, but with the new baby on the way he and Lesley decided to give up the bungalow and move into the farmhouse with George and Margaret. With seven bedrooms, two en-suites and a separate bathroom, there was plenty of room for them all. There was even room for 'stuck up Brenda' to come to visit and stay over at weekends. So it guaranteed Lesley all the help support and company that she needed while.

John was working away in Liverpool and with the new baby on the way that was their top priority.

"You've got her pregnant again? Jesus John, you're quite the randy bastard aren't you". He deliberately hadn't mentioned the new baby on its way to anyone in work as he wanted Rene to hear it from him first. Now that she had he wasn't sure if Rene was messing or mad, but he was dead certain she was jealous.

So he reassured her in the best way he knew how. Making mad frantic love to her and it still thrilled her like it did the first time. In the few years they'd been meeting up once and sometimes twice a week, she'd taught him everything and she'd taught him well. No man before him had ever made her feel so desired, so irresistible, so alive. They knew it was wrong on Lesley but they eased their conscience by telling themselves it wasn't like her marriage would ever be was at risk.

John loved Lesley and nothing would stop that. But they did feel the weight of guilt from time to time, but it would never be enough to stop them seeing each other; they both knew that, but just like the word love it was never spoken between them.

Things were moving fast. The Board of Directors liked what they heard and agreed to get in a local building company with a good reputation. Ray Hall and Terry Humphries proposed Brossly Homes, stating including land assets they were valued at around one million pound, so would prove an asset and get CIDC off to a flying start. As the local people wouldn't realize they were dealing with an out of town company so would be more inclined to trust and buy.

Add to that fact they could offer low mortgages because they owned the Jersey Building Society, meant they would make an absolute killing. Edward Burgess was fired up and so too the Financial Director so they decided to go to Liverpool on a business trip of their own.

John was making the most of what holidays he had due to him before all the madness started and he was back on forth to Liverpool on a plane. So he invited his brother Jimmy and the rest of the lads to come over from Liverpool for a week, and George and Margaret would put them up in their boarding house at a massive discount.

Jimmy wouldn't leave Jean caring for his mother for a week. It was enough that she was a nurse looking after others. So he stayed back at home while the rest of the lads arrived in Jersey in high spirits and ready for a good week together.

Much to John's surprise Rene invited them all for a two day trip around the Spanish coast on board The Blue Lady. There was no getting away from it; the weather was perfect for it. But John felt uncomfortable because Lesley was so far gone carrying their next baby. But what Rene wants, Rene gets. She spoke to Margaret behind his back "It really would be in his best interest to be there Margaret, and to be perfectly frank, Edward is putting so much faith in him it wouldn't be a good look if he wasn't there".

No more needed to be said. She knew Margaret would spell out the importance of it being a business trip to Lesley, and had just guaranteed herself a two day jolly with John and the Liverpool lads.

Lesley walked into the kitchen to where John was sitting by the window starring out across the farm. She dropped his kit bag down in front of him. He looked at her confused "What's tha for?"

She gave him the smile that he never tired of seeing "You've got about two hours before they sail, now get yourself to the harbor and go have some fun". He was genuinely shocked as his intention was stay with her

"But worra bout the baby?"

She laughed "I'll be fine. Look its business so you can't afford not to be there".

He wasn't sure "yeah but" she stopped him "Stop worrying. Mum and Dad are here and Brenda will pop in too". He joked "We can always rely on good old stuck up". Even after all this time he still couldn't get close to Brenda, but he respected she was Lesley's best friend and she'd leant to laugh at his nick name for her.

"Go on, you better make a move or you'll miss out on all the fun". She kissed him. He stood up from the chair and held her close and kissed her "I love you Mrs Davenport-Kelly".

"Fuckin hell, you couldn't sail tha in the bath, it's massive!' As a former British soldier Big Harry had been around and seen a bit, but nothing compared to this magnificent and glamorous vessel. The rest of the lads remained speechless as they stood on the quayside gazing in awe of The Blue Lady.

When a top of the range Mercedes pulled up alongside them and a Chauffer got out of it and opened the door on the passenger side, and out stepped Rene "Hi boys, come, follow me". After they gave each other grins and knowing looks they eagerly followed her up the gangplank, and aware they had a direct view of her rear end she made sure she put some extra sexy wiggle into her moves.

Once inside the lounge everyone put their bags down and looked around in awe of the exquisite interior, as Rene picked up the phone and summoned Ingrid, who was visibly shocked when she entered to see Rene standing with four huge and rather hard looking men.

She was just about to be instructed to show them all to their cabins when in walked John with a huge smile on his face.

"Hey, you don't think you can get away from me that easy do you".

The atmosphere immediately lightened and the lads roared with laughter as they all moved forward to hug him and pat him on the back. Everyone was delighted but none more so than Rene.

"We thought you were staying with Lesley because of the baby?"

Danny was speaking for them all as John laughed it off as he walked towards Rene "Nah, she was glad to see the back of me". He put his arms around her and gave her a hug as he kissed her briefly on the lips. She responded by putting her arms around his waist and pulling him closer as she kissed him back for just a second or two longer. Long enough for them all to quickly give each other a knowing look. John turned back to them saying to Ingrid "Don't worry love, they're all house trained", giving everyone a much needed laugh in an otherwise awkward situation.

After everyone had been shown to their cabins and changed they returned to the top deck where Ingrid had laid on a light buffet with plenty of cold beers and champagne. And as they pulled out of port they were amazed and felt like VIP's as crowds of people gathered along the harbor to watch them sail out of sight.

As soon as the harbor was out of sight, Rene joined them all in a daring black bikini and white sarong. Her figure and dark sun tan looked amazing as did her hair and makeup. There was no getting away from it, she was as sexy as fuck and she knew it and so did the rest of them.

John grinned handsomely as she confidently made her way over to him and picking up the bottle out of the ice bucked asked "Champagne anyone?". After an amazing day this was the first time he and Rene had spent a full night together since he married Lesley, and not one second of it was wasted as they made love and spoilt each other all night long.

Chapter Seventeen

To run a development as big as the one in Croxteth Country Park, a reputable security company was needed to patrol it. The problem there was only two companies were operating in that neck of the woods, and between them they seemed to have the city stitched up. They covered all the large building sites, the hospitals, and all the night clubs. But the main problem was that they were all known gangsters and ex-cons.

So it was odds on they were on the take and thieving more building materials than the so called robbers, then supplying the smaller building firms. It was common practice with bent firms. So Rene had an idea and that's what this little two day jolly with John was all about. She'd met all the lads at John's wedding and could see for herself they were strong hard men and very loyal and protective of each other, qualities she liked and was impressed by.

Since then from conversations she'd had with John, she knew Big Harry and Dominic McGuire were doing so well with their security business they wanted to expand, but they didn't have the money they needed to do it.

Renee enquired "Anyone ever heard of Acer Security and Panama Security?"

They were all on the top deck sunbathing with a steady supply of ice cold beer from Ingrid. Everyone sat up "Bad companies run by bad lads, why?" Big Harry's shit detector was on alert. "Have they ever posed a problem to you and Dominic?"

Big Harry laughed as if the very idea of that was fuckin ridiculous "They're not brave enough love, why?" He wanted her to just get to the point. "Could you ever envisage a time when they might be a problem?"

Aware Big Harry was getting frustrated with the way she was dragging out whatever the fuck she wanted to say. Dominic interrupted, "Between us we've got a lot of contacts in the Huyton area who we can call on for back up, if needed, and now you're "one of the lads" so to speak.

They all laughed, "I'm sure Arthur here won't mind me tellin' you when we need a little info on someone, we can always access it through him". She liked what she heard and offered them the security contract for the Croxteth Country Park Development there and then adding "I know you're looking to expand and with a contract such as this I'm sure that won't be a problem for you. Now, let's talk about Brossly Homes".

CIDC had made Brain Brossly several very good offers, so good in fact they were over the market value, to buy his business. But he'd turned down every offer out of hand. Research on him showed he was in his sixties and had built up his business over twenty five years. He was a widow of ten years and had no son to pass the business on to, two daughters who held no interest in it, four grandchildren who he adored and a golden retriever called Guy who he loved and took everywhere with him.

The problem was during the land search carried out by the solicitors it was discovered that one piece of land in the Country Park development did not belong to the Council, it belonged to Brian Brossly. He'd bought it many years earlier off the church with plans to develop it into a health spa for his wife and daughters to run. But once his wife died, the dream of that died with her.

It wasn't a big piece of land but it was enough to cause major problems because CIDC needed two access roads to conform to the Fire Service stipulations. Without that land they were left with only one access road and the knock on problems from that would be endless and take up a lot of time.

The Council had said they'd put in a compulsory purchase order on it so it wouldn't be a problem. But resentment had built up towards them for the sale of Lord Sefton's estate, because it was such a beautiful green belt area. So they were dragging their feet and potentially that meant it could take months if not years, and that would fall right into the hands of those strongly opposed to the build.

"If Brian Brossly doesn't sell we can't take a chance on the City Council coming through, so we need this situation to be resolved in the next four weeks or the whole deal will be off". Rene gave each one of them a look of steel as she finished her sentence and without uttering another word, they all understood exactly what she wanted.

They sailed into Puerto Buena. John noticed a policeman waiting at the dock and as the gangplank was lowered he came on board, and after speaking with Rene for just a few minutes he left. Rene then walked towards John with an unfamiliar sad expression on her face and took his hand "John darling, poor old George has died, a heart in the early hours".

He and Rene flew back to Jersey immediately and left the lads to follow them on, and when they arrived home Lesley and Margaret were both still in shock and 'stuck up Brenda' was there helping out with baby Rebecca.

In the week that followed everyone walked around in a daze, and John helped Margaret to sort out all the necessary arrangements. He was glad that he and Lesley had moved into the farmhouse now. At least they could support Margaret as much as she supported them with the baby and would with the one on the way. Then he suddenly heard his mother's voice in his head "When God gives one, he takes one away". He'd always thought stuff like that was a load of crap. Now he wasn't so sure and just hoped his baby would be born healthy.

When the day of the funeral arrived it was like the whole of Jersey turned out to show their last respects. Rene was there with Edward and even the lazy fat bastard Rupert turned up. And John could feel him starring and watching his every move. So much so he wanted to snot the fat bastard, but now wasn't the time or the place, it would keep.

John's family flew in from Liverpool on a return flight the day before the funeral, and the lads had made it back in time on The Blue Lady, but they were flying back home to Liverpool with Mar Kelly, Jimmy and his missus Jean, straight after the funeral. They had business to sort out for Rene and they had a four week dead line to do it in. So they had no time to stick around to for all the pleasantries and do the sympathy bit.

Lesley was tired and heart sore and just wanted the day to be over and everyone to go home. And poor Margaret was utterly heartbroken and felt much the same way. She wanted to be left in peace to think and mourn and yell at God "why?" And understanding her pain, John just held her close and comforted her as she sobbed into his chest. And as she did it opened up every old wound from the loss of his dad and how he'd been cheated out of the chance of attending his funeral. And he'd fuckin have Eddie D for that and every other cunt that'd hurt him and his dad.

Lesley gave birth to another beautiful baby girl named her Georgina after her father, and just like Rebecca she was blond haired blue eyed and the image of her father who fell in love with her at first sight. But again John was gutted that he hadn't been blessed with a son. Something he longed for now more than ever. Lesley understood his longing and promised they'd keep trying until it happened, but it was blow and that's for sure.

Back in Liverpool Big Harry and Dominic McGuire had failed to uncover any skeletons in the Brossly family closet, and Arthur McNabb hadn't found anything they could use on him. He was as clean as a fuckin whistle. So they put him under surveillance and established his routine. On his daily walk around the big field on the left side at the Muirhead Avenue entrance to Croxteth Country Park, he let Guy off his lead and he ran ahead enjoying himself.

Brian was lost in thought he walked around the field, and barley noticed the two men who walk passed Guy and made their way to the small car park. Then he suddenly became aware of Guy lying down on the grass and he called out to him, but Guy lay motionless. So he rushed forward and was horrified as he reached him. His head was blood soaked, so he got down on his knees and held his head on his lap "Oh no, no boy, come on, Guy, it's me, dad. Come on boy, wake up". But it was too late. Guy was as dead as a fuckin Doe Doe.

Shot just like that at close range and right under Brain Brossly's nose. And as he looked around in shock he glimpsed the two men that had walked passed him, and they were grinning at him from a distance through the wound down car window as they sped away in the direction of Muirhead Avenue and the notorious Bootle estate.

Three days later as he sat in his office staring at the framed photograph of his faithful companion, his Guy who he took everywhere with him and was now brokenhearted and lost without. The phone rang. He lifted up the receiver but before he got a chance to speak he heard a man's distorted voice on the other end "Sorry about your dog. Still, it could have been worse. It could have been one of your grandkids. Sell your business". The phone went dead and Brain Brossly stood trembling with the receiver in his hand, then slammed it down and immediately rang the police.

It was no coincidence that Arthur McNabb was sitting with Brian Brossly in his office, taking notes "So let me get this straight Mr Brossly. You're claiming a person or people unknown are acting on behalf of Channel Island Development Corporation, to intimidate you into selling your business to them?" Brian was nodding.

"Yeah, yeah, that's exactly what I'm saying. As I say they shot my dog and they've threatened my grandkids and everythin". Arthur remained professional and stern "These are very serious allegations Mr. Brossly. So what I'll do now is take them back to the station and run a few checks on CIDC, and make a few enquiries at Croxteth Country Park to see if anyone seen anything suspicious on the day you say your dog was shot…" He deliberately stopped mid sentence and looked him in the eye with a long hard stare for a few moments to unsettle him "I'll be back touch. So, have you anything else to add before I leave?"

Brian's nerves were in shreds "No, other than I thought things like this only happened in movies". Arthur again looked him in the eye convincingly "Try not to worry Mr. Brossly, I'll give the matter my full attention".

True to his word two days later Arthur McNabb was sitting back in Brain Bossly's office holding a photograph Brian had just handed to him of his grandchild's school gates. "This picture you say you received through the post this morning doesn't actually prove anything Mr. Brossly".

Brian Brossly was still in bits and his voice was trembling a little "Well I think it proves I'm being intimidated and my grandkids are at risk". Arthur put the photograph back in its envelope and placed it inside his work file "It seems to me that you're probably the victim of a malicious prank, perhaps somebody you've upset in the past and forgotten about. As our enquiries show Liverpool City Council intend on serving you with a compulsory purchase order at an undisclosed date in the future, at which point its CIDC intention to buy you out legitimately. They're quite open about that fact".

Brian was a bit stumped for words. "So, it's probably best if you have a good think about your situation before you start making serious allegations of intimidation. CIDC are a huge and very powerful organization who always set out to get what they want Mr. Brossly, and they don't take kindly to having their name and reputation discredited in this manner. Brian went to speak, "but" and Arthur spoke over him "I suggest you save yourself a lot of grief Mr. Brossly and just sell to them now rather than waiting for that compulsory purchase order to be slapped on you...".

He then tucked his work file under his arm with the photograph still placed inside it. "I'll see myself out" and walked out of Brian Bossly's office with it. And there in stunned silence it hit Brian Brossly like a ton of bricks that CIDC had the police in their pocket and he was well and truly fucked. So when the call came through from CIDC a few days later with an improved offer, he accepted.

Edward and Rene were thrilled that everything was going ahead. "You wanted the deal wrapped up to a four week dead line, and that's what you got. That's all you need to know" said John, who was as happy as everyone else. Brian Brossly had agreed to sell his company for £1.2 million, and he accepted the position of MD for one year after the sale with a handsome salary.

Rene pushed it, "I do hope it wasn't too unpleasant, what the boys done to get the sale?" John wasn't proud of what Brian Brossly had been put through. The poor old cunt couldn't eat hadn't slept for days and was now frightened of his own fuckin shadow. But it got the result they wanted and even Brain himself had to admit that in the end, he'd come out of it smelling of roses anyway. "Ask me no questions and I'll tell yeh no lies".

Rene smiled satisfactorily, she knew waiting for that compulsory purchase order to be served would have cost them time and money and the whole deal would have gone down the pan. But now, thanks to the lads in Liverpool, and John, the sale of the Croxteth Country Park went through in record time and it was time for everything to swing into action "Thank you John, you're a darling".

The work force and office staff at Brossly Homes was unsure and concerned at being invited into a meeting with Brian Brossly, one of his site agents and three of his foremen.

"I've invited you all here today because I've got some good news… and some bad". The whole room fell silent.

"The bad news is I've sold the business".

Immediately everyone looked at each other in shock and thought redundancy.

"The good news is everyone's job is safe".

The relief could be felt right around the room.

"The company that's bought me out has got huge projects in the pipe line, so staff will be increased greatly and I will be staying put in the role of MD, for one year only, to make sure the transition runs as smoothly as possible".

Everybody was more than pacified. They were also excited by the changes that lay ahead.

Chapter Eighteen

Lesley not only seemed completely untroubled by the fact that John would be working away from home in Liverpool for two weeks at a time. She actually seemed to look forward to it. But, with her mum still grieving and two little ones to care for she did have more important things on her mind to worry about. That was why she was grateful that 'stuck up Brenda' was moving in for a while to help her out. John was grateful too because at least she'd have company with someone her own age, and that made him feel a lot better as he headed off for Liverpool with Ray Hall and Rene.

They booked into the Adelphi Hotel on arrival and the following day they done a whistle stop tour of the whole development area, including the former Gate Keepers cottage. It was a listed building and couldn't be demolished and it was ideal for what Rene had in mind.

Once back at the Adelphi, Ray announced he was going to the Empire to take in a show and asked if they fancied joining him. John had already arranged to meet up with the lads in Franco's Italian restaurant in Castle Street

"Italian? I love Italian" Rene said.

That was it then. Ray was given the knock back and John was as pleased as he was relieved that Rene wanted to join him. Rene was a terrible flirt he knew that, but there was nothing more galling than when she done it under his nose, as she did lately with Ray Hall, all the time. It was fuckin annoying. That sort of thing played with a man's mind and he wondered how the fuck Edward had ever managed to put up with it.

John annoyed himself too for being so jealous but when all said and done, they'd been sleeping together for several years now and she'd taught him everything he knew between the sheets. He'd done things with her that he still hadn't done with his own wife. Though that wasn't for the want of trying, but Lesley wasn't adventurous. She wasn't even very sexy, if he was honest with himself. She was predictable, some might even say boring. But she was a fuckin good wife and mother and he wouldn't have a wrong word said about her, but he hoped and wished she'd bless him with the son he so much longed for.

When they arrived at Franco's, Rene looked like a million dollars in her top of the market evening wear diamonds and fabulous hair style. And as the waiter led them to their table she oozed confidence and wealth, and typically all the lads jumped up to welcome her, and just as typically she was like the cat that got the fuckin cream with all the attention. During the meal she changed the tone of conversation to business "Sorry to mix business with pleasure boys, but how far down the line are you all with expanding your Huyton and Knowsley Security business?"

They were caught off guard and the answer had to be due to stretched finances they still hadn't got very far "Well, I've got just what you're looking for" and true enough she had. It was the former Game keeper's cottage. It had several bedrooms making it ideal for night patrols, a pig pen just the right size to knock into a kennel big enough for two Alsatian guard dogs, and a barn that was big enough to convert into a garage for two patrol vans.

"To round everything off nicely gentlemen, if you're both willing to move into it I'll waver all rent and throw in the two patrol vans, with Huyton and Knowsley security printed on the side of them of course, as part of our deal".

Rene had a knack of making offers that couldn't be refused and this was one such offer and Big Harry and Dominic McGuire were ecstatic.

"Gentlemen, call it a bonus, for getting such good results from Brossly Homes".

She teased, "The rest of you will get your reward in kind".

And as they all laughed, John couldn't help feeling a bit pissed off with her and she knew it. After she left the table to go to the ladies he asked if anybody still went to the She Club. It was his way of asking if Eddie D and Dot still drank there. Arthur McNabb got on to him straight away "They don't drink there anymore John". John pretended not to understand "Who?"

Arthur gave him a knowing look as did the rest of them.

"Eddie D and Dot. They drink in the Golf Club all the time now mate".

John nodded "Thanks" that was all he needed to know, for now, the rest would come but all in good time. And he had plenty of that because he was on a twenty year construction job, a development that would offer him every opportunity that he needed to bring them down. To make them suffer as they had made him suffer. To ruin their lives as they had once ruined his.

He was back and it felt good. Back in the city he loved. Back in his own back yard where he understood the rules and knew how to play the game. Back in his beloved Liverpool, the place he loved more than any other place on the planet. The city them pair of conniving cunts forced him to leave. Well that would never happen again because he wasn't that young wet behind the ears schoolboy leaver now.

He was a man, a ruthless man, and a man who not only knew how to get the best from people. He also knew how to deliver the worst on them. And by the time he'd finished delivering these two cunts with the worse they'd curse the day they were born, and he would do anything to bring it all to and.

The ringing of the phone woke John out of a deep sleep, he couldn't remember what time he'd got back to the hotel with Rene, but it was definitely the early hours. He fumbled for the phone

"Hello?"

The voice on the other end was full of the joys of spring.

"Alright Kid, what time d'yeh want me to pick you up?"

He'd completely forgot that he'd agreed to go to Jimmy's to have his Sunday dinner, or lunch as he preferred to call it these days, with his mum and the rest of the family. He tried to sound enthusiastic but with the hangover from hell that wasn't fuckin easy

"Call it one o'clock Jimmy".

After dragging himself out of bed and standing in the shower feeling like shit and promising himself never to drink champagne by the gallon again. He suddenly remembered not only did Rene decline the offer into his room, she didn't invite him into hers either. She just thanked him for a lovely night and kissed him, nothing else, just a kiss, and that struck him a very fuckin odd.

Then as he stood pondering on it all, while waiting for Jimmy to pick him for lunch. He was completely taken aback when out walked Rene all glammed up and linking Ray. He tried not to show his shock or his anger for that matter, but it wasn't easy, and he fumed as they walked away across town together looking like and old married couple.

"See you later John, enjoy your lunch darling"

Cheeky bastards, behaving like that right under his fuckin nose. Then again he behaved like that in front of Edward all the time, and with Rene, it was just possible there was nothing in it and she was playing one of her games. She was a fuckin nightmare at times and Ray was being a bit of a twat for playing along with it. As Jimmy drove them past his mum's old house in Bruton Road, he was shocked at how rundown it was and how the road looked much rougher than he remembered it.

He was glad she didn't live there anymore. Glad she was living with Jimmy and Jean in the house Jimmy had built for them on Stanley Road, but not just for her sake. He'd be embarrassed for Lesley to see this, his kids too. He wouldn't want them visiting a place like this. He'd rather Jimmy bring his mother and Jean to visit him and his in Jersey. He'd moved on from all that life now. He loved coming back and he loved the city with a passion. But he was upwardly mobile and had climbed up the social ladder, and he wouldn't live here now for a house rent free. He was happy where he was thank you very much, and he didn't miss this one bit.

Once they stepped foot inside Jimmy's and he set eyes on his mum he was shocked. Although it was only months since he'd seen her at Georges funeral, he hadn't really noticed her decline. She'd aged; really aged, she was an old lady, a proper old lady standing right in front of him now and he could hardly believe his eyes. He knew she was getting older, of course he did. But he hadn't seen it until now, as she stood there in front of him with her white hair and looking frail.

"Oh Mam, come here, you look great".

He opened his arms wide, but when he wrapped them around her in a loving hug her tiny frame just felt like a bag of bones in his arms. The guilt washed over him and it hurt as the lump in his throat made his voice thick with emotion

"It's good to see you Mam".

She swelled with love and pride and was teary eyed "You too son".

He should have made more of an effort. He'd left everything to Jimmy and Jean, it was wrong and he knew it. And throughout dinner, not lunch, he looked at her with love and he could see the sadness in her smile when she looked back. Jersey had robbed years from them both and none of it could be got back, because even if he did want to live back here now. It was too late, because he had a wife and a family of his own to think about.

But all of them would always know how much he loved this old lady sitting in front of him. How proud of her he was. How she was his mother and had gone without to make sure he had plenty. How she had nursed him around the clock when he lay battered and broken in intensive care, and after praying to her beautiful Virgin Mary for his full recovery. She told everyone he was her miracle boy because all her prayers were answered as she sat holding his hand so he could feel her love and wouldn't be frightened. She gave him her strength to fight and survive and all the time she was grieving for his dad.

She was a mother in a million and always had been, not just to him and Jimmy but to Big Harry and Dominic, Danny and Arthur McNabb too. She never turned anyone away and was loved for it, loved in Burton Road by neighbours who were the salt of the earth. He'd make sure his kids knew that too and he cursed himself for feeling embarrassed earlier. For feeling he was the 'bees knees' and a cut above. He'd been away too long and sampled the good life and it had turned his head.

But seeing his mother had brought him back down to earth and without saying one word she'd reminded him who he really was, John Kelly, not Davenport-Kelly. John Kelly working class lad from Huyton in Liverpool, and he was ashamed he'd let himself forget it, and knew his poor dad must of turned in his grave when he did. He missed his dad and never more so than when he was with his mum.

And he would argue with any cunt who said time is a great healer, because 'no it fucking isn't' he thought. Because it still hurts and that emptiness it left behind could never be filled. He'd just had to get on with it and learn to live with it, that's all. Here for Sunday dinner with the smell of cooked lamb wafting all around the house, and his lovely old mum sitting facing him and listening to all his stories about Lesley and the kids, and life in Jersey.

It had brought everything back and he was heart sore and hurting thinking about how devastated Margaret was over loosing George, and how he comforted her. How his mum must have been that devastated when she lost his dad, but he wasn't able to comfort her, it had all been left to Jimmy who was a good brother and a fuckin good son. It was sinking in deeper and deeper. He hadn't been able to give his own mother one crumb of comfort when she lost his dad, and that was down to Eddie D paying the Higgnet twins to see him off, and it was one more bastard thing he'd pay for fuckin tenfold.

The office staff at Brossly Homes' proved to be a great bunch. Kate was in charge of sales and doing the hand overs on completed properties. Nigel her partner, was in control of buying all materials and land for future developments. Kate was in her thirties with dark brown eyes, black shoulder length hair and an hour glass figure. She was stunning. What the fuck she seen in Nigel was anyone's guess. He was at least ten years older, stood no higher than five foot six and weighed in around ten stone wet. He was a weasel of a man and how the fuck he managed to pull a stunner like her was a mystery. Carl was the Draftsman, Carol the book keeper and Jenny the receptionist, they were all pleasant enough but Kate and Nigel were the main players.

The first phase in the development was up and running with access roads and sewers being done, to be followed by the first houses going up. But there was a fly in the ointment, so Rene called a meeting with Big Harry John and Dominic McGuire in the lounge of the Adelphi Hotel.

"We have a problem Gentlemen. CIDC have been informed that a local security firm is putting the strong arm on sites all around the city and charging them extortionate rates… And now that the Croxteth Country Park Development has been covered by the Liverpool Echo, it's only a matter of time before they call on us, and clearly they won't know or care that we're intent on working with Huyton and Knowsley Security for the duration".

Big Harry asked the question "Right, have you got their names?" Rene handed him a slip of paper with the name on it "Will they be a problem if they turn up on the site wanting to take it over?" As an expert in martial arts and a former British soldier who was trained to kill and had done just that, he resented the question.

Dominic knew it so he jumped in first "Look Rene, me and H can handle anyone who tries to muscle in on the development". He looked at the name on the slip of paper and put it back down on the table. "We can find out all we need to know about know about him and his firm from Arthur. The fact is Rene, you hired us to do a job and we're up for tha regardless of what it takes to do it. Do you understand tha?"

Rene appreciated straight talking and the fact was Dominic was far better at it than Big Harry "Oh good. Yes. Yes I do. Now, what can I do to help you get rid of the problem?" The lads were glad of the opportunity to remind her of what she'd promised them over their meal in Franco's "We're gonna need to hire extra security guards to cover the different sites, and we could do with those vans you mentioned to be honest"

Rene immediately picked up the phone and rang a Fords Dealer "Rene Burges here, the two transit vans with Huyton and Knowsley Security to be put on the side… Oh good". The call was short and sweet "I'm pleased to say your vans will be ready for Friday". She then got a huge bunch of keys out of her bag and pushed them across the table "The cottage is ready to move into".

Rene had set up a main office for John and Ray to operate from in the Corn Exchange building in the city centre, where they were both sitting at their desks going through lists of contractors. One name in particular jumped out at John and he banged his hand on the desk.

"Got yeh!"

Shocked, Ray looked across to him "Got what?" John had waited a long time for this so he wasn't gonna fuck it up now, so he faked a laugh "Dirty little fly on the desk, I just squashed it". Ray shrugged then carried on going through his lists but John had just found the contractors he wanted and he put a big red circle around them, Edward Decker & Son, painting and building company. Before now Eddie D had never referred to himself as Decker but with his dad as the senior partner in the business he probably didn't have much of a say in it.

They were up to date with all their tax returns and payments and their workforce were cards-in, no subcontractors. They ticked every box for CIDC, and CIDC had set up their payment schedule that leant itself to their company perfectly. They would have to pay in all invoices twenty eight days from the end of the month, they were submitted.

So invoices for the first month put in at the beginning of the second month, would take twenty eight days from the end of that month for the first pay cheque. Things were about to get interesting as John, at long last, was about put a plan into action that would create havoc in the life of that cunt, Eddie fuckin dead man walking, D.

John thought his position was to be confirmed as one of the site agents, but Rene had other ideas "You have got bigger fish to fry mate, you're the new Contracts Manager and I am the new works Director" said Ray. They were both as pleased as punch and laughed 'When you went to Jimmy's for Sunday lunch and seen me and Rene heading out for ours to a local restaurant. That's what it was for. It was a business lunch".

He laughed. "By the way, your face was a picture that day but you do know she was just using me to wind you up, don't you?"

John grinned "She's a fuckin nightmare at times".

Ray nodded in agreement then spoke about his wife. She was in ill health and that meant he wouldn't be able to spend as much time working in Liverpool as he'd like. He didn't know it, but he'd just give John an even better opportunity to give it to Eddie D right up the fuckin arse. But before he did, he swung it for Jimmy to have one of the site agent's jobs, and arranged for Danny Owens to be brought over from Jersey for a permanent plumbing contract on the Croxteth Country Park development. Thus ensuring all the lads where finally back in Liverpool at the same time, and would act as a ring of steel for each other that nobody would be able to penetrate.

It had been a long two weeks and John couldn't wait to get back home to see Lesley and the kids. He'd missed them more than he thought possible and knew it was going to be really tough on them all to adjust to him working away. But it was an opportunity he couldn't let pass him by and Lesley understood that and supported him.

He was over the moon when he walked through the door and they met him with kisses and hugs all around, and Margaret did look a lot better than before he'd left for Liverpool. But 'stuck up Brenda was her usual cool and stand offish self when she smiled politely "Nice to see you back". He wondered why the fuck she even bothered because it was clear she didn't like him, and truth be told he didn't fuckin like her very much either. He tolerated her for Lesley's sake, as they'd been best friends from when they were little girls.

After the excitement of the day settled down and kids went to bed, Margaret and the other stuck up cow went out for the night, so

John and Lesley made up for lost and made love. But the rest of his time at home flew past and before he knew it he was heading straight back to Liverpool.

John instructed Brian Brossly to deal with the painting contract being given to Edward Decker & Son, and told him to make sure they came in to sign their contracts when he wasn't around. "Can I ask why?" Brian liked John, as it was he remembered his dad and knew him to be a genuinely hard working and all round nice fella. So he put store in that and figured John was probably a chip off the old block. But still, this was a bit of an odd request. John told him he had history with Eddie D and if he had his way Edward Decker & Son would never have got the contract. But Ray Hall insisted they were the best for the job, so that was that. But that couldn't be further from the truth, he was just setting out to cover his tracks right from the very start.

Later on in the day as he sat in the Brossly site office trying to look over some site costs, he became increasingly aware of Nigel going on and on to Carol in the background. So he stopped what he was doing to listen properly "I don't care, it's cold and tastes like piss!" he banged his mug down on the desk. "Now go and make me another one". The poor woman fled the office in nearly in tears and John felt like punching his lights out as he looked across to Carl "Is he always like tha?" Carl laughed "You should see him on a bad day. He can be a right nasty bastard".

In the couple of weeks that followed John witnessed Nigel flexing his muscles time and time again and no one stood up to challenge him, not even Brian Brossly who'd worked over him for years. He was as arrogant as he was sly. So sly in fact he'd already tried to get the staff to tell him how much salary John was on, and if he got paid through Brossly Homes or CIDC. He was an all-round snake in the grass. A scrawny little bastard, whose gob was bigger than him and like the coward he clearly was he enjoyed bullying people with it.

John was sat at his desk reading lists of new suppliers to go to tender, and again Nigel's voice came bellowing out of his own office "You can't kid me you lying bitch, It's not fuckin Nescafe!" John couldn't stop himself as he stood up from his desk and looked across to Carl "That's it. I've had enough of listening to this shit every day".

Carl grinned as John stormed his way to Nigel's office, marched through the open doorway and straight up to him and took the mug of coffee out of his hand and banged it down on his desk "Listen shit head! If you don't like the way she makes coffee, make it your fuckin self!" He then turned to Carol 'In future you don't do another thing for this prick, unless you want to, understood?' She stood with her mouth open and nodded and Nigel nearly burst a blood vessel as he stood up

"Who the fuck do you think you're talking too?"

John saw red mist. He promptly kneed him in the balls sending him to the floor in agony then looked around the office at everyone "I'll be in the pub across the road if anyone wants me" he walked out and slammed the door shut behind him.

Brain Brossly couldn't believe the dramatics, as Nigel stumbled into his office

"I've just been assaulted by John. I want the prick sacked for gross misconduct, and call the police cos I want him charged. Carol is a witness."

Brian didn't respond.

"Well? What are you waiting for?"

Brain remained calm. "Sit the fuck down Nigel and behave yeh self. I can't sack him cos he works for CIDC, and they, as you know, bought Brossly Homes off me six months ago".

Nigel sat stumped for words for a few moments.

"Why the hell did you sell to them Brian? You don't need the money".

Brian smiled "Let's just say they made me an offer I couldn't refuse... if you know what I mean? And I've got a sinking feeling that John is somehow involved in all that. So forget me sacking him and forget the police Nigel, cos they work hand in glove with CIDC". Brian was tired of it all and he was tired of Nigel and his abusive outbursts. "Besides, you had that one coming to you. So take it like a man for fucks sake and let it go". Nigel was gob smacked as he left Brains office in a state of disbelief.

Ray Hall had to fly back to Jersey to be with his wife as her illness had worsened, leaving John in complete control. And as he sat behind the desk in the site office mulling over paperwork, in walked Kate with a face like thunder 'Where do me and my husband stand with your future plans?' John grinned. He definitely liked this woman, she was feisty.

"Sit down Kate" John calmly said.

She pulled the chair back and plonked herself down on it "Why can't your husband speak for himself?" She was livid. Mostly because she knew herself that Nigel was a gutless bastard. He had been since the day she married him, in Los Vegas, and God knows she didn't do it for love. She didn't even fancy him for fucks sake. That side of things was a chore at best but more often than not it was a fuckin endurance.

She'd just had one too many shit relationships, been hurt once too often by men promising her the world and giving her fuck all, unless you count the odd slap because she'd had plenty of them. But never off Nigel. Nigel provided her with a flash car, a five bedroom house and plenty of money in the bank. She could live with that until something better came along. But no matter how much of a gutless bastard he was, he was excellent as his job.

"After what you done to him yesterday you're lucky he hasn't gone to the police, never mind talking to you" she spat.

John definitely liked this woman. She was smart she was stunning and she was very fuckin sexy.

"What stopped him?" She was thrown for a second.

This fucker was sitting here across the desk and grinning in her face

"Brian stopped him, but never mind that, he's good at his job but he just gets a bit wound up at times, that's all".

He admired her loyalty, but she was a bit too quick to brush off the suggestion of the police and a bit too desperate to save his job. Something didn't feel right here and gut instinct told him he'd have to watch these two, and in the case of Nigel, that was going to be an absolute pleasure.

"Wound up or not it's got to stop… tell him his jobs safe, yours too".

They both smiled and in that one instant it was like an electric current between them.

Chapter Nineteen

Before flying back over to Jersey, John was looking through the suppliers list and noticed one company supplied everything from bricks to pluming and everything in between even window frames. So he raised it as an issue with Brian Brossly, who told him it was because they had the most competitive prices. He decided to raise it as an issue with Rene at the first available opportunity.

But for now he was back to Jersey to spend time at home with Lesley and the kids. Who were all waiting at the airport for him as he came through customs, and run at him before jumping all over him with hugs and kisses. This was what it was all about; this was what he worked his bollocks off for, family, and nothing else even came close and absence really did make the heart grow fonder.

Stuck up Brenda had moved back into her parent's home as her and Lesley had had some sort of a row, but fuck getting involved in that. He'd learnt from very early on it was best to leave those two to sort themselves out, and they always did in the end. Besides, he was glad to see the back of Brenda for a while. She was great with the kids and he couldn't deny they did love her, but there was no love lost between him and her.

Margaret on the other hand was doing great and coping much better these days, helping Lesley with the two little ones. They'd been her saving grace since losing George and had literally given her a reason to keep going. Which was just as well as much to the delight of everyone Lesley had announced she was having baby number three.

It's a funny thing life, full of twists and turns and most of them we never see coming. And John was pondering on just that as he sat with his eyes closed relaxing in his favourite armchair. He never imagined his life would turn out like this. As a kid growing up the Huyton, he never once thought he'd ever leave the city of Liverpool. Now he couldn't be happier that he did because he'd met and married Lesley, his wonderful wife, and had his two beautiful daughters, Rebecca and Georgina.

They lived in a luxurious farmhouse with acres of land and a string of family business that George had left to them all, and stuck up Brenda with all her business acumen helped them to run. He also had a fantastic career that took him back and forth to his beloved Liverpool and he thrived on it.

And he still had Rene as a lover. She'd taught him the value of having an affair and the art of never letting it get in the way of a good marriage. Now he had baby number three was on the way and he was still only thirty. Life was amazing and he had everything he wanted except the one thing that would make it all perfect, a son. He wanted that more than he'd ever wanted anything in his life and the older he'd got, the more important it became to him. He longed for it, yearned for it, and dreamed of the day it would happen.

He was desperate to have a son and heir to carry on his name and his father's name before him. Davenport was a good name but it was Lesley's name, not his. It was her father's name not his. He wanted the good name of Kelly to be carried on into the future, and he wanted a son of his own to do that for him.

All too soon John was on his way back to Liverpool and looking forward to it because until Ray Hall returned he remained in full control. When he arrived at the airport he was met by Rene. Edward had gone to New York so she decided to join him to oversee everything on the Croxteth Country Park development, and have some overdue quality time with him.

As she sat next to him on the plane, she played footsy with him as he told her about the warehouse where all their materials were kept from the one supplier. Adding he proposed they build a secure compound on one of their own sites and have all the materials transferred to it, following a complete stock take.

But she was only half listening as she rubbed her fingers up and down his thigh. As he tried to continued, it wasn't easy "We could save on the rent and rates of the warehouse and make things more efficient at the same time, because all materials would be readily available when needed". He looked her in the eye and grinned.

"Wha' D'you think?" She grinned back "I think you know what I think". He could feel himself getting more and more turned on.

"Yeh, but do you agree?"

She leaned into him and whispered "I agree" then added

"I've leased us the penthouse suite at the Atlantic Tower Hotel, overlooking the river Mersey… I want you; want us, to be comfortable when we're away from Jersey Working in Liverpool". Having to spend what little spare time he did get with Lesley and the kids had kept them apart for far too long, and they missed each other like crazy. Nobody could please him like Rene could and nobody could satisfy her as he did. They needed each other, and he wanted her right there and immediately started to get hard. So she put her hand on his crotch and squeezed whispering

"That's the first thing we'll have to take care of when we arrive".

And they did, as no sooner had they stepped through the door to the penthouse, they were passionately kissing each other all over as they frantically ripped the clothes off each another as they made their way to the bedroom.

They spent the following six hours making up for lost time. Pleasing each other with every move, every kiss, every touch, feeling and tasting every part of each other, gasping and moaning in pleasure and ecstasy of it all.

The following day Rene insisted they stayed away from the Corn Exchange office "I'm taking you clothes shopping darling".

He was a bit thrown and not too sure if he should be offended or not.

"Hey, I'm quite capable of sorting out my own wardrobe thank you" he added.

She smiled 'Oh don't go all macho on me darling, humour me instead".

She quickly kissed on the lips "Come on, let's go and have some fun".

Before he knew it he'd been measured up by the best tailor in the city for three suits made from the finest material, with another three off the peg, he had a dozen shirts, half a dozen ties and six pairs of shoes. And when the shopping spree was over they had a very long and enjoyable liquid lunch.

"Right, now it's time to visit the Corn Exchange".

John was confused "But I thought".. She stopped him mid-sentence and smiled "I want to show you something. I also want to drop in on them all unannounced".

It was mid-afternoon when they got there and the young girl on reception smiled "Hi John, Brian's already left".

She didn't even look at Rene and Rene did not like that one bit.

As they made their way to Brain's office they passed by Nigel's office, and he and Kate were also gone. The only people around was Carol and Carl, who both stood up when they walked in the room.

"John, Mrs. Burgess, nice to see you again, would you like tea or coffee?" John smiled and thanked her for two teas then they continued to look around Brain's empty office Rene seemed to be in a mood.

"Are you ok?"

"What sort of a stupid question was that? No. I am not. The bimbo receptionist should address you as Mr. Davenport; she's not your best mate for God's sake! And it's only just turned three o'clock and the rest of them have gone home…"

She pulled open the draw on Brain's desk and took out a cheap bottle of whisky "Christ! What kind of a set-up is this?" she was *furious* "It's not good enough John, you won't have a cat in hell's chance with this bunch of amateurs".

Carol had walked in at that point and heard every word as she placed the cups of tea down on the desk, and she couldn't get back out of the office quick enough. Rene actually looked more upset than angry now.

"I feel like the whole day has just been bloody ruined".

He was shocked to see such a rare show of emotion.

"Hey, come on, it's not that bad".

She looked at him upset. "Follow me' and he did straight to the boardroom. Only now it was no longer the boardroom, it was his office. Rene had even had the locksmith in to change the lock and the sign writer in to remove the boardroom sign from the door, and replace it with Mr. Davenport.

She smiled and handed him the keys "All yours Mr. Davenport" and as he opened the door and walked inside the whole room had been furnished out to his requirements, right down to a framed picture of him with Lesley and his two daughters sitting on his desk. She shut the door behind them as he looked around in stunned surprised taking in every last detailed change, she smiled "Do you approve?"

Approve he did and walked over to where she was standing and after looking into her eyes for a few moments, with love, they kissed. A long sensual love filled kiss that expressed what they both felt but never once dared say to each other.

Back at the penthouse after agreeing things needed to improve, Rene finished off her rant "Remember, familiarity breeds contempt, and don't rely on other people to give you the stats. It pays to have your own, just keep on top of things John", and John smiled "What? What are you smiling at?" He knew how much she loved him and how much she wanted him to succeed.

John looked into her eyes "Stop worrying, I know what I'm doin and I won't let you down, okay?"

She smiled back at him and knew he was right, he did know what he was doing; she also knew he would never let her down because he loved her in that same unspoken way that she loved him.

Things were hotting up on the security front as Brian Brossly was approached at the site office by a huge black guy calling himself Omar Wakeem, of Omar Security. He was straight to the point advising he was taking over the security contract at Croxteth Country Park Development.

"Ah sorry mate, but that's already in the charge of Huyton & Knowsley Security. They got the contract for the duration. It was awarded before we were even up and running".

Brian couldn't have been any more respectful and clear, but this big bastard wasn't listening and handed Brian his card, "You will need me Mr. Brossly".

It was a blatant threat and Brian was worried, he'd seen this kind of thing many times before and knew how dangerous it could get. He immediately informed Big Harry and Dominic McGuire straight away over the phone. But they'd already had Omar Wakeem checked out by Arthur back at the station, and were confident if he was stupid enough to take them on; they would completely obliterate his business and so called hard man reputation.

Two JCB's were vandalized in the early hours and a small portable cabin was set alight. Followed by a phone call the next day from Omar Wakeem.

"I've checked out Huyton & Knowsley Security Mr. Brossly, and they're crap. I hear they couldn't even protect your JCB's and portable cabin. Now you should get shut of them and bring in Omar Security. That way you're guaranteed no more problems with vandalism".

This was not good, and Brain wanted fuck' all to do with it. He was relieved to be able to pass it on to Big Harry and Dominic McGuire. If the truth be told, he felt too old for all this malarkey and couldn't wait to retire and get the fuck out of the whole construction industry.

Following a meeting with John, Danny Owens, and several security guards that they'd hired, it was agreed that Big Harry and Dominic McGuire were right. They needed to retaliate and hit Omar Security so hard, they'd completely destroy him overnight and instill fear into every other wannabe gangster right across the city at the same time. So this was now being viewed as a mini war, and it was vital that they win it.

They knew it was only a matter of time before one of the main firms came in sniffing for a slice of the action. The needed to end it swiftly; ensure any other deluded cunts with ideas above their station where taken out of the picture. They would be badly mistaken and stopped right in their fuckin tracks so to speak. So Big Harry and Dominic set in motion a series of events to be carried out with military precision.

It was set to completely destroy this amateur cunt' Wakeem and obliterate his Security Firm clean out of existence, in a way that would send out a clear message. It would guarantee no other gangster would take up the challenge and try to oust them, and it would still be talked about in all the local pubs and clubs long after Omar fuckin Wakeem was kicking up the daisies.

It was five am when a loud explosion quickly followed by several smaller ones rocked the buildings in Isaac Stet, blowing out all the windows in the properties there. Omar Wakeem jumped out of bed and stumbled across the room hopping over the shattered glass strewn all over the bedroom floor. The room was already aglow from the fires raging outside.

The net curtain was shredded by the huge shards of jagged glass still sticking out of the window frame. It was flapping and blowing out into the street as he stood bollock naked gaping through the huge hole where only seconds earlier the window had been. In a state of shock he watched his Jaguar, his pride and fuckin joy, now a heap of twisted metal and ablaze. So too was his firm's security van that was parked right next to it, and he couldn't do a thing except stand and fuckin watch as the distant sound of police sirens and fire engines started getting closer.

It was a similar scene in other districts right across the city; Kensington, Wavertree, Old Swan, Garston, Aigburth and Speke. All of them targeted, as every fuckin' security van belonging to Omar, the cunt who'll never take the piss again. Wakeem was blown up at five am outside the homes of the security guards that drove them, and who's names and addresses had been sourced by and courtesy of Arthur McNabb.

At seven thirty am, John was enjoying full English breakfast in the penthouse with Rene as they sat watching the local news television. The newsreader was standing with the fire brigade behind him, still dousing smouldering vehicles as he spoken "At first it was feared the IRA may be responsible as several vehicles exploded all over the city at five am, but police now believe it's the work of gangland fractions fighting for control in the city, and say it's a miracle that no one has been injured or killed".

That was no miracle, five am in any district was deserted, and that's why they picked it. The last thing they wanted was a fuckin murder enquiry chasing at their heels.

John picked up his cup of tea, "Looks like the lads have had a busy night".

He then took a slurp and put the cup back down on the table and began cutting into his bacon like it was an everyday occurrence.

Rene sat in stunned silence unable to eat. She knew there was a darker side to John and "The lads" as he always called them. In some ways that was part of the appeal but she'd only ever seen glimmers of it before now and it was exciting. She liked it if she was honest, even when her grandson Rupert cautioned her to be careful because he thought John was nothing more than a thug; she laughed it off, and why wouldn't she?

Rupert was no more than a coward and a bully himself and interested only in protecting his inheritance. Nothing else mattered to him. He was greedy and spoilt and suspected she was sleeping with John, so perceived him as a threat. But who she slept with had nothing to do with him. It was a private matter and one that she and Edward found no difficulty in living with.

But this matter was genuinely shocking and had her in a state of fright. Not just by the nature and extent of the activities carried out by "the lads", but by John's ability to view them so matter of fact. He was completely unfazed and acted like it was the most normal thing in the world. But it wasn't and she had no idea that things would get this dangerous when she gave him and "the lads" Omar's details.

To be fair she knew they weren't going to invite him around for tea and biscuits and a cozy chat. When she quizzed John about what they did have planned, like he always did when he wanted to protect her from something, he looked her straight in the eye and said

"Ask me no questions and I'll tell you no lies".

So deep down she did know things would get serious, she just didn't think it would be *this* serious. It was a shock being hit in the face with it like that on breakfast news. Still, as the newsreader said, nobody had been hurt or injured… and Harry and Dominic were definitely professional enough not to make mistakes and bring trouble back on them… back on John, back on her and CIDC.

So that was that then. It was done and couldn't be undone, so she decided not to say another word on the matter. John was right, she really shouldn't ask questions on these matters. Now seemed like the perfect time to fly back to Jersey in time for Edward coming home from his New York trip.

John was in the Corn Exchange office and asked Carol to pull out twenty random invoices to see if they matched what had been quoted in tender. She did and they were full of some glaring discrepancies with cement being quoted at one pound a bag, but the invoice claiming one pound twenty, twenty percent more. So he told her to get the supplier in to see him immediately. A couple of hours later Denis Simmons of Parr Building Supplies walked through the door looking very nervous as he offered his hand to John.

"Mr.Davenport, pleased to meet you".

John grinned in his face as he shook his hand

"Sit down Dennis, and call me John".

Dennis relaxed but not for long.

"Right, no point beating around bush… I've been going over your last set of invoices and the amounts tendered are different to what's on them. Can you explain that?"

Dennis was visibly uncomfortable and fidgeting in his seat before clearing his throat and trying to waffle his way out of the situation.

"Ah hum. Erm, that's our early payment discount, and erm, if you settle your account within twenty eight days you qualify".

John gave him an icy stare.

"Then we've got a big problem here Dennis… I've gone back over the past three years invoices and we have always paid you in full, within the twenty eight days settlement period, but, we haven't had one penny discount".

He held his stare accusingly, and Dennis, it's fair to say, was clearly shitting himself and drained of all colour with fright.

"Dennis me old me mate," John was mocking him now because he knew he had him banged to rights, "Your company owes my company two hundred and thirty two thousand, five hundred and eighty pounds. But, our book keeper is going back over the whole eight years we've done business with you… So tha' looks set to become a lot more".

The poor bastard looked like he was about to faint but he tried to hold his nerve and act dumb.

"Erm, I don't understand this John, how have you worked that out like?"

John immediately pulled a document from out of his case and handed it to him. It was dated three years earlier and was an agreement between Brossly Homes and Parr Building Supplies. Highlighting twenty percent would be given on all quotes, where a payment was made within the twenty eight day settlement period, and it'd been signed by Nigel and Dennis. Panic was setting in now and the paper was still shaking in his hand after he read it and became defensive.

"Er, hang on, you got your discount in the form of materials".

Now this was very fuckin interesting.

"I hope for your sake you've got documented proof of tha', as all our materials and invoice records tally. So Dennis, I'll be fixing it for the company auditors to team up with CIDC quantity surveyors, and let them source where almost a quarter of a million pounds worth of materials have been used?"

The poor Bastard sat trembling, "You need to talk to Nigel". In a nanosecond John went from plain speaking to banging his fist on his desk and raising his voice "For fucks sake! Somebody's screwing the company big time and I'm givin' you a chance to be straight with me here!"

He glared accusingly "But if you're not interested you can get out and expect CIDC to sue you as well get a visit from the police. Right now Dennis, you're lookin' more and more like an accessory".

Dennis sat chewing on his bottom lip anxiously at he stared at John. It was obvious he wanted to spill his guts on something or someone. So John changed tack and went all softly-softly catchy-monkey on him.

"Look, to be honest mate, I can make all this go away as far as you're concerned…. But, you've gorra tell me everything".

That was all the gutless bastard needed to hear, that he wouldn't be implicated when the proverbial shit hit the fan. So he let the fuckin lot go.

Nigel had always been in charge of placing orders and for five years he'd had a nice little arrangement going on. Guaranteeing all Brossly Homes orders went to Parr's but in return, instead of Brossly Homes getting the early payment discounts, he took it all in materials. And that was what he built his big posh fuckin house with.

But after the house was completed he got greedy and met with the gaffer at Parr's and made a new arrangement. Thereafter all materials were delivered to a legit warehouse that doubled up as small builder's merchant, and were put down as cash sales under different names. He then sold on to small builders and local people into DIY and business was fuckin booming. But Dennis was shafted by them and was now out of the loop.

John listened to every word with pictures of the sly weasel-faced cunt Nigel, who liked bullying women, going round and round in his head. No wonder Kate was quick to squash talk of getting the police to John for assaulting him. No wonder she panicked to save their jobs. These two robin bastards were making a fuckin mint, but their days were numbered now and he'd have them, big time!

"So, I presume Kate is involved, but what about Brian Brossly?"

Poor old Brian Brossly didn't have a clue, but Kate was a real asset behind the counter every Saturday. Moving her sexy curves and flirting with the punters to make them stick around and spend more money.

John got more information from the land registry and sure enough, Nigel's house was registered. But the best piece of information was that two years earlier he'd applied for planning permission to demolish a small factory and build eight luxury apartments in its place.

The right thing to do now was tell Rene and Edward everything, but where was the sense in that? This had been going on for five years under Brian Bossly's nose and he didn't have a clue. Rene and Edward didn't suspect a thing when they bought him out and took things over. So apart from Dennis, who was scared of his own shadow and guaranteed not to say a word, there was only the other two scheming twats. And they were in it up to their necks so had no choice but to keep their big gobs shut.

This felt like a plan coming on and if he played his cards right everything could work to his own advantage here. It'd be tricky of that there was no doubt, but it was doable, if he weighed things up long enough, really took his time to get it right. The prosperous and booming business trade at the merchants could and would be all his.

If he renewed the planning permission application as well, he could build the eighty luxury apartments for himself. It wasn't robbing off Rene and Edward, as much as preventing that greedy cunt Rupert from getting his hands on it all. That was Rupert's only conversation, it was all he ever spoke about, his inheritance "One day all this will be mine". He said it time and time again to anyone who'd listen, adding he'd sell the lot and fuck off to the states to enjoy a jet set lifestyle with the rich and famous.

But this was one little slice of his very big fuckin cake that he'd never get his hands on, and for that reason alone no matter how long he had to sit tight and work it out for. John would make sure this plan came together, and in a way he was doing Rene and Edward a favour really, because he'd never piss it up the wall like Rupert would.

Chapter Twenty

Lesley had the baby. A healthy seven pound seven ounces bouncing baby girl, and they called her Mandy. But John was gutted and he was angry too. He loved the child, of course he did, but she didn't and could never fill his longing for a son. But this time around Lesley wasn't as sympathetic or as understanding. She'd had a difficult pregnancy and long labour over this one. She was exhausted and had been sick every day for the whole nine months.

Morning sickness, afternoon sickness, even bloody night sickness. And she was glad it was finally all over saying "Never again!"

It had put her off wanting another; she couldn't go through all that again. Wouldn't go through it all again, no matter how much John wanted a son. She'd done her bit now and enough was enough. The first two had been a joy and a doddle throughout the whole nine months and the birth, but this time round ranked as one of the worse experiences of her life.

So no matter how disappointed and angry John was, he'd have to bloody well get on with it. Besides, he was hardly ever at home anyway. He spent more time in Liverpool than he did with her and the girls. So it was a good job she could rely on Brenda who had moved back in to help out.

Her mum was wonderful, a great support, but she was no spring chicken. Brenda on the other hand was fit healthy and very hands on, an absolute God send and part of the furniture now, part of the family. John needed to respect that and stop calling her stuck up because she wasn't that at all. She was just quiet and reserved, and she worked bloody hard to help them run the boarding house, farm and shops.

So it was time he stopped it, besides, if he didn't it was only a matter of time before the girls copied him and repeated it in front of Brenda. That would be deeply embarrassing and quite hurtful to her. No, it had to stop. Brenda had no children of her own but she loved these three little ones. They made up for her not having any of her own and she loved them dearly. They loved her too, and at the end of the day that was what mattered.

Lesley was being very offish towards John. She had started wearing more cloths to bed than when she was out and about, a housecoat as well as pyjamas which was a bit over the top even by her standards. A point John was making to Rene after they had just had another energetic bout of love making.

"Give the girl a chance John, she has had three children in four years she will need to be given time". That's what Renee was saying but what she was thinking was 'all the more for me, her loss my gain'.

This time as John got ready to return to Liverpool, it felt as if Lesley was relieved to see him going back. Not like his eldest Rachel, she clung on to him saying "Love you daddy". This brought a lump in John's throat and he gave Lesley a look as if to say she loves me. It was at that point that he made his mind up that he would make sure that what was ever going on in Lesley's head, he would get to the bottom of it next time he was home.

Jimmy called up John and told him he was in town and he had something he might find interesting, and he was going to drop it off. As soon as John opened the door at the penthouse, Jimmy walked through it and handed him a large brown envelope "Look what I found when I was sortin' out some of me mums stuff".

Confused John opened it and took out an official letter and read it before looking back at him gob smacked.

"Wow, after all these years".

It was the Huyton and Knowsley Golf Club letter sent to his dad confirming the two thousand pound late penalty clause they screwed him for, and the poxy one thousand pound payment. And all those involved were named in it, but old age had already seen two of them off and they were kicking up the daisies in West Derby cemetery. That left Peter Finch and Eric, "Cunt features" Decker, and chairman of the of the housing committee Mr. Brain Read. Everything came back to him and he felt the hate and the anger soar through his body.

"That bastard family! So Eric was in on it too, screwing dad of his hard earned cash, while Eddie was screwing Dot at the same time! If it's the last thing I do I'll crucify these cunts!"

Also in the envelope was the picture of him and Dot in the Liverpool Echo under the caption '*Pair of winners*', they looked so happy young and carefree. But he was too angry for fuckin' nostalgia, so he put it in his briefcase.

"Ring the lads and get them all round here".

Within the hour Big Harry, Dominic McGuire, Danny Owens and Arthur McNabb were all sitting in the penthouse wondering what the fuck was so urgent. Jimmy sat with them in silence as John poured out the drinks then sat down with them

"Right, it's time to make some serious wedge on two new projects"

They were all ears.

"Project one" He handed the letter to Arthur "Pass it round when you've read it". Everyone was as shocked as Jimmy and John when they realized Eric Decker was in on Joe Kelly being shafted out of his retirement money. Holding up his glass of whiskey he glared at them.

"We sort these cunts out once for all, agreed?"

They all raised a glass 'agreed' they also agreed to bring the world of Peter Finch crashing down around him.

"Project two, Nigel Anderson and his extremely fit wife Kate, have been creaming it off Brossly Homes for years, and have continued to cream it since Brian Brossly sold the company to CIDC".

He proceeded to give them chapter and verse on every detail of what they'd been up too. Then he grinned.

"So, I think it's time we had a bit of fun and set a few plans into action". Danny Owens was a little unsure.

"Where does Rene come into all this, mate?"

John made himself very clear on that matter.

"Look, her and Edward haven't got a clue they're being ripped off, and as long as we go about things in the right way, they never will. Besides, they'll never even spend what they've already got for fucks sake, and in a way we're doing them a favour".

Everyone looked confused and Jimmy asked the question -

"How do you work that one out John?"

John mischievously smiled "It'll stop that greedy cunt of a grandson Rupert getting his hands on it and pissing it up the wall, so let's do it, yeah?" They all laughed as he raised his glass "Cheers!" and in turn they raised theirs, "Cheers".

Like every other Friday, the staff at Brossly Homes finished early and went for a few drinks to the Corn Market pub. But this particular Friday, John followed on to join them. Kate spotted him as soon as he walked through the doors and waved "Come and join us".

He nodded got a pint, then weaved his way through the punters and sat next to her. The place was heaving and smoke filled with the usual Friday revelers being rowdy above the sound of the juke box, and raucous laughter reverberated around the place. Kate was all smiles and tits as she raised her voice to be heard "How come you followed us on?"

John kept a straight face leaned forward and whispered loudly in her ear.

"I need to talk to you and Nigel".

He looked around the place then back at her.

"Somewhere quieter and more private".

She was totally unsure "About what?".

John glared at her accusingly "The warehouse and builders merchant business. Follow me outside".

He downed his pint in one go then left the company and within less than five minutes Kate and Nigel had followed him outside. They were both bungled into the back of their own car by two security guards wearing balaclavas. As the car sped off, they protested in panic and fear. The security guard sitting in the front passenger seat turned around and leaned over to the back, and put a gun in Nigel's face "Shut the fuck up".

Kate and Nigel were driven into a warehouse that was overlooking the river Mersey; it was huge empty and very cold, and in one of the far corners was a dimly lit office with the blinds closed.

Not too far away stood a bare table and three straight back chairs. With the gun still firmly pressed into his temple, Nigel and Kate had no option but to do as they were ordered and walk towards them and sit down. They were left sitting there as the guards walked back to sit in their car.

Then they heard the sound of footsteps as John walked through the doors they'd been driven through and closed them behind him, before slowly walking towards them, pulling back a chair, and sitting down with them. John then looked at them both with a blank expression and his usually bright blue eyes were dead and so cold, they chilled them both to the bone. He held his stare and the silence was as terrifying as it was deafening.

"What's all this about John?"

Her face was white with fear and her voice quivered when she spoke, but for all her fear he knew she'd be the first one who found the balls to speak. Then as casual as you like he told her

"The quarter of a million pounds you've creamed off Brossly Homes and now CIDC" He then pulled a hand full of rolled up papers out of his jacket pocket and pushed them across the table. It was a summary of all the figures and discounts, *not* received

"Now if you add on top of tha' little lot the labour costs used to build your big posh house, and the wages you pay your staff at the warehouse and building Merchants… who know what the final sum will come to?"

Nigel was visibly terrified and to coin an old phrase was 'shaking in his fuckin Hush Puppy boots'. Kate looked confused as well as frightened but she held her nerve

"So what are you proposing John?" He liked this woman a little bit more every time he was with her, she was too good for this gutless prick that's for sure. But he didn't answer. He just nodded towards their car and signalled to the driver with his hand. Once again the silence was deafening and they watched in fear as their car was driven to the very far end on the warehouse then stopped.

The security guards got out and unlocked two huge doors that opened out onto a sudden sharp drop right into the river Mersey. They then got back into the car and drove it to the absolute tip of the edge.

"These are your options".

John was nonchalant now.

"One, we bring in the police and on conviction sue you for return of all monies, plus interest of course. But I doubt selling your house and the building merchants would cover all that, besides; tha' would all take time and drag on for years".

Nigel was wide eyed and trembling like a rabbit caught in the fuckin headlights.

"Option two" He paused just for dramatic effect', after leaving suicide notes at your home telling family and friends how you couldn't bare losing your home, your business, and your reputation in the city, you're both found in your car".

He nodded to their car precariously parked at the edge of the river "In the bottom of the Mersey of course. Then with all the evidence we've got, we just make a claim on your estate after your death. And with the sale of both house and business will recoup at least some of the cash for us".

Kate couldn't stand it any longer. She was shaking with fear but her nerves got the better of her and she couldn't stop herself from gobbing off.

"So go on then big man. What's option three?"

Her sarcasm was duly noted.

"Hand over the deeds to your house and the Builders Merchants" He paused *and* the cash you've salted away in the bank".

He stood up at that point.

"I'll leave you to think about it and talk it over"

Then walked away from them and went straight into the office.

"Did you get all tha?"

A microphone had been fitted underneath the table and Big Harry and Dominic McGuire were monitoring every word that was being said "Shhhhh" John grinned as he pulled up a chair and sat with them as they continued to listen to Kate and Nigel having a domestic.

"So much for telling me everything you done was a big tax fiddle, you lying bastard! This lot means business and we're in deep shit here, and you haven't done a fucking thing to protect me!"

The sound of a loud smack could be heard connecting with Nigel's face, and they all put their hands up over their mouths to stifle the laughing.

"How much have we got? And I want the truth!"

Now this was what they wanted to hear so it soon shut the laughing up as they listened to Nigel reluctantly speak.

"Just over forty thousand".

She sat fuming as she starred at him for a few moments.

"Right, when we get out of this mess. You go the bank and get the fucking lot out. Then we go to my sisters in Kent, We sell the house and business in the auctions and move to Spain as soon as we can".

It was clear to all concerned she hadn't been in on the scam, and they couldn't help but be impressed and admire her ability to think on her feet.

"You had me thinking my life was on the up in the house of my dreams and being in charge of the sales in a big company. But you've fucking ruined everything like you always do!"

John stepped back out of the office and joined them again.

"Well, what's it to be?"

Nigel looked down like the coward he was, so Kate looked him square in the eye.

"Well as we've got no real choice in the matter. We'll hand over the deeds and ten grand in savings that we've got".

John smiled. She was still edging her bets, trying to keep some back for her and shit head. But that was never going to happen. But he liked her style for trying. She was definitely the kind of woman he'd like on his side if he ever came unstuck. Yeah, she was wasted on this gutless little shit and better by far, too good and too smart for him in every way.

"No. You'll give us the full forty grand and the deeds, and on Monday morning Nigel will go to the bank and put all tha' in motion".

Nigel looked up and agreed straight away "Does that mean we can go now?"

John grinned "You can. But after the conversation you've just had about fuckin off to her sisters in Kent, she stays with me until Monday".

They were over a barrel and there was fuck all they could do to change it, Kate expected Nigel to at least put up some sort of objection, but Nigel didn't even try and as he walked away without as much as one backward glance. It hurt her big time and was the defining moment that made her promise herself if she ever got out of this unscathed and alive. He was fucking history.

A heavy silence hung between them as John drove to the penthouse and they never spoke one word when they stopped in the underground car park of the Atlantic Tower Hotel. Mentally her head spinning and she planned how she'd fight him if he tried to rape her, but that would be a waste of time he would be much too strong for her she resigned herself to her fate.

Then as they stood alone in the lift together she avoided eye contact with him, and she couldn't step out quick enough when it finally stopped on the top floor and the doors opened automatically. There were just two suites on the whole of the floor and as John turned the key in the door to one of them. He nodded for her to enter ahead of him.

Once inside he nodded for her to sit down and as she did he picked up the phone and ordered them something to eat from room service. Then he opened a bottle of expensive wine that he'd finally acquired the taste for, and poured them both a glass "Look, I don't want you here under these circumstances any more than you wonna be here, but its business, big money… You're a smart woman Kate, you must understand tha".

She didn't look at him or say a word as she sipped at her wine. Hoping it would help to take away the fear and sickening feeling she had in the pit of her stomach. He knew she was frightened and he didn't like himself for that. But business is business and with these sums of money involved he couldn't afford to be sentimental. Still, he didn't want her frightened. He didn't want any woman to be frightened of him.

"I'm trying to say is, this isn't personal Kate so you can relax, cos I'm not going to hurt you love. That room over there' He pointed to the spare room 'is yours, it's got a lock on it so you can feel safe, ok?" She didn't look at him but she felt some of the tension and fear she felt inside draining away as she nodded, and he knew he'd just made a break through".

The following morning he ordered them both a breakfast from room service as if it was normal to do that for your kidnap victim. Then he sat eating his like he didn't have a care in the fuckin world. She'd rather him have breakfast and be nice to her than anything else, so she ate. He mopped up the last of the brown sauce on his plate with his bacon butty then stopped just before biting into it "Oh yeah, I didn't know your size but guessed you're about a twelve. So there's a sports bag in the bathroom. You'll find all the changes of underwear you need and a couple of tracksuits too, that'll get you through to Monday". Then he bit into his bacon butty and scanned the morning paper like she wasn't even there.

This guy was unbelievable. One minute he was putting the fear of God into her, the next he was ordering her breakfast, and now he was making sure she had all she needed to get her through the weekend. But by Monday he planned to destroy her life by taking her house, her career, and every penny she owned. He was one scary fuck, an unknown quantity, probably a fuckin psychopath.

Kate was confused. In work he was a good laugh and got on well with everyone, apart from Nigel, who now made her sick to her stomach. But there was no denying that John was fair to everyone and was actually a really warm and likeable fella, when he wasn't being threatening.

Even when she heard him speaking on the phone to Lesley his wife, she was struck by how loving he was towards her and his kids. In fact under different circumstances she knew he was the sort of fella she'd really get on with, not least of all because he was exciting and really sexy too.

Chapter Twenty One

Paula Harris was a stunning looking twenty three year old mother of two children under the age of three. Life had been unkind to her when the father of her two girls had been killed in a building site accident. The fact that he was paid cash in hand meant he had no insurance so Paula not only lost the love of her life, but she had lost her sole provider.

In order to keep the roof over head and put food on the table she had turned to the oldest profession in the world and had only been on the game two weeks when she had been given a police caution. One day as she was getting her two kids ready for bed there was a knock on the door of her two bedroomed flat. When she opened the door she did not know the person standing there. When he introduced himself as detective sergeant Arthur McNabb from Merseyside police, she insisted on seeing his identification.

Reluctantly, she let him in, not knowing what he wanted and she was thinking it was for the unpaid fines she had been given for soliciting. She told him to take a seat while she put the kids to bed and when she returned to the living room she was all ears.

Arthur got straight to the point when he started the conversation when he said

"Paula I have got a business proposition for you. How would you like to make a lot of money".

"Doing what" she replied "and How much" she replied.

"Ten grand plus bonus and expenses".

"What the fuck do you want doing for that type of money".

"Get me a coffee and I will explain" was his reply.

Two hours later shook hands with Paula and gave her a thousand pound down payment.

Less than two weeks later Paula was sitting in the office of Brian Read, the chairman of the housing committee. It is amazing how splashing the cash can move you up the housing chain. It was a break she needed.

With a brand new sexy short dress she looked good enough to eat, the way she sitting she was making sure that the councillor was getting a good eye full, and Brain Read was taking full advantage.

The councillor picked up the papers from his desk, he looked at them then said to Paula "Well Miss Harris I have looked at your application to rehouse from your flat to a house and you are way down the list and you just don't have the points on your account that the council use to rehouse people".

Paula parting her legs slightly said "Mr. Read I will do anything to get out of that shithole of a flat, I now live in I fear for my children's health, the place is so damp, if you came to see it personally I am sure you would agree and make me the exception".

"Let me check my diary to see when I am free" as he looked at it he could fell himself getting aroused by the site of this young beauty sitting before him. Not being the type that let the grass under his feet, he thought no time like the present.

"I am free this afternoon, I could call around then say 1 pm?"

Paula knew she had him on the hook "That sounds great, I will be waiting for you".

As she got up to leave Brian Read could not take his eyes off Paula's backside. She was not the first one that had offered sex in exchange for being rehoused, but she was by far the most stunning.

One o'clock sharp, Paula opened the door to her flat and led the councilor in to her home. She did not beat about the bush, she just led him strait to her bedroom. They both knew why he was there.

Some two hours later, it was a very happy Brain Read that left Paula's flat. The wild uninhabited sex he had just had blown his mind. It was the best he had experienced in years and he was going to bend every rule in the book to get this girl rehoused. He did not want to let this beauty slip away, he would call in every favour he was owed and then some. He had swallowed every word that Paula had told him when she said that she preferred older men, especially successfully ones like him.

She had fed his ego to a tee, and from that point on Brain read called to her apartment every morning and stay for between one and two hours. What he did not know was every time he called his visits were being monitored by a local reporter who also worked free-lanced for the News of the World Sunday national newspaper.

Joan Peters had been sitting at her desk in the Liverpool Echo office, where she worked as an investigating reporter. She was in the process of opening her mail and one piece in particular had caught her attention. It was a letter claiming that a Knowsley councillor Brain Read had been giving council homes to single woman with children, in exchange for sexual favours.

The article detailed how his latest conquest entertained him every Monday, Wednesday and Friday mornings in her flat in Sledgely Walk, in Longview Huyton. He usually arrived at around ten am and left at twelve. Enclosed were a dozen photos of the councillor going in and out of Paula's flat on a regular bases. There were even snaps of them in one or two restaurants.

The sender informed the reporter that Miss Paula Harris had been offered a three bedroomed house in the popular Knowsley Lane, and at this very moment the council are in the middle of completing a total refurbishment on the property. Paula Harrison was going to be moving in when she came back from a council conference, which was taking place next week in East Bourne, where she was accompanying Mr. Read for the three day event as his guest.

The Echo reporter lost no time in finding out which hotel was hosting the event and Brain Read was in fact booked in to the Hilton for four nights. Joan the reporter was confused when she found out that he was booked in to a double room with another male college.

Her boss had her and the photographer booked in to a local Hotel in East Bourne to make sure the story was true.

The first thing Joan did was take all the information to her boss, who in turn brought in the legal department. They reiterated the seriousness of the claim and that they had better get the facts right before they could publish anything. The paper's leading photographer was allocated to the case and Joan was told to do as much background checks on councillor Brian Read, to see if he had any other skeletons in his past.

As arranged Paula Harris met with Arthur McNabb in the Hanover Hotel in Liverpool City centre. She was keeping him up-to-date as to the progress she was making. Handing over the sixth payment of a thousand pounds he told her "It will not be long now, you move into your new house after you get back from the conference then we will have the bastard".

"I hope so he repulses me, he must be four stone over weight and when comes to the flat he makes sure he gets his money's worth. To think I have going to spend four days and four nights with him, the pig - I am starting to wonder was this all worth it?"

Arthur had expected something like this, so he told her about the other sweetener he had planned for her if she pulled what they had started off "How long did you say that you worked as a barmaid?"

"Four years, why?" Arthur took out a photo of a pub and put it on the table.

"Do you think you could run your own place?"

"No problem, it's a piece of piss, why?"

"Well here's the deal, this pub The Nags Head is located in Southport. The lease has ten years to run and has been prepaid for three years you and you kids will be li-ving there when the shit hits the fan. The fact is you could never have lived in that house in Knowsley lane, once the story broke in the papers". There was a long silence. Paula did not know what to say when she did speak all she said "You're not taking the piss are you".

"No I told you this prick has upset some very influential people and its pay-back time".

Paul looked relieved "Tell you what, next week he is not going to know what's hit him. I am going to screw the brains out of him. This is just the thing I needed to put a spring back in my step".

This was just the reaction Arthur was waiting for. He also knew it was best not put all his cards on the table when he first met Paula in case she lost interest. He then took out another picture this time it was one of Joan Peters the reporter.

"This woman is a reporter. There is a good chance she will approach you when you're in East Bourne. It will probably happen when the councillor is in conference and you are on your own. Do not tell too much, just tell her you're a with a friend with benefits so to speak.

You don't have to tell her who you are with, she already knows. Make sure to tell her about the tragic death of you boyfriend leaving you high and dry with two young kids. If she asks you how come you're here, just sometimes 'a girl's has got to do what a girl's got to do' and leave it at that and get up and go to your room".

"How can you be sure she will contact me."

He explained "She is very good at her job. She will not let it go at that, she will almost certainly bump into you again. This time you be a little bit more friendly, tell her about your job as a bar maid, and only left you just above the poverty line living from hand to mouth. She may think what a load of bollocks when she looks at the way your dressed, so you need to be convincing of the truth".

"Why should I tell her that? Would it better to just let her do her job without me getting involved?"

"No, I want her to really go for it. She will have a story that has everything, sex corruption. Abuse of power, a young beautiful 23 year old victim and an old overweight sixty year old politician taking advantage".

Paula was starting to worry, just what the fuck she had got herself into. It was obvious that Arthur was just a front for and whoever it was they must have some clout the way they were splashing the cash.

After leaving Arthur, Paula made her way to the post office and placed most of the money she had just been given in to her post office savings account. She had built up a tidy nest egg just in case this Arthur was bullshitting her. She would need to move fast when the shit hit the fan.

That night the lads got to gather and Arthur reported that everything was in place and Mr. Brain Read was being set up for the biggest fall of his life. He told John that the little carrot dangler of an offer of the tenancy of a pub in Southport made Paula all the more determined to go through to complete the task at hand.

Brain Read was disappointed when Paula turned up at the hotel as he had made his way to East Bourne with the rest of the councillors. Paula had followed him by train. Paula had dressed down on the advice of Arthur, as he wanted her to give off the image of the girl next door type not some brass.

It was the second day of the conference. Brain was in attendance in the main conference hall. Paula had been to the hair dressers, she had made her way back to the hotel and made her way up to bar and ordered a large gin and tonic when a voice next to her say is that a Liverpool accent?

Paula turned to face Joan Peters the reporter. It was just as Arthur had warned her, this would happen. Paula smiled and said "Huyton" picked up her drink and turned and took a chair at a table near the bar. Joan followed her and pointing an empty chair said "Do you mind?"

Paula shook her head and Joan sat down, who wasted no time in engaging Paula in conversation "So you here on holiday or work?"

"Sort of, I am with a friend just staying a few days. So what part of the pool are you from?" Paula asked.

"Crosby".

"So how come your down here" asked Paula.

"Work I've got an interview with a local hotel as an assistant manager".

They chatted for a while, Paula telling Joan about the death of her husband and how she was struggling to bring up two kids. Joan could not believe her luck in getting so much back ground information.

The morning session in the conference room had finished for a lunch break. Paula spotted Brain heading her way and she got up from her chair turning to Joan saying

"Ah well a girls got to do what a girls got to do" she then walked over to Brain and made her way to the restaurant for lunch. As soon as they vanished Joan jumped up and made her way to her colleague who had been sitting some way of taking pictures

"Did you get any good ones?"

"Sure did the one with his hand planted firmly on her arse. It's a cracker"

"I felt a bit sorry for her having to give herself to that grease ball, just to get a bloody decent place to live. She obviously does not want to be with this creep" she commented to her colleague.

Chapter Twenty Two

Joan Peters' boss was really pleased with her. She had got her story all finished and ready to publish. She had only had been on the case for four weeks and she had Brain Read 'bang to rights'. Normally this type of investigation took months, if not years. The photos of Brain Read helping Paula to move into her three bedroomed house, and coming and going as he pleased with his own key, along with all the East Bourne pictures, proved beyond any reasonable doubt that he was a manipulative evil man.

It was a Monday morning when Paula's doorbell rang when she opened it she was surprised to see Joan Peters on her doorstep. Paula pretended not to recognize her. It was Joan who spoke first, "Hi, I don't suppose you remember me from East Bourne do you? We need to talk."

Paula invited her in.

"Look I will come straight to the point. I wasn't telling you the truth when I told you I was searching for work, when we had a drink together. I am really a reporter working for the Echo newspaper group"

"So what's that got to do with me?" Paula asked.

"I am here to warn you that we are running a story line on Brain Read" Joan told Paula.

"When is it going to hit the street?" Paula pretended to look shocked and angry.

"Tonight. I would have liked to have given you more warning, but I could not take the risk. This way you can at least lay low until it blows over. This place will be swarming with reporters and police. I'm sorry to do this."

They chatted some more and Paula wanted to bring this to a swift end.

"Thanks for the tip off, I need to start packing ready to get the fuck out of here". She led Joan to the door. Paula could not help herself, causing a bit of mischief as she was closing the door she said to Joan "By the way which of the photos are you going to use. Did you catch him leaning over the table trying to kiss me, or the one where he had his hand on my rear end when I first met you? You should tell your photographer to be a bit more discrete now. Bye" she closed the door on Joan.

It hit Joan as she sat in her car that Paula had known all along that she was a reporter. If that was the case, then it was odds on she knew the person who gave her the tip off in the beginning.

Brian Read was in his office when he received a call from his wife screaming at him calling him a low life cheating bastard. The echo had him on the front page exposing him for the pervert that he was. No matter how many times Brain told his wife that the story was not true, she was inconsolable. Angrily she told him that she was packing a bag and going to stay with their eldest son who lived in Wales.

Brains heart was racing, he felt sick and his head was spinning. He was feeling like his world was closing in on him. Just as he thought things could not get worse, it did. As Brian was about to leave to get a copy of the newspaper, in came the Leader of the Council, followed by two of his colleagues. One who was from the legal department, in his hand was a copy of the Liverpool echo. There was nowhere to hide from this. On the front page, a full picture of Brain outside the Hilton with his arm around Paula, whose face had been blanked out of the photograph.

Sweating and pointing to the paper Brian said "This is a set-up, I'll sue the bastards"

His boss quietly replied "I think you should read the article first. What the hell were you thinking of?"

"It's not what it looks like ok. I have had an affair, but I am not the first and won't be the last" Brain said trying to play down the situation.

"Then how come she ended up in a three bedroom house, in a sort after area and how did she jump to the top of the housing queue. I have called an emergency meeting this afternoon. We need to get to the bottom of this. You are suspended" Turning to Brain he said "If I was you I would get a good solicitor".

Rupert wasn't best pleased and complained loudly at being instructed by Edward to spend more time in Liverpool overseeing their investments. But as Edward was back and forth on business trips to New York, he gave him no option "I can't be in all places at all times Rupert, and Rene does her share in Liverpool. So you can too. So sort out it out man, and stop complaining".

That was that, and Rupert seethed with resentment. He didn't want to go to Liverpool because he couldn't stand John Davenport. He was an opportunist who just got lucky getting involved with his grandparents, and he'd be dammed if he'd let John wheedle his way into the Burgess empire as well. As that was all his, every last penny of it, and John Davenport would be history the day he gets his hands on it and takes over the running of CIDC.

As just like every other Scouser, he'd ever met, John was as thick as pig shit and just a thug. It never crossed his toffee nosed mind, that John was actually already worth a fortune in his own right, and he didn't have to be separated from his wife and kids and work his bollocks off week in and week out.

John did so because he liked to work and provide for his family, regardless of how much they already had. Unlike Rupert who enjoyed sitting back on his big greedy fat arse, being fuckin spoon fed. Besides, like it or not, his grandmother actually loved John and she had his grandfather's blessing on the matter, and John in his own way actually loved her too.

Big Harry was waiting for Nigel outside of the bank and warned him not to try anything foolish or Kate would suffer. He nodded in acknowledgment of the warning and entered the bank with Harry almost stuck to him he was that close. While Dominic McGuire was ransacking his big posh house looking for any other stashed cash.

Kate was beginning to relax, despite the absurdity and seriousness of her predicament. She knew how to keep a cool head and play the game. She and John were even managing to have a laugh over breakfast with radio city playing in the background "Listen, I've gorra proposition for yeh". It killed the laughing dead, and she immediately tensed "Here we go, I sleep with you and you'll reconsider things?"

He grinned "A business proposition soft girl… if you and Nigel play ball and do what I say I'll let you keep the deeds to your house, and I'll let you both keep your jobs".

He had her full attention and her face softened, so he continued

"I've gorra very old score to settle with someone who shafted my arl fella out of a very serious wedge years ago. Interested?"

If it meant she could keep her beautiful house and her job, of course she was interested. Her life savings would be gone after today and she was in no position to turn this down. So she was all ears as he explained…

He'd applied to renew the planning permission on the site Nigel had never got around to building on, but the deeds remained in Nigel's name. "Once the planning permission is granted, Nigel will be approached by a building developer who'll offer to pay for all the building costs, and split the profits fifty-fifty on completion. Nigel will accept that offer but the site will never be finished".

She was holding on to his every word and truth be told she was excited

"I want the people you'll be dealing with to cut corners, and don't worry they will because they always do. And they'll be dead easy to tempt on board with the sums of cash they think they'll make".

He was confident and had everything worked out. But he kept the last details back, for now, and she was up for it. She'd make sure her gutless snake of a husband would be too, and she quite liked the fact that whatever it all turned out like in the end. It wasn't for money and it wasn't for sex either. It was for something terrible that had been done to John's dad years earlier. And she liked his style because she'd do the same if someone hurt her dad.

All weekend Nigel toyed with the idea of going to Lime Street station and getting the first train out of Liverpool. And it wasn't the thought of leaving Kate who had been kidnapped and the fact that she could have been beaten raped or even killed that stopped him. It was the sure knowledge that John and his band of men would track him down and kill him that made him stay. He was now a quivering nervous wreck as he sat on the luxurious white leather sofa in the penthouse, with eighty thousand pounds spread across the smoked glass coffee table.

Brian was surrounded by Big Harry, Dominic McGuire, John and Kate all starring at him accusingly.

"You lying gutless bastard! I could kill you myself!" Kate flew at him and John dragged her back but not before she managed to land one on him right in the kisser.

Dominic McGuire had found an extra forty thousand pounds he'd stashed away right, under Kate's nose in a safe under the floorboards in her bedroom. The atmosphere was tense and Kate was white with temper and upset so John took control.

"Look, I'm gonna cut you a bit of slack here Nigel. I can see you've had to try to keep something back".

Almost mocking now he added

"We'd of done the same wouldn't we lads?"

Big Harry and Dominic played along nodding in agreement and Nigel seized on it

"I was just trying to secure me and Kate future, because you're taking everything from us".

He was a coward and weak and John looked at him with disgust

"You're a greedy cunt Nigel, who was tryin' to shaft your own woman as well as us"

Nigel was shitting himself and his eyes widened the size of saucers with fear.

"But, there is a way back from this Nigel" John leaned over the table counted some of the cash then pushed ten grand across to Kate "that's now all hers, ok?"

Nigel nodded "Good… but if I find out you've spent as much as one penny of it I'll stamp all over your fuckin head till your brain bursts, gorrit?"

He got it all right and nodded so much his fuckin' head nearly fell off.

"I'm glad we understand each other Nigel, cos now you're gonna sit and listen to how you're gonna earn the deeds to your house back, as well as your job".

Chapter Twenty Three

Rene kissed Edward, "Don't work too hard". He kissed her "You too darling, let Rupert do his bit for a change". She smiled "Don't worry I will. Now go before you're late". She gave him one last peck on the cheek, "Safe journey darling". Then she stood and watched as he walked several yards away before turning around to give her one last smile and a wave. She smiled back as she blew him a kiss before he finally walked out of sight, to their private plane that was waiting on the runway ready to fly him to New York.

Francesca had made sure Rupert had everything packed and ready for his business trip to Liverpool with his grandmother.

But Rene had no sooner walked through the door when the phone rang. Edward's plane had crashed before it had even flown out of Jersey and Edward and crew were all dead.

John flew back to Jersey immediately and was met at the airport by Lesley without the kids. But she didn't throw her arms around his neck and greet him with her usual hugs and kisses. This time she was cool and stand-offish and greeted him with no more than a polite kiss on the cheek. He put it down to the shock of Edward dying and on the drive home asked if anybody knew what caused the crash.

It hadn't been confirmed, but it seemed to have all the hall marks of pilot error and was probably just a tragic accident. Rene was in terrible shock and heartbroken, so Rupert had taken control of things and was asking everyone to respect the family privacy and stay away until the funeral.

John was not best pleased by that, in fact, he was very fuckin annoyed and worried sick about Rene. He had no option but to be seen to respect Rupert's request. The funeral was a grand and lavish affair with family friends and business associates flying in from countries all around the world to be there, making it impossible for him to get close to Rene.

Sitting next to Lesley in the church he gazed across to where Rene sat. She looked like she'd aged over night and was truly devastated, and that hurt. Even though he knew she and Edward loved each other dearly, she never rubbed it in his face. Just as he never flaunted what he felt for Lesley, but now it was right under his nose and he could see the depth of that love and the loss, and it wasn't comfortable.

He still wanted and needed to hold her and comfort her, but with Rupert playing the devoted grandson that neigh on impossible. Especially as Rupert and Francesca, took Rene out a cruise on The Blue Lady the day after the funeral to help her to recoup.

Lesley was still being distant and very cool and was clearly pissed off over something, so putting his concerns for Rene to one side he decided to confront her, and she tore into him

"You can neglect me and this marriage as much as you like! I really don't care. But you will not neglect the girls! They miss you and really look forward to you coming home every two weeks. But you're disappointing and hurting them every time you cancel yet another weekend at home with them, for yet another weekend of business in Liverpool, and for what? It's not like we need the bloody money!"

It was true he'd cancelled quite a few weekends home with them lately. But he could hardly tell her it was because he'd kidnapped a very sexy woman and held her hostage in his penthouse. Or that he was up to his neck in gangland style shenanigans and was about to wreak some long overdue havoc in lives of those cunts who wreaked havoc in his and his family's life many years earlier. And they'd been stupid enough to think it was all forgotten about and over, so wouldn't see what was heading right in their direction like a fuckin' torpedo.

So he smoothed her over because when all said and done, she was his wife and the mother to his kids, She was good a mother too and that counted for everything. Regardless of the fact that she was never interested in sex these days, and when she did let him close she was still boring and lacked that fire possessed by Rene, that chemistry, that passion. That same passion he felt when he looked at Kate.

In the cold light of the day, he knew in his heart, Lesley and the kids were the best things that had ever happened to him. They were his pride and joy, his very life. The life he kept separate to his one in Liverpool. The life he kept separate to his life with Rene. So he took what she dished out and promised it would change once Ray Hall's wife was better and Ray was back at work in Liverpool. He'd then take some time off to spend at home with her and the kids and spoil them all rotten.

Rene spent all of her time in her cabin heavily sedated, while Rupert spent all of his time drinking with his wife, Francesca.

"Darling, when CIDC and the rest of the Burgess Empire is in my control. I'll waste no time in winding things down and selling off most of it. So we can finally enjoy the jet set life style in America that we deserve"

Francesca was a docile woman who catered to his every whim and obeyed his every command

"But how can you be so sure that everything will be in your control by the end of this trip?"

Rupert shook his head in frustration of her stupidity. He'd bullied her into getting tranquillizers for herself off her doctor. Then instructed her to take them out of the box so they couldn't be identified as hers, and give the strips to an Ingrid to administer to his grandmother, who was already being administered her own prescribed tranquillizers, and was now being slowly and very deliberately overdosed by an unsuspecting Ingrid.

"Try to keep up darling. Grandmother thinks we're on our way to the Canary Islands, but I've instructed the Captain to change course for Florida. We'll be calling into port in France to take on the extra fuel we need to cross the Atlantic".

The penny was a long time dropping "Yes, but I still don't understand".

The naivety of the woman annoyed him immensely

"Darling do you practice at being this stupid or does it really come naturally?"

She looked at him startled and hurt and he gave a huge sigh of exasperation

"Look, in the time it takes for us to reach Florida. Grandmother will have slipped into a deep coma… Don't you see? It will be too late to save her and everybody will understand her not wanting to go on without Grandfather… I will then be granted power of attorney and everything will become ours".

She was wide eyed with shock and very frightened, but neither she nor Rupert realized that his every word had carried, and was heard quite clearly by an equally shocked and alarmed Ingrid who was in the galley.

Ingrid hid every tablet in her own cabin and pretended to medicate Rene, who regained consciousness within two days and was horrified when Ingrid told her what Rupert was up too. Petrified she told Ingrid to instruct the Captain to wait until night fall when Rupert would be drunk and asleep, then change course and head straight back to Jersey.

Renes also asked Ingrid to get an urgent message to John right away for him and the boys to be waiting on the harbor when they arrive, and not take no for an answer but come straight on board. In the meantime she pretended to be sedated, especially when poor petrified Francesca popped into her cabin and asked Ingrid to stop administering the tables, but not tell Rupert.

All crew were warned not utter a word to Rupert that they'd changed course, and after receiving his message John telephoned each of the lads in Liverpool, and told them to drop everything and get the first flight over to Jersey because Rene was in trouble.

Realizing they were heading back to Jersey and were probably no more than an hour away from Port, Rupert stormed up to the Captains bridge to ask what the bloody hell was going on. But he got the shock of his life when he flung the open the door, and seen Rene sitting there with a mug of tea in her hand, "Grandmother!"

She put her mug down and after giving him the filthiest look she could muster, she pushed passed forcefully and walked out onto the deck. Where Francesca gasped with shock and relief and rushed towards her with a warm embrace "Oh thank God you're okay". As Rupert looked on seething as the sound of the gangplank could be heard hitting the harbor floor, and John and the others immediately stepped on deck.

Big Harry and Dominic stayed at the entrance, but Danny Owens Arthur McNabb and John walked straight up to Rene. She looked terrible; her hair looked like it had never seen a brush or comb and she was pale and thin, and though John and the others still didn't have a clue what had happened. They knew enough to know whatever it was, Rupert would be behind it and they were truly concerned and upset to see her that way, but none more so than John

"Come on love, let's get you home" she smiled and forced a joke as she linked him "I knew my cavalry wouldn't let me down".

John asked the lads to give him some time alone with Rene and back at her home she told him everything. How Rupert had pressured Francesca into getting the same tranquillizers she had been prescribed when Edward died. How he destroyed the box that identified them as Francesca's, and put the strips of tablets with hers then instructed Ingrid to administer her double the dose four times a day.

It wasn't the brightest of plans and Ingrid was uncomfortable administering such high doses, but did so thinking she was following medical instructions passed on by Rupert. So she was slowly being overdosed until Ingrid overheard his conversation that terrified the life out of Francesca.

"Ingrid immediate stopped administering all the pills and in so doing she undoubtedly saved my life John, as I was slowly slipping into a coma. And I have no doubt no matter how amateurish it all seems; Rupert would have explained it all away to convincing effect".

She was very shook up and John was too and wanted the greedy cunt handed over to the police after a fuckin good kicking. But he was her step grandson and more importantly, he was Edward's natural grandson.

"Poor Edward would turn in his grave and never rest if he ended up in prison John".

She couldn't do it much as she knew he deserved no less. But she didn't want him anywhere near her either. So John agreed to Ray Hall remaining in Jersey, even though his wife was well enough for him to return to working in Liverpool. Rene needed to feel safe and have someone she could trust to be around her at all times.

That meant the greedy posh cunt Rupert, who sounded like he was choking on his fuckin big silver spoon every time he opened his even bigger fuckin mouth to speak, would be moving to Liverpool in Ray's place, where he'd be forever under the watchful eye of John and the lads.

While Rene tired with never really being able to trust anyone fully, except Edward, and perhaps John, decided it was time to close down all the CIDC offices in New York and run everything from the Jersey head office.

Chapter Twenty Four

No sooner had John arrived back in Liverpool, when he had Kate and Nigel following his every instruction to draw in Eric Decker and his son, Eddie fuckin D, into the "deal of a life time" that would bring their world crashing down around them. As Big Harry, Dominic McGuire, Danny Owens and Arthur McNabb followed his instructions to bring down Peter Finch.

And as those two birds were being killed with the one stone, he was keeping his eye on the ball at work on the Croxteth Country Park construction site. And making sure Rupert and Nigel didn't get too close and form an unusual alliance, because if they did, Nigel would spill his guts and that was one very messy fuckin headache he could do without.

Two hundred and fifty hardcore blue movies including some really fuckin nasty specialist ones had all been distributed to every video shop belonging to Peter Finch, local Councilor, respected lay preacher. He was the one time cunt who shafted poor old Joe Kelly.

Big Harry and Dominic had done the sales chat and conned every video shop manager owned by Finch, into taking them as under the counter merchandise. On the promise they could keep all the money they took in the first month as an incentive. It worked like a dream.

Arthur McNabb informed the Head of Vice at work, saying he had information from a reliable source that Councilor Finch sold porn over the counter at all of his video shops. "It's not fucking on.

The dirty slimy bastard is a Councilor and a fuckin lay preacher!" he told the squad leader.

It was now time for step two to be put into action. It was the day the Vice Squad was due to raid the home and every video shop belonging to Peter Finch. Danny Owens sat in his car waiting outside Finches big posh detached gaff in Roby Road, until he left for work at his usual time 8.30. Then he got out of his car and rang the bell on the front and put on a professional smile as the door was opened by Mrs. Finch.

"Good morning Mrs. Finch", he handed her a sealed parcel.

"Delivery for Mr Finch, I was supposed to drop them into one of the video shops, but haven't got the time to be honest". She smiled "Yes, of course", He smiled back "Thanks ever so much' and off he walked back to his car with a grin from ear to ear.

Less than fifteen minutes later, the Head of Vice and thirty police officers with warrants raided Peter Finches home and every one of his video shops that were dotted all over the city.

The reporter Joan Liggett from the Liverpool Echo was ecstatic with the tip off. She had been by the same person who had marked her card about the 'homes for sex scandal'.

When it was leaked, the specialist stuff was child porn and part of Peter Finches personal collection, the Echo made it front page news and covered it for nights, and that was before it had even got to court. It was not long before the story made the national news and it was all over for him.

His wife walked out on him. His Labour Party cronies fled like rats off a sinking ship. As the police and reporters did the rounds for more information on him, all the hyper-critical arse' kissing phonies denied knowing him that well. They watched on as he was crucified, with name, reputation, career and a life destroyed forever, as he faced the public and prison alone.

Joan Liggett was on a roll, last week her information source had given her one of the biggest stories in her career. Now she was in East Bourne on another lead that could possibly be bigger than the last one. Her gut feeling told her the two were tied together, corrupt bastards the lot of them.

Rupert was too close for comfort living in the penthouse facing John. But needs must and at least this way he could be watched. Equally though it meant he could watch John, and for the first time that had John feeling vulnerable.

Because at best the money he took off Kate and Nigel really belonged to Brain Brossly. At worst it belonged to CICD, and if Rupert got wind of that from the gutless Nigel, he was fucked, because embezzlement warrants a nice tidy long stretch. And that's without kidnap and a long list of other shenanigans. So it was time for him to hold his nerve and watch Rupert, and Nigel, like a hawk as him and the lads drew Decker & Son into a false sense of security. He would completely destroy them with the help of Kate, and Nigel, whether they liked it or not.

Sunday night in the Golf Club and Eric Decker got the surprise of his life as he stood at the bar waiting to be served, and Danny Owens struck up conversation with him "You made a nice job on them show houses you last worked on".

Shocked Eric replied "We aim to please. I heard you got the plumbing contract with CIDC". Danny smiled "Yeah, should make a good few bob with it too".

Then he walked away from the bar with his pint. Leaving Eric Decker thinking the big freeze over his cunt of a son, Eddie D, paying the Higgnet twins to work John over, had finally after all of these years just turned into the big thaw.

A few weeks later they met again in the Golf Club. Only this time Danny had Kate and Nigel with him, they sat talking over a bevy for a good half hour before shaking hands with him and leaving. Danny then got up and went to the bar and stood next to Eric Decker and his cunt of a son, Eddie fuckin dead walking.

"Rubbin shoulders with the management eh, bit out of their neck of the woods drinkin here though isn't it?" Eric Decker had been in the construction business a long time and he knew almost everyone else who worked in it. Danny smiled again because this hard faced cunt was taking the bait, hook line and sinker.

"Yeah, but it's proved to be a bummer really because they had a business proposition for me, but to be honest it's out of my league".

Eric Decker was all over it wanting to know the ins and outs of a cat's arse.

"Well they've got land with planning permission to build eighty apartments on it. But, they haven't got the cash to develop it. So they asked if I wanted in on it and split the profit right down the middle. Chance of a life time really, it's estimated worth is two mill. So I'm gutted to be honest, but there's no way I've got the sort of cash needed to develop summit that size". He then picked up his pint and after a friendly nod left the bar smiling.

Back in the Corn Exchange office on the Monday morning, John double checked with Nigel that the land Danny had baited Eric Decker with, had been landscaped seeded after the demolition of the wearhouse and named Talbot Court. It had indeed, and the grass was already starting to grow.

"Good, now make sure when Eric Decker and son ask about it, you just happen to have a set of these plans with you". He then slid two sets of development plans across his desk. One set for Nigel to study and the other for Eric Decker. Nigel picked them up "How can you be so sure they'll definitely go for it?"

John grinned, "Greed my friend, greed".

Danny Owens was in the show house with Nigel and Kate looking over the development plans for the eighty apartments on Talbot Court, when just as expected Eric Decker walked in with Eddie D carrying a tin of opened paint. She'd deliberately marked a wall in the show house, so it needed a quick repaint. Then fixed it for the job to be given to Eric, knowing he'd turn up with his son, Eddie D, to have a fuckin good nose around.

Then while she took Eddie to the room where the marked wall was, Danny engaged Eric "Hey, you might be interested in this Eric?"

He pushed the plans across the desk "It's the proposed development on tha land Nigel owns, isn't it Nigel". Nigel done his usual nodding dog act and played along "oh yeah, yeah, it is. I'm trying to work out what the overall cost will be".

Eric seized the moment "I can ask my lad Eddie to tha for yeh if you want? Cos that's his job like." Nigel put on his grateful face "Oh that would be excellent. Here, take a set of plans to show him, and let Kate know when you can meet up to give me an idea". Kate walked back in all curves tits and smiles with Eddie "All done" And Eric Decker couldn't get out of the show house quick enough to show Eddie the plans.

Kate and Nigel were still being kept in the dark by John and just following orders, but whatever it was that he was setting up they were just glad they weren't the ones on the receiving end of it.

Eric and Eddie wasted no time and made their way to the site where the apartments were to be built. They were impressed. It was a prime site, in a good residential area with good access for construction. So they checked out all the local estate agents and got excited. The luxury apartments would sell for between eighty-five and a hundred grand each, and that was a potential to make seven or eight million.

So they visited Wilson & Associates, the architects who looked after all their plans and costing, and one phone call later they'd established the cost to develop the site was estimated somewhere around the one million. So it was definitely a big project, but it had the potential for massive profits, too massive to let it slip through their fingers.

Kate sat behind the desk looking like a picture of sincerity as Eric Decker told her he'd been to view the development site and wondered what she thought the sale price of the apartments would bring in?

"Well, I don't really know the area, but Nigel said he's been told they could fetch between fifty and sixty grand each".

He couldn't believe what he was hearing. They were that fuckin' thick they hadn't even worked out the real value yet.

"How come you're not financing it yourselves love?"

It was time to remember exactly what John had instructed her to say. So she waxed lyrical on how Nigel's granddad died and left him the land years earlier, along with a plot in Southport that they built a big detached on. But they borrowed off the bank to do it.

"One thing and another though it took two years to complete instead of one. So we had to keep going back to the bank for more money, and it destroyed our credibility to be honest" she acted embarrassed "Poor Nigel wasn't that experienced at the time".

How the hell had these two got to work for CIDC? They were a pair of numpties, absolute fuckin' amateurs. She was no more than a hot arse sales woman and Nigel a glorified gofer.

"So you see, we're not in a position to finance it ourselves". He was determined to take advantage of these soft pair of bastards and they deserved all they got for being so flaming thick.

"It happens to the best of us love. Tell yeh wha' why don't we all discuss this further over a meal?"

Bingo! It was now a done deal.

Before their meeting in the restaurant, Eric clued Eddie in on everything.

"Listen, this is a once in a fuckin lifetime opportunity that's gonna make us millionaires".

He'd already been the bank

"We put everything we've got up for security. The two detached houses, the building yard, the painting and decorating firm and small builds' contracts company. It's fuckin doable son and this is my last chance Eddie. Let's face it I'm getting a bit old for this game son, I need this deal. We both do".

Over their meal Nigel acted out his role to perfection and truth be told it made Kate sick. She couldn't stand even being in the same room as him anymore. Yet here she was playing the dutiful wife over a business deal that was as bent as fuck. But as she had very little option in the matter, she competed for the Oscar that up to Nigel winning hands down.

"No, I've had enough of self-build to last me a bloody life time, and anyway, CIDC would fire me on the spot if they got wind I had a project this big being developed. No, what I need is somebody with all the right references and enough cash to complete the project. Then following a deduction of all the legal fees and construction costs, we split the profits fifty, fifty".

Eric Decker smiled as he offered a handshake to Nigel across the table

"You've just found your man".

Eddie D and Kate sat weighing-up each other and the situation as Nigel and Eric shook hands on the deal and agreed. Decker and Son would be responsible for all construction costs, including the utilities, landscaping and footpaths. While Kate and Nigel would be responsible for taking care of all the sales, and as that was set to save them the two percent normally charged by the estate agents.

Eric was delighted. Then following John's instructions to the letter, but as yet still not fully understanding why, Nigel was very specific and drove home the fact the Eric Decker and Son, must agree to carry out the contract to the exact specifications stipulated by the architect. It was in order to get the National House Builders Certificates, so they could sell the properties.

Decker and son produced all the required references for Nigel and had the money in place ready to start on the development. John had instructed his company solicitors to do the contracts and instructed Nigel to give Eric Decker a copy of them, to take to his solicitors to be proofed approved and amended if necessary. And while all of this was going on he was taking a break back home in Jersey with Lesley and the girls.

Lesley was a different woman these days. No longer the shy young girl he met all those years earlier. She was confident and strong now and loved being a mother and running the family business with the ever faithful Brenda, who still got right up John's nose even if he didn't say.

Their marriage had grown predictable and boring, especially in the bedroom department. That was all down to her not him, and she just wasn't interested in him if she was honest. The years of him working away in Liverpool and missing weekends at home with them all had taken its toll, and he still put pressure on her to try for a son, and that didn't help. They still loved each other, of course they did, and in fact she knew he loved her deeply, but she wasn't kidding herself. She also knew that was more to do with the fact that she was a good mother to his three beautiful daughters.

A fact she knew guaranteed she'd always hold first place in life and nobody would even get to be a close second, because for all his secretive ways that she turned a blind eye too. She knew in her heart of hearts that he was a damn good father and provider, and family when push came to shove family would always come first. So the gulf that was between them in the bedroom was left to go unspoken about.

John and Rene had met up. It was so relaxing just the two of them being back on the Blue Lady together without Rupert lurking somewhere in the background.

"How's he doing with all you Scousers keeping an eye on him?"

John laughed "He's coping". It was six months since Edward had passed but he knew his loss had already changed Rene forever. She hadn't spoken about it, nor even shed a tear in front of anyone. She was quieter somehow, always more deep in thought and pensive.

"Penny for them?" said John.

Rene smiled at him "Oh I doubt they're even worth that much darling"

She poured herself a glass of wine and held up the bottle to him "Another?" He smiled "Best not. Don't want to roll home too drunk". She didn't even try to coax him. He leaned forward and grabbed her hand "You ok, Ree?"

The warmth in his voice and understanding in his tone, his concern and unspoken love reached the depth of all her pain and she broke. This powerfully strong and indomitable woman gasped for breath as she sobbed, and as he lovingly held her in his arms she whaled loudly into his chest for the loss of Edward her dearest love and friend. She sobbed for the loss of all their future plans together. She sobbed at the unfair and cruel finality of death.

She rocked with emotion as he held her close to him and lovingly kissing her on the head at first. Then as she looked at him heartbroken he wiped her tears gently with his thumb and kissed her sorrowful eyes "Shhhhh shhhhh everything's gonna be ok".

Somehow in that painful loving and grief stricken moment, when both their hearts were hurting they kissed, gently at first, loving and reassuringly, then slowly and passionately and they made love for the first time since Edwards death. And it was sensitive considerate and gentle, it was also love filled beautiful and soul healing, and afterwards they both cried.

While John was away in Jersey, Eric Decker had got his solicitor to look over the contracts, and he was happy that as long as he kept to the materials stipulated by the architect, everything was pretty straight forward. So he and Eddie met with Nigel and Kate at the Corn exchange office, where they each had a copy of the contracts to be signed by all four of them.

But as they needed to be witnessed, Kate scooped them up off the desk "Wait a mo. I'll just go and get one of the staff to come in and an independently witness it for us", everyone agreed. She them left the office and headed straight into the next office where she swopped the contracts for four identical ones with an extra clause added. She then joined the others again with a Finance Manager in toe, who witnessed Eric Decker and son signing their horrible life away.

Now John was back, and he was chomping at the bit as he sat talking in loud whispers to Jimmy after just finishing a lovely big Sunday roast. His Mum was fast asleep in the armchair bless her, and Jean was washing the dishes

"The Decker deal is on!"

Jimmy snarled "It's been a long time comin' John".

John couldn't agree more but the best things are always worth waiting for. The beauty with this was as he gave it to Eddie D right up the fuckin arse, he got to shaft his cunt of an old fella at the same time.

"Yeah, just like he shafted me dad".

Jimmy was as ready and up for it, as John. So they agreed to wait a couple of weeks then swop all the specified expensive paint that was being used on the Croxteth building site for the much cheaper stuff, making sure to pour it into the expensive tins so it wouldn't be noticed. Then spray one or two walls in every house that brossly homes built with a chemical. So within months all the paint would start to flake.

That meant the contractors would have to go back and carry out maintenance work on them, and when that happened they had reason to hold back all payments due to fuckin' Decker and son.

John was over the moon as Kate told him Decker and son had taken advantage of the offer of a cheap mortgage, and refinanced their two houses to the hilt with the Jersey Building Society.

And the guy who processed their applications told them he was launching a fantastic new opening deal on cars, and then talked them into exchanging all Decker and son company vehicles, and their own cars, for new lease hire ones. Thinking they were in the money they couldn't resist so went for the whole deal replacing their own cars with two top of the draw Jaguars.

They also unwittingly agreed to work with the very bent Parr Building Suppliers, to take advantage of their three months to pay on invoice offer.

"Kate, you are a diamond! Now how about letting me take you for a meal to celebrate?"

The Shangri Palace was situated at the pier head on the banks of the river Mersey and its views were stunning as ships sailed in and out of the harbor, especially as the sun set over Liverpool bay and shimmered over the river. It was one of John's favorite Liverpool settings and definitely his favorite Chinese restaurant.

As the wine flowed and they enjoyed their meal they relaxed into each other's company.

"Eddie's wife, Dot, has been into the office to introduce herself to everyone, and she's been passing on all their sales enquiries to me. So I've sent them all information packs."

John's heart nearly came out of his chest when he heard Dots name

"Oh right, wha did you think of her?"

Kate thought a second and smiled

"She seems a dead nice woman to be honest, quite sharp too."

John went quiet then took a sip of wine before speaking

"There's a story behind all this y'know."

Kate was all ears and he told her the lot. How Dot used him as a cover while she was seeing Eddie D cos he was older. How Eddie paid the Higgnets' to leave him for dead while he eloped with Dot to Gretna Green and married her. How his dad was shafted by Eddie's dad, Eric, before suddenly dying of a heart attack that was probably brought on by the stress of it all. How he didn't even get to go to his funeral as he was still in hospital fighting for his life.

And after all that how Dot had the fuckin audacity to turn up at the hospital when he was still in recovery, and dared to say sorry then tell him she was pregnant with Eddie D's kid.

"So yeh see, I've made it my life's mission to destroy the fuckin lot of em, and you just watch cos I'm gonna do it fuckin grand style".

Kate was stunned "Oh my God".

They sat in silence for a few moments.

"I don't know what to say John' and she genuinely didn't. As much as she felt so sad for him wanted to hug him, she also felt frightened of him. Frightened of his capability, frightened of his utter ruthlessness, frightened too that whether she liked it or not she was also involved in it now, right up to her pretty neck.

John changed the subject

"How's posh boy getting on with Nigel?

He was relieved to hear they couldn't stand each other and Nigel gave him a wide birth as much as he could.

"What about you, do you like him?"

She nearly choked on her drink "Rupert? Oh my God! You're joking me aren't yeh, he's an absolute tosser! Always going on about how he'll be a multimillionaire when he grandmother dies and he inherits everything".

John's stomach turned

"He's a complete fuckin arse wipe!"

She laughed 'No love lost then, but I won't tell you what he calls you."

John laughed "I can imagine."

She laughed too then rambled on about how he always talks to her boobs and not her "He makes my skin crawl". John was fuming but tried to control it, "If he gives you any problems let me know Kate, cos the guy's a slime ball, a total fuckin sleaze."

Feeling heady with the wine she laughed some more "Oh I can handle the Rupert's of this world John, don't you worry about that."

John laughed then suddenly went serious

"I'm sorry we had to start, under such bad circumstances y'know Kate. But I hope you know me well enough by now to know, I would never have hurt you. I'd never hurt any woman love."

It never crossed his mind that kidnapping her and frightening her half to death was hurting her. But she understood that. She understood that even though he had total control over her and she was kept a prisoner and powerless in his gaff, it was all about getting the money out of Nigel. It was business and not personal. That's why he treated her well, with respect even, so when he said he'd never hurt a woman. She totally believed him.

And now it was her turn to be honest

"I haven't slept with Nigel since that night. I still can't believe he didn't even try to protect me. Don't get me wrong. We've never been madly in love with each other but what we had suited us and it worked, if you know wha I mean, but, whatever it was that we did have… It was killed instantly that night."

John put his hand across the table and held hers "I'm sorry love."

She pulled away, "Don't be. You've done me favour."

They looked at each other in the eye and for one brief moment it was again like electric. So it was on the cards and it was always going to happen. They both knew that.

As Big Harry and Dominic McGuire stood drinking coffee with John in the penthouse kitchen, they got the surprise of their life when in walked Kate straight out of John's bedroom wearing nothing but John's shirt and a smile "Any coffee going spare?"

John nearly choked on his coffee, because he thought she'd stay out of the way until they all left for work.

"We had too much to drink and she missed the last train home to Southport."

They all burst out laughing including him and Kate, as Big Harry quipped

"I'm sayin nothing, but I'll tell yeh what, she looks ten times better in that shirt than you ever did."

As they finished their coffee and breakfast John doled out the orders, "Kate, get Nigel to find out who is doin' the groundwork on the apartments, and out of the seventeen enquiries Dot's give you. Tell her we've got ten interests, six with holding deposits and four on the way with full deposits on exchange of contracts. I'll give you all the details you need and a queue for when she comes into the office, so tell her all ten have applied for mortgages and their applications look really good.'

He looked at the lads and grinned, "Now, let's get this show on the road."

Danny Cain was the boss of the contracting company that developed the Croxteth Country Park foundations and drainage, his father had been a lifelong friend and work mate of old Joe Kelly in his younger days. John's brother Jimmy asked him to give Decker and son a very low labour quote to ensure his company got the work. Danny knew exactly what was being asked of him, "Consider it done Jim."

The foundations had been excavated and passed by the local building inspector and were ready to have concrete poured the next day. So after all the contractors left the site for the day, another set of workers turned up and were let on site by one of the security men working for Big Harry and Dominic McGuire.

They went straight to work putting a connection to run from the water mains all the way up to the east gable end foundation trench. Then it was fitted with a stop tap that was buried and marked for future use. Following this, a foot of organic compost was laid all the way along the trench then two foot of dry sand and stone was added without cement. Finally it was topped off with a thin layer of concrete, making it look as if the whole trench was full of concrete, even at the ends of the trench where shuttering had been fitted.

So when the shuttering was removed it would still give the impression the whole trench was three feet of solid concrete. The following morning when the men turned up to work they were met by a note pinned to the site office door by the security guy "Concrete turned up after you left, so told driver to pour into nearest footing and leveled it as best I could. You owe me a pint!"

Back in the Corn exchange office John gave Kate a folder containing ten applications with names addresses and details of family and friends on them, and attached to each was a cheque for five hundred pounds.

"Contact Dot and give her that lot and tell her it looks like four more are in the bag."

This guaranteed Decker and son would work their bollocks off to complete the apartments as fast as they could, and that meant they'd cut corners. And sure enough they worked full steam ahead for three months and the apartments were flying up, even with the roofs on and the tiles up.

An independent surveyor made an inspection of the site to make sure all the work carried out was exactly to schedule and the materials and workmanship were to the correct specifications. John was completely pissed off that everything had conformed, except for the problem of flaking paint on the site in Croxteth.

So he ordered the site agent to take samples of the paint and put them into separate containers and date them for future analysis, but instructed him not to tell anybody.

Unknown to the site agent, John had the quality paint swapped for a much cheaper paint. He also had coated two to three walls in all the new houses with a solution that would make sure it would peel and flake, that would give John a good reason for holding back any payments to the Decker family.

Chapter Twenty Five

As John and Kate were sat side by side in the office looking over paper work together, Rene walked in unexpectedly and John got the surprise of his life and jumped up "Rene!"

He hugged and kissed her on the cheek then smiled

"You do know Kate, don't you?"

Kate smiled as she stood up and offered her hand to Rene "Pleased to meet you Mrs. Burgess."

Rene completely ignored her hand.

"Be a darling and put the kettle on, I'm parched."

Kate tried to hide her shock and annoyance, as she walked out of the office with a fake smile on her lips "Of course."

Rene couldn't help but weigh up her hour glass figure in her tight pin striped pencil skirt and crisp white blouse. She instinctively knew Kate was John's new bit on the side and she had been replaced for a younger model. She also knew if he wasn't carful this new bit on the side, she would posed a threat his marriage with Lesley.

Once Kate brought the coffee in she left them to it. But it wasn't just Rene's visit that shocked John, she'd lost at least two stone in weight and didn't look well.

"You look like you need a good pan of Scouse down yeh".

Rene laughed, "Don't fuss darling, I'm fine."

She'd been feeling under the weather a lot lately. Not ill, just something she couldn't put her finger. She undergone a lot of tests and was awaiting the results, but she didn't want John knowing.

She'd never been the same since losing Edward, so John convinced himself it must be down to that. Truth told she was feeling quite lost in Jersey without Edward and she was missing John lots too.

"I'm not here on business or to check on the County Park Development. In fact, I'm very happy with the way that is going" John looked at her quizzical

"What are you up too?" She smiled "You know me too well darling…. Let's go on a cruise around the Med for a month. Me, you, Lesley and the girls, and let's take Lesley's mum… and Grace my sister… and even the dreaded Brenda. What do you say?"

John looked at her shocked. It was all a bit random and a little out of character, and the last thing he wanted was to leave the Decker and son problem in everyone else's hands "But worra bout work Ree? I can't drop everything for a month just like tha love."

She looked at him disappointed and even a little lost and desperate. "I can get Ray Hall to leave the Jersey office and cover Liverpool for you, his wife is well enough…"

He wasn't used to seeing her like this "Why would you want Margaret to go and your sister to go?"

She smiled "Because I want all my favorite people with me."

He looked at her disbelievingly 'Since when did stuck up Brenda become one of your favorite people?'

She laughed. "Well is she one of Lesley's favourite people, so that's good enough for me. Besides, she'll be a great help with the girls."

She teased him "You know I'll make it worth your while, and you'll enjoy it."

For the first time, that meant nothing to him and he was shocked and didn't like himself for it, but she'd changed, she'd aged.

He knew as much as he loved her to bits… he didn't fancy her anymore, but he'd never admit it and hurt her. "Okay then, a month around the Med it is, but give me a couple of weeks to tie up a few loose ends on the sites here." She was delighted.

Dot unexpectedly turned up at the sale office at Tablet Court with Eric and Eddie, and they were like the cat that got the cream as they looked over all the sales and wall charts.

"Is there a specific reason why most of the first sales are for the east side of the development?" Eric asked Kate, John had warned Kate he'd ask this so she replied as she'd been instructed "Selling this way means we can complete a section at a time and hand it over, so it brings the cash in sooner. If we sold them all over the development, we'd have to wait until the whole site was finished before the money came in."

Eric was satisfied and muttered to Dot out the side of his mouth as Kate put the kettle on "I underestimated her, she's quite switched on really."

So far he hadn't spent a penny on advertising, yet the sales were flooding in. Kate looked at Dot differently now that John had given her the rundown on things. She could see she'd been a looker, when she was younger and despite everything she did actually seem like a nice woman.

But him, Eddie D, he was just a male chauvinistic pig who spoke to her terribly and she was so used to it she didn't even notice. He was all beer belly and bald and bit crude with it. It was a mystery what she seen in him really. His dad Eric wasn't much better, but then that's probably where he got it all from.

Including the big fat belly Eric stood pushing out as he boasted "Well, I think six months tops and we'll all be home and dry and millionaires a few times over." They didn't have a clue as to what was about to hit them.

John was happy he'd agreed to the cruise now, because the kids were bursting with excitement and everyone was in good spirits. Even stuck up Brenda cracked a smile. And the fresh sea air was bound to do Rene the world of good, especially as she'd lost even more weight since her surprise visit to Liverpool. He was glad her sister, Grace, had joined them too. Having her around would also do Rene good, as nothing can beat having family close by when you're not at your best.

They spent the day's sunbathing on deck and having fun with the kids, and the evenings relaxing over good food and wine and sharing stories of days gone by. They openly shared happy memories and some sad ones too; funny times and times of great struggle and hard work. By the end of the night when they were all a little bit worse for wear, they even enjoyed a good old sing-along together. It was all lovely and relaxed and special in a way that it hadn't been before. Perhaps because this was the first time they'd all been together without lovely Edward and the dreaded Rupert.

Everyone was making an extra effort for Rene to feel good about life again, and it was working because none of them wanted the holiday to come to an end.

It was early Sunday morning and the yacht was tied up at the quayside, and they were in Malta. The weather was gloriously with blues skies all the way and the sun was beating down. So Grace and Margaret decided to take the children ashore with Lesley and Brenda, to go looking at all the churches and light candles for Edward.

That wasn't John's thing and Rene was feeling too tired for all the walking, so John opted for staying on board to keep her company. As they all left for shore Rene called out to Grace "Light a candle for me too darling."

John laughed, his mother had lit candles all her life to the Virgin Mary, but he never imagined that Rene would hold any store in any of that. They were on the top deck taking in the sun and the scenery as they watched them all walking slowly up to the high street

"You have a lovely family John..." He smiled then reached out squeezed her hand "I know. Thank you, cos you've given me the chance to have the kind of life that I could only ever of dreamed about..." He stared into her eyes "I love Lesley, you know that, but the love I have for her has never been like the love..."

She immediately pressed her finger on his lips "Shhhhh don't say it. Don't'. They had never said out loud what they truly felt for each other. Action speaks louder than words and everything they'd ever done for each other said what they felt deep down. But this love had changed now. It had shifted since Edward had died, and Rene knew it was to shift even more for lots of reasons, including Kate. "I want you to know I know you've slept with Kate" said Rene softly, but matter of fact.

John was shocked and the panic shot right threw him as he drained of colour "Worra you talking about Ree?" She gave him a smile full of wisdom and knowing.

"Darling just be careful, you've got three beautiful daughters a good wife and you're all very wealthy… She has that weasel of a man Nigel and probably a modest savings account, am I making myself clear?"

She starred at him and he starred back at her and for once he was stumped for words. She laughed a little, "Darling don't look so worried, I can see the attraction, those curves of hers would drive any man wild."

He was very uncomfortable now and continued to struggle for words "Rene, she's just someone I work with love."

She laughed out loud, "Oh John darling, Lesley isn't interested in sleeping with you anymore and look at me, I'm twenty years older than you, I've turned into an old bag of bones, and I've past my sell by date." He was shocked 'Don't! Stop it! Don't talk like tha Rene, please.'

She was hurting and sad but she was a realist and had never been one to shy away from a tough situation. "I'm trying to tell you, I understand. I'm telling you to be careful and protect your marriage and family John… I'm also trying to tell you that you have my blessing." She looked straight into his beautiful blue eyes and not only did he see the full depth of her love for him, he felt it deep in his too.

They'd almost finished the second bottle of wine when Ingrid appeared and asked if they would be eating on deck or inside. Rene joked "This fella has just said I need a good pan of Scouse inside me."

She was surprised and delighted when Ingrid said her husband was from Liverpool and could make them a lovely pan of Scouse. John was pleased too and couldn't stop laughing at the idea of sitting on yacht eating a bowl of Scouse made out of the best prime beef, while drinking an expensive bottle red wine. "It's still no match for my mother's Scouse though Ree, cos she makes the best pan of Scouse in Liverpool!"

The heat, the food, the wine and all the talking had left them both a little drunk and shattered. So John picked up the third bottle of red and as Rene put her arm around his waist he put his around her shoulder and they helped each other to the master cabin, and Ingrid rushed to inform the deck hands to keep a look out for the shore party returning and inform her immediately when they were spotted.

The third bottle of red was left standing on the bedside table untouched as John lay gently snoring with his arms wrapped protectively around Rene, as she snuggled into his chest weeping silently because all her test and scan results were and showed she had lung cancer. It was aggressive. It was advanced. And it was terminal.

She this strong and dignified woman had told no one, except Edward when she whispered to him in her prayers and asked him to be waiting for her. This cruise was all about giving them one last time together to be happy. It was all part of putting her house in order. It was about letting go, saying goodbye and leaving them all her love. Unlike them she knew her time for leaving them all forever was very close at hand.

Ingrid smiled. Rene was snuggled up into John's chest and fast asleep, and John was still holding her protectively. It took a minute for him to wake up from Ingrid gently shaking him. "John, John, quickly, your wife and children are making their way back down the high street to the gangplank." He was startled "Oh, okay Ingrid. Thanks. I'll come right up."

Chapter Twenty Six

Eric Decker was not a happy bunny. He'd just been given a written warning by the CIDC site agent about the continuing faults being filed on the flakey paint, stating if it wasn't sorted CIDC would hold a bigger retention to cover future maintenance costs and bring in new contractors. He couldn't understand why it was happening, but consoled himself with the thought if CIDC did get shut of him; he still had his own development going on at Talbot Court that was set to make him millions.

So he decided he wasn't going to lose any sleep over it. The site agent up called up Ray Hall on the matter and acting on John's instructions, Ray sent the paint samples off for analysis to see what the problem was. They withheld all payments due until the results came back. If they proved unsatisfactory, all payments due for the contracts he'd worked on would be withheld for six months to cover maintenance costs that might arise in the future.

The sales at Talbot Court were going so well over sixty percent had been sold, in addition to the ten that John had taken on the east gable end. So Eric planned to hand over all the completed apartments within six weeks, thus making him a sure three million before tax.

He was on a permanent adrenalin rush and had even started looking for more land to develop once this one was completed. He was forever back slapping Eddie "There's no stopping us now lad. Decker and son are moving up in the world!"

His bank manager was chuffed as well. Half a million was the biggest risk he'd ever taken in his twenty years banking, and he'd extended the overdraft far more than was usual because he'd been to the development and could see for himself how impressive it was. So it was just as well the first big cheque was due in from CIDC.

There was a huge material bill pending, so it was all a bit of a tight squeeze for him and Eddie even had to pay their mortgages. But Eric laughed it off with yet another back slap, "Don't worry about son. It'll all be sorted in a matter of weeks then the good times are a coming." Truth be told though, Eddie D was worrying and he was starting to fear they'd bit off more than they could chew.

John was back on site, all sun tan smiles and speaking to Ray Hall "You lucky sod! You look great, how's Rene?" John was glad of the opportunity to talk about her

"Not good to be honest Ray. She's never been the same since she lost Edward, and between me and you she couldn't even give a shit about work and board meetings at the minute. She's terrible and you should see the weight she's lost."

Ray had a lot of time for Rene and he was sorry to hear all that.

"How about Rupert, is he keeping an eye on her."

John almost spat in his eye

"Don't get me started on tha' greedy prick. The only thing he gives a shit about is his inheritance."

Ray nodded in agreement, as Rupert would tell anyone who'd listen what he stood to inherit once Rene was gone.

"Make no mistake about Ray, that spoilt posh cunt can't wait to see the back of her, an if she didn't care about him so much, I'd give him a fuckin good kickin."

Ray laughed "Well if you ever do, stick one on him give him one for me while you're at it."

They both laughed then John asked if the report was back on the paint used by Edwards and son. Sure enough it was and it confirmed they'd been using a cheap alternative. John nodded, "Just as I thought to be honest Ray. So as of now their painting contract with CIDC is terminated for using substandard materials that don't conform to specification. Suspend all payments due to them and fax me a copy of the lab report to show them."

Following this he went to his office and rang Big Harry "Go to Talbot Court and turn on the secret water supply that leads under the foundations on the east gable end. I want all the peat washed away as soon as possible."

His next call was to Dominic McGuire to inform him everything had gone to plan and he was instructing the site agent to remove Decker and son off the CIDC Croxteth site. It would be without any of their materials, on the pretense of they were evidence of inferior materials. "I want you there with Big Harry and some of your security lads just in case it kicks off. Then once Decker and son are out of the way I want you to move all their materials back to the farm house security base… I wonna strip these two cunts bare so they've got nothing to work with and can't make money elsewhere."

There was no chance of that though Decker and son had maxed up all their credit with the building suppliers and others suppliers around the city. John had made sure that every possible avenue of them getting finance was well and truly closed to Decker and son. And with both of them being mortgaged to the hilt they were in very deep shit.

His final call was then to Kate "Fancy joining me for a lovely meal somewhere?" She was thrilled and couldn't wait to see him.

Once all his calls were out of the way, he held a framed photograph from the cruise of him Lesley and his three daughters, taken at the Trevi fountain in Rome, and he hung it on his office wall.

Then he stood back admiring it, with pride but deep within his yearning for a son still gnawed away at him. He had so much in life and was lucky, he knew that. Lesley was a good and beautiful wife, as was his three daughters, who all took after him for their blond hair and blue eyes. He had a fabulous home and career and he was also an extremely wealthy man.

He'd even had a love affair all his married life with a very beautiful rich and powerful woman for God's sake, and she'd just given him her blessing to trade her in for a much younger model in Kate. The truth of it was he really did have everything in life except for the one thing he truly wanted more than anything else, and that was a son.

A son who would carry his name and fathers name before him, the proud name of Kelly, instead he got three daughters and a wife who was no longer willing to try again for a son. And he resented her for that, and the fact that it was on his shoulders the name of Davenport was being carried on for her father George and business reasons.

John had just finished going over the Decker and son invoices' for twenty two thousand pounds that they'd never get paid, when Kate buzzed through to his office.

"Eric Decker is on the other line demanding to speak to Mr. Davenport." John grinned, put him through "This is Mr. Davenport speaking, how can I help you Mr. Decker?"

Eric Decker nearly came through the phone, "Don't give me all tha; you know quite well why I'm ringing. You've just had me and twelve of my men thrown off the Croxteth Country Park site and I want an explanation now!"

This was making John's day, "Sorry to disappoint you Mr. Decker but I've been away for the past month and only been back in the office for a few hours. I think you should to be speaking to Ray Hall."

His calm and smug tone only served to push Eric's buttons further, "Listen, I don't think you realize who you're dealing with here, so if I don't get some answers soon I'll be down to tha posh fuckin office of yours, D'you understand me?" The threat was loud and clear, but just made John grin all the more.

"Feel free to come down whenever you want Mr. Decker. I'm sure the security people you've already met will have no problem in throwing you out on your arse."

Decker wasn't expecting that, "Give me Ray Hall's number now!"

John had him over a barrel and was enjoying every minute of it.

"I'll do better than that Mr. Decker, I'll give Ray Hall your number and get him to ring you." Eric slammed the phone down much to John's amusement.

Ray Hall didn't have a clue about John's vendetta, but he was a long standing friend and in the construction business and that meant you stuck together. He also knew the construction law, and wasn't averse to enforcing it. So the first thing he done was fax a copy of the lab report to Decker and son, after underling the part that read "Inferior paint not suitable" and putting a big red circle around the part that read "Traces of Asbestos."

Then ten minutes later he followed it up with the call, and by the time he's finished speaking, Eric Decker believed he'd be lucky not to get sued for thousands "But unless someone has deliberately sabotaged me by using my good paint and replacing it with their crap stuff, I genuinely don't understand how this has happened." The call ended on a much more serious and quieter note, and Eric was sick as a pig.

Ray Hall called John and let him know it was all sorted as he'd attached a form to the lab report, which he'd borrowed from a different site mentioning asbestos in the paint. Ray told John he had he had told Decker a team of experts were heading to Liverpool to go back to every house owner who'd complained and test for asbestos.

He laughed, "I told him his only saving grace was the fact that the defective walls had now been painted with normal paint, so fingers crossed the Asbestos would be sealed in." John laughed, "Nice one Ray, I owe you one."

Chapter Twenty Seven

When Kate walked into the Lounge Bar wearing high-heels and a black low cut figure hugging cocktail dress, John almost fell off his bar stool "wow, you look absolutely stunning." She smiled seductively as she sat next to him with her hair and makeup done to perfection, and the smell of her perfume adding lingering in the air.

Then after just ten minutes of small talk and a swift drink, they got a taxi to the most expensive restaurant in the city. John couldn't take his eyes off her as they ate; her eyes shone like diamonds and her smile lit up her whole face. He shocked himself at how proud he felt, especially when seeing the admiring glances she was getting from the other men there.

"Where did you tell Nigel you were going dressed like tha?"

He almost choked on his drink when she said, "I told him I was meeting you and not to wait up cos I wouldn't be home."

She laughed out loud at his reaction and he laughed out loud at her nerve, then she told John they'd agreed that once the Decker malarkey was out of the way and they were free of all John's "business ties" they'd divorce. That little nugget put a slightly different tone on the rest of evening and John decided to do a bit of straight talking as soon as they got back to the penthouse.

She linked him as they walked towards the lift, and once inside it she rested her head on his shoulder. Until he put her straight on a few things he held back with the affection. Once inside he put some relaxing background music on and poured them both a glass of wine as she kicked off her high heels and sat seductively on the white leather sofa.

He sat next to her but he didn't make a move. So she ran her slender finger along his thigh, her well-manicured nails gently stroking him. But he simply lifted his glass of wine to his mouth and drank.

"Well, I know you find me attractive, so what's up?"

There was no point in pretending, "Kate, I do think you're stunning, I think you're intelligent and funny too… and I love being with you." This was starting to feel uncomfortable. Kate quickly said "Just get to the point John."

So he did. "Look, I love my wife Lesley and my three kids and I won't ever leave them or put my marriage at risk." She smiled, "Well I've already worked that much out… I'm going into this with my eyes wide open John. I've got no expectations. I won't make any demands…"

She laughed, "I pretty much know my place in the packing order" So stop worrying because I'm not here to rock the boat or threaten your marriage, ok?" He starred into her eyes then smiled as he pulled her towards him "Come here" and kissed her passionately. She stopped him "Wait!"

Then she stood up and went to the bathroom and two minutes later came back out with the zip on the back of her dress already down. Then she very slowly slipped the shoulders off one at a time and let the dress drop to the floor, before stepping out of it very sexily, walking towards him in time to the music. Not having a care in the world, he allowed himself to indulge in a long and passionate night.

The next morning over breakfast Kate told John something that had made him sit up and take notice. What Kate told him was that Nigel and Rupert were getting a bit to palsy, and they had even gone for a pint together. Everything had been going to plan. If that little shit spilt the beans to Rupert, he would be ruined.

Nigel was standing on his own inside one of the newly build houses on the Croxteth Country Park estate waiting for John. He still didn't know why he'd been summoned but he knew better than not to turn up. He was looking out of the kitchen window deep in thought when he sensed someone standing behind him; he turned around to look and seen stars, "Gerrup you slimy little prick!"

John was peering down at him on the floor with big Harry and Dominic McGuire standing close by. Nigel struggled up dazed "As of today Kate will be living with me in the penthouse, got it?" He nodded slightly as he tried to stem the flow of blood from his nose

"Good. Now get this next bit into your horrible thick skull very carefully. Don't ever think of gettin clever and tryin to pay me back by cozyin up to Rupert and tellin him about the Decker and son situation"

He glared at him for a moment "Cos if you do, I swear to God you'll be wearin a concrete fuckin overcoat, understand?" He never uttered a word just blinked in acknowledgement as he gave another slight nod.

"Good… Now just carry on playing your role in the Talbot Court deal and do everything I say without fuckin up, then when it's all over, I'll sort you out with enough to make a fresh start elsewhere." He mocked as he shook a hanky at him to stop the nose bleed "See, I'm not all bad am I?"

Nigel took the hanky without saying a word as all three of them laughed, then John looked at the others "Come on, we're done here." It was a real piss take and a fuckin liberty really, cos Nigel couldn't punch his through a wet echo. But they had to come down hard on him to make sure he didn't fuck up or spill the beans to Rupert on the Decker and son deal.

They stood to lose millions if he did and a fair old spell in clink and that wouldn't do at all especially if all their efforts to bring down Decker and son and destroy them were thwarted.

Good as her word, every night when John rang Lesley to say goodnight to her and his daughters. Kate didn't even show a hint of jealousy. She simply acted like it was any other call, knowing if she didn't she'd be straight out of the door because his wife and family would come first every time. She knew he didn't love her; he was in lust with her, she was sex on legs as far as he was concerned and he loved their wild romps and the admiring glances she got from other men when they were out.

While Lesley on the hand, though still predictable and unadventurous in the bedroom, was graceful with an air of confidence and her respectability shone for all to see. Somewhere between the two of them he really did have the best of both worlds.

As he knew it would, the constant running water under foundations at Talbot Court had washed away all the peat and was starting to show huge settlement cracks to form in the plaster work and brickwork. Even the most lay person could tell they had problems big problems with the development.

As instructed, Nigel was sitting in the office of one of the most powerful solicitor in the north west of England. He signed papers that were to be served on Decker and son the following day, giving him a chance to meet them and point out settlement cracks.

He was instructed to go missing until he was next called on by John, and he couldn't wait to get out of the line of fire. The first ten apartments were due to be handed over to Decker and son, thus easing their cash flow problems. But the running water under the east gable end of Talbot Court had done its job.

Kate made the call to Eric "We've got a problem Eric, some of the clients now want a full structural survey done before they'll complete because settlement cracks big enough to fit a pen in have appeared."

She then arranged for him and Eddie to meet with her and Nigel on site after lunch, and when they arrived both her and Nigel played naïve in not understanding the full implications of the cracks. Relieved Eric and Eddie fed them a load of old bull shit about it all just being shrinkage and nothing to worry about.

Nigel humored them "I trust you Eric, so if you and Eddie say it's nothing to worry about. That's good enough for me. But please, don't let me down boys because I need to complete this as soon as possible. I've got a lot of commitments to sort." Eric was back to thinking him and Kate were total fuckin idiots because they hadn't even noticed the outside brickwork cracks. But he didn't give a shite because him and Eddie were desperate to get the first apartments handed over to the clients, so they could get their hands on the installment payment.

"Don't worry Nigel, I'll have a team here first thing tomorrow to fill in every crack and repaint all the rooms." Mission accomplished, so Nigel and Kate left them to it, and Eddie breathed out a big sigh of relief. "Dad, the foundations are fucked, so as soon as we get some cash we're gonna have to excavate to find out what the problem is" Eric nodded in agreement "I know son. I know in all the forty years I have been in the construction buisness. I have never seen a building go from being perfect to a total disaster."

John sat listening to every word that Kate was telling him, "To be fair Nigel played a blinder and it went just as you said it would, they were full of bull shit and thought me and Nigel were a right pair of idiots. So they've got a team going in tomorrow."

John laughed as no amount of plastering or repainting could hide the fact the gable end was structurally defective. And a structural surveyor had already been in and confirmed it looked like subsidence. They had started proceedings to have the foundations checked, and the concrete testing group had already taken samples for analyzing. And to top the lot, Decker and son still didn't realize all the apartments on the east gable end had only ever been sold fictitiously. So they were up the preverbal creek without a paddle and well and truly fucked!

Eric and Eddie arrived mob handed at the Croxteth Country Park site with a lorry to get the remainder of all their painting materials. They needed them to work on the Talbot Court Project. But Talbot Court had already been boarded up. Big Harry and Dominic McGuire had erected an eight foot fence around it with the help of their security lads, and they'd dumped all Decker and son materials and machinery on the car park for them to collect.

Ray Hall told them all their materials from the Croxteth site had already been taken away for testing and the entire team moving them wore protective clothing in case of Asbestos. Eddie completely lost his rag swearing and shouting like a fuckin lunatic as his dad dragged him back to the lorry.

Copies of the structural reports were in the hands of Nigel, Kate and the litigation solicitor. Nigel as ordered, had gone to ground staying in his brothers in Scotland, because Decker and son were about to have papers severed on them. This included a restraining order, keeping them away from the Corn Exchange Office and the Talbot Court site.

John checked, and as instructed Kate had cancellation letters ready from the ten fictitious buyers for the Talbot Court east gable end apartments. Each one had been written on different paper with a different pen, and three had been type written.

All letters stated they'd been strongly advised by an independent surveyor not to move in because of extreme structural defects that put the properties in danger of collapsing. They advised of the return of deposits, some adding they now had no option but to put their furniture in storage and would bill Decker and son for all charges incurred.

Her next instruction was to post one letter every day over a period of ten days to Decker and son. John grinned, "I love it when a plan comes together." Kate smiled but truth be told this side of John frightened her. She had no idea how he made the full extent of it all happen and she didn't want to know either.

Instead she just accepted it, as she wanted to stay in a relationship with him and carry on living with him in the penthouse. These were the sort of shenanigans she just had to learn to turn a blind eye too or pack her bags and get out. That was easier said than done, because no matter how unintentional in the beginning, she was now up to her pretty little neck in the shenanigans herself. However she couldn't deny that she did enjoy the luxurious lifestyle it all gave her.

Decker and son could try to fight this as much as they liked, but the truth was with no cash they'd never be able to afford the lawyers' fees. Even if by some great miracle they could, John had covered every base so the end result would still be the same. They'd lose everything. So the east gable end of Talbot Court was going to be demolished, the defective foundations removed, and it would all be rebuilt in under a month and was set to make John an absolute killing. He winked, "Now that's what I call a result."

Kate was sitting in the show house on one the Croxteth Country Park developments waiting for the Decker clan to arrive. As soon as they walked in she went into action and played a blinder screaming "Well you've got some nerve showing up here! You cheating shower of bastards! You've ruined me and Nigel, ruined us! Why didn't you do what we asked? We could have all made a fortune! Instead of fucking up so bad the site has got to be demolished"

She didn't stop and convincingly raged "I've been threatened with violence by some of the clients, and Nigel has had a fucking melt down and gone missing! Having a fucking breakdown while I sit take every bit of the shit, and for wha? Fuck all, that's what! After working so hard for so long" The look of shock on all their faces was clear but it was Dot's quiet tone that calmed things down.

"Kate, I'm so sorry, we all are, and we honestly still don't know what went wrong. But we will find out and fix it, that's a promise and we'll make it up to you and Nigel.

They had no chance, because the clause sneaked into their original contracts stated Decker and son would forfeit all interests in the development of Talbot Court, if they failed to keep to the agreed specifications of contract. They were now in breach of contract and had therefore lost all rights to everything. It was the performance of her life and she deserved a fuckin Oscar. The Decker clan left convinced, her and Nigel were as screwed as they were.

Chapter Twenty Eight

It was six in the morning and Kate was in bed with John and shaking his shoulder "Wake up, John, wake up it's the phone." Half asleep he reached out and picked up the receiver his voice groggy and deep "Hello". It was Lesley

"John, it's me love, we've just had a call from Grace. Rene passed away a few hours ago".

He was devastated. Kate did not know what to do. John was sobbing openly, all he kept saying "She's gone she's gone. Rene's gone." His outburst left her knowing that John and Rene had been lovers and John had loved her.

Rupert flew back to Jersey as soon as he found out in the early hours. But John stayed around to break the news to everyone before he left. All the lads were shocked and genuinely gutted but none more so than him; he was heartbroken, but he would never be able to let it out in front of Lesley or Rupert.

The lads supported him as he went about business as usual with one of the site agents "Everything on the Croxteth Country Park estate is running smoothly and to schedule, so you shouldn't have any problems while I'm away."

Then he spoke with the lads telling them he'd decided the Decker clan could sweat till he returned from the funeral.

"I'm gonna wrap everything as soon as possible after tha, cos when Rupert gets his hands on CIDC I'll be out on my arse and the penthouse will be gone."

The lads agreed and as he flew back to Jersey with Ray Hall. They said they'd follow him over for the funeral

The funeral was a grand and somber affair with family friends and business guests from all over the world and there was hardly a dry eye in the church. Even the Liverpool lads shed a tear or two, but posh boy Rupert sat like the cat that had got the cream with not a tear to be seen.

When the service and cremation were over and everyone was mingling over drinks and a bite to eat. Rupert made everyone sick with disgust as he made his way to John who was standing with Ray Hall and the Liverpool lads talking shop.

"I've just been speaking to the Mr. Finny, the family solicitor" he looked straight at John "He's already told me I've been left grandmothers shares in CIDC and the subsidiaries. After the reading of the will there will be a lot of changes, starting in Liverpool."

John turned white and leaned so close into his face his spit landed on Rupert's cheek, as he spat out his hurt and grief in hushed anger. "Listen to me you greedy insensitive cunt, nobody gives a flying fuck what you've been left, what's in the will, or what fuckin changes you're gonna make. So show some fuckin respect, got it or I will deck you here and now where you stand!"

Ray Hall pulled him back by his arm and the Liverpool lads stepped into Rupert's personal space. So he quickly walked back to Francesca his wife, his aunt Grace and her son Tony, leaving John shaking and upset with temper, and still trying to take in the shock that Rene knew she had lung cancer yet she never said a word about to him.

The next day the atmosphere was awkward and tense as everybody sat in the large study of Rene's home waiting for the solicitor, Mr. Finny, to begin. Rupert and Francesca sat centre room while Rene's sister Grace and son Tony distanced themselves and sat towards the back of the room, where John, Lesley and Margaret were also seated.

Several members of staff had also been invited to attend. Mr. Finny made the customary opening speech and continued by explaining those happy with their bequest sign an acceptance form, and those unhappy sign a form to contest "Does everybody understand?" He looked around the room and as no objections were made he began.

Rene's driver was left a vintage Bentley and several other cars for all his years of loyal service, her house keeper was left the small bungalow she been allocated to live in for the past twenty years and called home, they signed their acceptance forms. Sixty thousand pounds was left to Ray Hall for his loyal service too, and Grace and Tony were left one million pound each, and again they all signed their acceptance forms.

Bonds to the value of a half million pounds went to Francesca.

Then Mr. Finny looked up from his paperwork, stating Renees words "I leave Moonbeam to John and Lesley Davenport, so they will continue the good times with their family, as they did when sailing with Edward and I". Mr. Finny pushed the acceptance forms forward and they were all signed. He then cleared his throat before reading on "Finally, I leave all my shares in the Channel Island Development Corporation, the Bank of Jersey and the Channel Island Building Society and their subsidiaries, and my house to my Grandson Rupert Burgess."

The look of triumph on his face as he signed the acceptance forms was sickening, but worse still when he stood up after signing

"Right, is there more? Because I've got multimillion pound companies to run and need to be moving" All the staff gasped with shock and disgust and Grace was furious "Dear God, shut up Rupert and sit down!"

John had to contain himself because he was seated with Lesley.

Then Mr. Finny again cleared his throat and brought about a wave of silence in the room.

"Clearly you don't understand Mr. Burgess, but if you'll allow me to finish all will become very clear." Everybody looked at each other confused.

"The grand total of your Grandmothers shares in CIDC and subsidiaries is six."

The gasps reverberated around the room as Rupert stood up white faced, "What on earth are you saying?"

Mr. Finny continued "Your Grandmothers own words Mr. Burgess reads as follows: Rupert darling, I realize Grandfather and I spoilt you, so now is the time to stand on your own two feet. No more hand-outs, no more indulging your every whim, no trust fund, no inheritance, no place in the companies. Because my darling I know that you would simply sell everything off to live the life of the idle rich, and after mine and Edward's hard work and your despicable act after Edward passing and you took me sailing on Bluelady. I will not allow that."

Everybody was stunned but not more so than Rupert himself.

John swelled inside with pride at Rene's last strike back at the greedy cunt.

"But I don't understand, where have all the other shares gone?"

Mr. Finny continued "Your grandmother transferred ninety four percent of all her shares over six months ago to another party." He was furious "What other party? You should have announced that before I signed my acceptance form! I want to know who she's left it all too?!"

The atmosphere in the room lifted and amusement was being openly expressed, but Mr. Finny remained calm and composed as he picked up his papers "Ah yes, here we are. Everything had gone to Mr. John Davenport." The room fell silent as all eyes turned on John who was more shocked than them "Me?" Mr. Finny smiled "Yes Mr. Davenport, you now own it all, except for the six shares of course. Congratulations."

Rupert left ranting and raving with Francesca running after him "I'm taking legal advice!" But everything was in order and had been done in the correct and legal manner. So John was congratulated by everyone there. Ray Hall shook his hand and joked "So, do I call you boss now?"

Grace hugged him "Did you know?" She just winked at him and kissed his cheek then squeezed his arm before walking away with Tony who shook his hand. And as he watched them walk out of the room, it was like watching Rene walk away.

Margaret and Lesley stood looking at him in stunned silence then they all hugged until Mr. Finny imposed on the moment, "If I could just have some private time with you Mr. Davenport. I do have a lot of forms and papers for you to sign."

John told Lesley to take her Mum to the Rose and Crown and he'd follow on as soon as he could. Then once they were on their own Mr. Finny smiled and handed John a letter "Rene asked me to give you this in private."

He then left so John could read it in private, as he sat there in the quiet of the room his hands trembling as he opened the envelope and took out the hand written letter. He sensed her presence and could hear her voice in the clear of his mind as he read every word.

"Hello my darling, here we are again alone at last" He laughed a little out loud as the tears began to roll down his cheeks. *"I'm sorry I never told you how ill I was, but you do fuss darling and I didn't want that. What I do want is for you to be strong and not be daunted by the task that lay's ahead, because I have been mentoring you for this day for a long time. You can do it. And Mr. Finny and the Board of Directors will guide you every foot of the way"*

Her reassurance gave him instant relief, yet his sense of sadness engulfed him as he continued to tremble and cry *"Be happy with Lesley my darling, and do try to tolerate stuck up Brenda a little more."* He laughed again. *"People are seldom what they seem John and she is one of life's good guys."* He nodded in agreement.

"As for Kate, please, do as we have done and never allow it to threaten your marriage".

He continued nodding and he spoke to her as the tears just kept on rolling *"I won't Ree, I promise, I won't love."* Then he wiped his eyes with the back of his hand so he could see her words *"Besides Edward, you my darling are the only one who has ever loved me for me and not my money and that is a rare gift as you will learn a new'*

He gave a heavy sigh. *"Rupert is just a product of his privileged upbringing, and he is weak… don't be too hard on him."* He smiled *"Ok, don't worry I won't."* then read on *"Edward and I worked so hard to build up everything we had. Continue that work for us my darling and finish the*

Croxteth Country Park development just as we wanted it to be and make me proud, make yourself proud, and make your warm and wonderful city proud. After that, make your own mark my darling."

He whispered "I will Ree, I will". The ache in his chest felt like a ton weight and was hurting when he was taken aback by a stern warning *"But listen to me, that part of your life that's always gnawed a hole in your soul, let it go my darling because if you don't it will cause you great pain and sorrow one day."*

He knew she was talking about his burning need for revenge on Eddie D and everyone who shafted his dad and he resented it as he read on. *"And that side of your life that Lesley and I have always turned a blind to will also hurt you, so whatever it is that you get up too John, bring it to and end my darling or one day you may just go too far."*

That annoyed him because he needed to finish off what he'd started and destroy Decker and son, but his annoyance quickly vanished as he read on. *"I've had a wonderful life John and it has been made all the richer by your love, and for that I thank you and will love you forever."*

Then as he came to the finishing lines, he sobbed great sobs aloud and heartfelt as the pain of her final goodbye became unbearable.

"It's time John, time for me to go home to Edward… But don't be too sad my darling. I will always be close by and watching over you, so until we meet again be happy."

He clutched the letter to his chest, as he sobbed great loud sobs of grief because she had taught him much about life. They had shared something special and unique. But now she was gone and he was going to miss her more than he could ever admit to anyone. So he wiped away his tears stood up and inhaled deeply before he opened the door and walked out into his new life as very, very rich mean man.

Chapter Twenty Nine

In the weeks that followed, John met with the board of directors and had Ray Hall appointed as the new Managing Director. Tony appointed as the new Works Director and Kate appointed as the new Sales Director and kept everything else just as it was. The Croxteth Country Park was on target and going very well and Ray Hall had everything in hand. So John got back to the matter of Decker and son.

Eric, Eddie and Dot were all shell shocked because in a matter of months they lost their business and the building suppliers had served a bankruptcy order on them. They'd missed too many payments on their fleet of works vans and their two cars, they were in breach of the lease terms, so the company repossessed all but one of the vehicles. That was the Jag they'd managed to hide away on the Golf Club car park.

Their own reports on Talbot Court came back confirming they had used the wrong concrete on the foundations, and therefore had no case to make as they hadn't conformed to the terms and conditions of contract, so had to forfeit all monies due. They also owed HMS customs a fortune in taxes, and had been unable to pay any wages to their work force.

Kate had got them their mortgage with the Jersey Building Society. So Dot called into the Croxteth site office albeit filled with dread to appeal to her for help in getting more time on the repossessions of their homes.

Kate smiled warmly "Look, I'm due to have dinner with the owner of the Jersey Building Society. So I'll see what I can do because if anyone can help you, he can. He also owns the Bank of Jersey and CIDC who bought out Brossly Homes.

They agreed to meet us at the Corn Exchange office nine thirty prompt on Monday morning with Eddie and his dad. Dot was so relieved that Kate didn't throw up the fact that Nigel had never returned to her or Liverpool. She left the office feeling like a ton weight had been lifted.

At nine thirty prompt Dot, Eric and Eddie D were led into John's office by Kate.

"Mr. Davenport will join you shortly."

As they sat nervously waiting, Dots eyes were draw to the family picture hanging on the wall and every part of her froze inside. It was John Kelly with his arm draped over a very attravtive woman and it was obviously a family photograph as the three girls in it were the living image of him. Unable to speak a word, she looked to Eric and Eddie in shock as everything came crashing down into place. Then Kate opened the office door.

"Let me introduces you. Mr. John Davenport." Eric didn't realize who he was and stood up to shake his hand, but John walked straight past him and went behind his desk. The penny dropped and still standing only now with the look of shock right across his face, Eric blurted out the obvious "You're not John Davenport, you're John Kelly!"

John grinned "Davenport is my wife's name, but that's irrelevant. I believe you lot are in shit street and need my help?" Eddie D was white with anger and stood up trembling with controlled rage "You're behind all of this aren't you?"

Before John could even answer, Eric interrupted "Why would somebody with all your wealth go out of his way to put us all on the scrap heap? Surely you wouldn't hold a grudge for that long because Dot chose to marry Eddie?"

John carried on grinning at their obvious shock and distress then tut tutted "Eric, I fucked you over because you fucked my dad over all those years back, you done him out of his hard earned cash and retirement bungalow. So now I've just done the same to you." He grinned wider "Not nice is it."

Eric looked as Eddie in dismay and John continued "And as you were fucking over my dad, your cunt of a son was fucking over my girl and had me beat up and left for dead, and that stopped me from going to my dad's funeral. So you shower of cunts might have thought that had gone away with the passing of time… but I've made it my life's mission to bring every bastard one of you to your knees and completely destroy you all, and right now, I'd say that's mission accomplished wouldn't you?"

He looked them each up and down like they were the shit of his shoe, "Now get the fuck out of my office."

With Big Harry and Dominic McGuire standing close by they had no option but to leave as Dominic sent the boot in "Hope you've got bus fair, we've repossessed the Jag from the Gold Club car park."

Later, Dot returned very distressed and walked right past everyone and barged straight into John's office.

"I get it John ok! I get it! But you can't do this, you just can't!" Her voice was filled with emotion and her eyes were swollen from hours of crying. John just looked at her unmoved "I think you'll find I can and I have."

She stared at him appalled by his coldness "You don't understand."

She pointed to his family picture hanging on the wall. "You can't do this because I've got your son!"

Now it was his turn to be shell shocked. "He's the living image of your three daughters and you'd take him for your eldest's twin. You're not just destroying me Eddie and Eric; you're destroying your own son!"

Chapter Thirty

Alone in the penthouse John was shattered. Dot had got things catastrophically wrong. She genuinely had thought she was carrying Eddie's baby, but with hindsight and the passing of time she realized it was more likely to be his, but she never told a soul and let Eddie rear him as his own.

Yet years of trying for a second child she kept remembering what Eddies first wife had been telling everyone that he was firing blanks that sadly now seemed to be true and the only other explanation was John, and the older her son grew it was becoming more and more obvious.

It seemed the best thing to do at the time was to say nothing. But now the privately paid for results from Rodney Street clinic confirmed John was Michael's father and he was in turmoil. So too was Dot as she still had to tell Eddie.

The first thing John done was put the repossession orders on hold and Dot had the task of telling Eddie why.

'What did you have to do to get the horrible bastard to do that? Sleep with him!"

He was shaking with fury as she screamed back at him. "No I didn't! I told him Michael is his son!"

Michael was standing outside of the room listening to every word as she sobbed 'He paid for a private test and it was confirmed… I'm sorry Eddie ok, I'm sorry"

Eddie fell to his knees "No, no no no!!! Get out! Get out Dot! Get out!"

She wanted to hold him, to comfort him, but he was beside himself with the shock and rage and betrayal of it all, so she left with Michael who was still sobbing.

After spending several hours with his Mum and Nan, Michael was much calmer and wanted to back home to be with his dad. So Val Harper gave Dot her cars keys.

"Go on, go home to him love. He'll be much calmer now and he'll see it changes nothing cos he'll always be Michael's dad not matter what the results say."

Dot and Michael agreed and set off back home, but as they drove up Huyton Lane to Garth Close, a police car and ambulance were parked outside of their house and when they pulled up and got out of the car a policewoman stopped them from entering their home and led them across the road to Eddie's dad's house.

Their sense of confusion and concern exploded into raw grief as they walked into Eric's house and seen him sitting with his head in hands sobbing, because he had found Eddie hanging dead from the banister.

It was almost time for the offices to close for the day at the Corn Exchange, when in rushed Michael.

"Where is he? Where's John Davenport? I wonna see him now!" Kate was gob smacked and tried to calm him down telling him John was at home. "Take me to him now cos I'm gonna knock his fuckin head off!"

Everyone in the office was shocked and Kate gave one of them the nod to ring John, while she tried to calm the lad. However he wasn't having any of it "My dad has just hung himself because of tha bastard and I'm gonna fuckin have him!"

John gave word for Kate to get the lad to him right away. As soon as they walked through the door of the penthouse, he felt like he was looking in a mirror. "I'm gonna fuckin' kill you!"

The lad rushed at him and Kate screamed "Michael no!" But it was too late John was already wrestling on the floor. Put there by a son he longed for all his adult life and didn't even know he fuckin had until now.

His lad was on top of him now and trying to punch the life out of him. But John grappled with him and managed to hold him in a tight bear hug and unable to move the lad broke and sobbed in his arms.

John loosened his grip and sat on the floor hugging him "That's it, let it go, let it all go." Kate stood crying as she watched John's tears rolling down his cheeks as he silently cried with his son in his arms sobbing aloud for the loss of that cunt.

Eddie, who'd been the only dad he'd ever known and loved.

"We can work this out Michael. I can put this right. I promise."

It was the worst thing John could have said.

"How can you put this right yeh stupid cunt."

The lad had his temper and his tongue was sharp and even in the midst of this turmoil and pain he could see this was a son to be proud of. A son who knew how to stand up for himself and those he loved. A son who'd called another man 'dad' all his life and that other man was none other than Eddie D, the cunt who ruined his life! The lad was eighteen and sobbing like an infant for a low life.

"My dad's dead cos of you! He's hung himself cos of you! So go on, how you gonna put that right big man?"

John was completely shattered. He understood the lad's anger and his pain.

"Michael I didn't want this to happen son."

That was the proverbial red rag to a fuckin' bull.

"I'm not your son!!! Don't you ever say tha' again! Eddie's my dad, got it? You're just the fuckin sperm donor!"

John wasn't having that, no matter how much the lad was grieving.

"Now you listen to me for a minute! Yeah ok, I wanted to settle a few old scores. Things you don't know about, but I swear I didn't want things to turn out like this."

He pulled open a draw and got out a letter and a couple of old newspaper cuttings. One was the picture of him and Dot in Liverpool Echo, the other was the story about him being beaten up and left for dead, and the letter was attached to the invoice that Eddie's dad was one of the signatories on when his dad got shafted.

"Michael, I was in love with your mum, but she was using me as a cover cos Eddie was a lot older than her and she was seeing him. But he was jealous and paid to have me beaten up and left for dead by two men. While I was in hospital, your mum eloped with him and they got married."

But Michael wasn't interested in all yesterdays and ancient history. "It's all here Michael, in these cuttings and letters. Your mum came back and told me she was pregnant but to Eddie, not me, I was devastated… There's so much to tell you and it's all true. So yeah, I've have set out to pay Eddie and your Granddad Eric back, but I wouldn't have done that if I'd have known about you… I really didn't want it all to end like this."

Michael had stopped crying and was standing staring and listening to every word.

"You can stand there all night fuckin long doin' the poor old me routine if it makes you feel better, but it doesn't justify what you've put my mum through and won't bring my dad back. And no matter which way you wrap it up, *you killed him* and *I'll never forgive you for that*".

Michael was as cold as ice and he meant every word and John was at a complete loss. "What can I do Michael? What do you want me to do? Go on, name it and I'll do it."

He thought for a moment "Clear all my mum's debts and stop the repossession on her houses." John smiled "I've already put a stop on the repossessions, but I'll make sure I clear every debt for her too…. And I'll open an account for you cos you'll want for nothing Michael. I promise you that."

Michael shook his head in disbelief "You just don't get it do you? You can shove your money right up your fuckin arse' cos I don't want a penny."

He was a chip off the old block and John was bitterly disappointed.

Chapter Thirty One

It was six months since Eddie had hung himself, and John still hadn't heard a word from Michael. He'd done as he asked and paid off every one of his mother's debts as well as securing her houses. And despite Michael's protests, he'd opened a bank account for him with a hundred grand.

But true to his word, the lad hadn't withdrawn a penny. He wanted nothing from him. As he lay in bed unable to sleep, with Kate snuggled up next to him, he went over and over his life.

Poor Brian Brossly had retired due to ill health, brought on by the strain of everything he'd been put through. Once he was paid off Nigel never did return to Liverpool.

The Knowsley and Huyton Security business was thriving, because word went right around the city that Big Harry and Dominic McGuire put another company out of action in one night. So they were given all the doors on the night clubs in the city centre. Arthur McNabb was acting as their paid advisor and getting them all the inside information they needed from police files.

Danny Owens was running a very successful plumbing business, but was available at a moment's notice if John or the others needed him. All of them were married and all of them had a bit on the side too, that was just the way it was.

Jimmy had never cheated though. Him and Jean were still looking after old Mar Kelly and had finally become parents with a son who they named after old Joe Kelly, so the family name would live on. And that felt like a knife going straight through the heart of John.

John had given every one of them a two hundred and fifty grand pay-off, plus a four bedroom house each. They were all doing well and were really happy. But he'd never felt so unhappy or empty in all his life. He thought over Rene's words.

She said all this was *"Gnawing a hole in his soul."* She was right, because he had a fuckin' great big hole there now. She said it would all cause him great sorrow and pain one day, and she was right about that too. He should have listened, should have taken notice, and should have stopped then before it was too late.

He should have let it all go, but it was too late and revenge wasn't so sweet after all. It was hollow and left a very bad taste it did get rid of the anger but he was empty and he wished so much Rene was still here. She'd listen, she'd know what to say, know what to do. Kate loved him he knew that, but he also realised that there was different types of love. He had loved Dot like had never loved before, but he realised that that was puppy love first love. He had fell in love with Rene she had taught facts of life about sex about business and had passed on a wisdom.

Then there was the love he had for Lesley she had given him three beautiful daughters, been a perfect wife in every way, no man could ask for more. Whether it was love or lust he had feelings for Kate, he knew she had fell head over heels in love with him. She had told him that still accepting him on a part time basis would still be a million times better than the life she had before.

As Kate lay next to him in a deep contented sleep, he wished it was Lesley next to him. She understood him too and like Rene she'd know what to say. Lesley was devastated for him at getting so near yet so far to having his own son to carry on his name, but after she gave birth the doctors had told her that it would be a danger to have any more children and tied her tubes.

He wished more than he'd ever wished before that he hadn't wasted so many years resenting her for not giving him a son. He sorely regretted neglecting her for his work and shenanigans in the city, instead of spending more time with her and his three beautiful daughters and cherishing them more.

John wished he was safe with her and his three daughters right now. That it was Lesley lying next to him not Kate. That he was holding Lesley close, because he realised now more than he'd ever realised before, that Lesley was the true love of his life.

As he lay in silence thinking over all of these things, he reflected on how life had a strange way of delivering Karma.

Meanwhile back in Jersey, Lesley lay in her bed being held by her first love… Brenda.

Epilogue

The years that followed John inheriting the company, were good to him and his family and friends. Renee had been right in spotting his potential early and he grew into his new role, successfully leading CIDC he had kept all the directors and managers that had contributed to the success of the company.

His eldest had gone to university and got a degree in European economics and she had joined CIDC and was looked upon as a rising star. His other two had taken totally different routes. His middle daughter had married her childhood sweetheart and had two sons of her own. The youngest had started a career in modelling and was becoming quickly famous in international circles. As they say success breeds success and in Johns case it seemed to be true.

In Liverpool, Mar Kelly spent the last years of her life in comfort, living in luxury with Jimmy and Jean in their four bed-detached house. His son Michael never contacted him again, and the last time heard about him he had a successful career in computer programming. John by this time got used to living a double life. He used the name of Kelly when he was in Liverpool. He lived in the large detached house he had built with Kate, who had taken the surname of Kelly when she gave birth to the first of her two children ....both boys.